# the
# other
# side

**Also by Trice Hickman**

**Dangerous Love Series**
*Secret Indiscretions*
*Deadly Satisfaction*

**Unexpected Love Series**
*Unexpected Interruptions*
*Keeping Secrets & Telling Lies*
*Looking for Trouble*
*Troublemaker*

*Playing the Hand You're Dealt*
*Breaking All My Rules*
*The Other Side*

**Published by Dafina Books**

# the other side

## TRICE HICKMAN

KENSINGTON PUBLISHING CORP.

www.kensingtonbooks.com

DAFINA BOOKS are published by

Kensington Publishing Corp.
119 West 40th Street
New York, NY 10018

All Kensington titles, imprints, and distributed lines are available at special quantity discounts for bulk purchases for sales promotion, premiums, fund-raising, and educational or institutional use.

Special book excerpts or customized printings can also be created to fit specific needs. For details, write or phone the office of the Kensington Sales Manager: Kensington Publishing Corp., 119 West 40th Street, New York, NY 10018. Attn. Sales Department. Phone: 1-800-221-2647.

Dafina and the Dafina logo Reg. U.S. Pat. & TM Off.

ISBN-13: 978-1-4967-0932-5
ISBN-10: 1-4967-0932-2
First Kensington Trade Paperback Printing: October 2019

ISBN-13: 978-1-4967-0934-9 (ebook)
ISBN-10: 1-4967-0934-9 (ebook)
First Kensington Electronic Edition: October 2019

10  9  8  7  6  5  4  3  2  1

Printed in the United States of America

This book is dedicated to my father, the late Reverend Irvin Leon Hickman
Sunrise~ January 19, 1947 — Sunset~ February 14, 2019

Daddy, you were a friend to many, a pillar in your community, a dedicated pastor to your congregants, a humble servant to God, and a beloved husband, father, sibling, and uncle to your family. We all miss you terribly, but have comfort in knowing that we will see you again and will rejoice with you on the other side.

# Acknowledgments

Thank you, God, for allowing me to complete another novel. It is His grace, mercy, and love that sustain me and let me know that anything is possible if you have faith and hold on to His unchanging hand.

Thank you to my best friend, helpmate, and husband, Todd T. Hayes, Sr. You are an amazing, hardworking, God-fearing man who leads our family with love and courage. I prayed for you and God gave me more than I asked for. Thank you for believing in me, loving me, and standing by my side through whatever comes our way. Thank you to my industrious and hardworking son, Airman Todd T. Hayes, Jr., for being a kind and loving young man. I am so very proud of you! Thank you to my beautiful daughter, Eboni Hayes (my Sweetie!), for making me laugh, encouraging me, and being an awesome young lady! I am so very proud of you!

Thank you to my father, the late Reverend Irvin Leon Hickman, for loving me, teaching me valuable life lessons, and instilling in me a hard work ethic and love of God; I miss you dearly. Thank you to my mother, Alma Hickman, for always being by my side, nurturing me, loving me, supporting me, and showing me by example how to be a good wife and mother. Thank you to my sister, Melody Hickman, for loving me and making me laugh when I need it. We have shared special moments and built a bond that will live with me always. Thank you to my brother, Marcus Hickman. Thank you to all my aunts, uncles, cousins, and family friends who have supported me through the years.

Thank you to my fantastic agent, Janell Walden Agyeman: your wisdom, guidance and calm spirit have enriched my literary journey and life in more ways than you know. Thank you to my talented and skilled editor, Tara Gavin, whose suggestions, patience, and knowledge helped to make this story stronger. I truly appreciate you! Thank you to everyone at my publishing house, Kensington (Dafina Books), who helped bring this novel to publication. Thank you to the many bookstores and booksellers, event organizers, industry professionals, bloggers, as well as book promoters and marketers who connect my books with readers.

Thank you to my dear sister friends who lift me up and always have my back. You ladies are true blue, tight like glue; Vickie Lindsay, Sherraine McLean, Terri Chandler, Tammi Johnson, Jeneane Davis, Tracy Wells, Tracy McNeil, Kimberla Lawson Roby, Lutishia Lovely, China Ball, Renee Alexander, and Tiffany Dove.

Thank you again and again to the wonderful and dedicated readers and book clubs who support me and help spread the word about my books. Each and every one of you is phenomenal! I'm honored that you continue to hang in there with me book after book, and I hope you enjoy this one!

If I didn't mention your name, please blame it on my head and not my heart. There are so many individuals and organizations that contribute along the way (a lot goes into writing and publishing a book) and I'm thankful for each and every one of you.


XOXO
Trice Hickman Hayes

# *Chapter 1*

## BERNADETTE

*Five Years Ago*

Bernadette Gibson had suffered many disappointments in her forty-five years of living, but in all her experiences, she knew without a sliver of a doubt that Walter Pearson was her worst and most costly mistake to date. Their relationship was the reason why Bernadette completely understood how someone could be pushed to the brink of committing premeditated, cold-blooded murder . . . with one's bare hands.

Bernadette had met Walter at the Prince George's County Urban League's Annual Black Tie Gala. She had immediately been attracted to his engaging smile, witty conversation, and charismatic style, not to mention the fact that he was easy on the eyes, with the type of looks that could have easily earned him a spread in the pages of *Esquire* magazine. She'd thought his perfect diction, refined mannerisms, and air of entitlement were the telltale signs of a man who most likely hailed from a pedigreed family with good genes and deep pockets.

Bernadette had worked hard clawing her way out of the projects of southeast Washington, DC, for the opportunity to be in the company of men like Walter. She'd earned excellent grades in high school, which had given her a full ride scholarship at Georgetown University. Getting into such a prestigious college had allowed her to join the right social and professional organizations, and those accomplishments had provided her access to attend the right churches, socialize with the right people, and land the right, well-paying corporate jobs. This was all in an effort to meet the right kind of man with whom she could build a happily-ever-after life. Walter Pearson had checked off the boxes for what Bernadette had deemed a good catch, and from their first hello, she'd been determined to have him.

"He's perfect," she'd told her mother.

"Ain't no such thing as a perfect anything, let alone a perfect man," her mother had quickly rebuffed.

"Well, he's perfect for me!" Bernadette had shot back.

Bernadette loved her mother dearly, but she also felt that her mother's bitterness toward men often clouded her judgment. Bernadette's parents had divorced when she was five years old. Her father had cheated on her mother for years before finally leaving her for a much younger woman, the pain of which her mother had never overcome. Growing up, Bernadette couldn't recall ever seeing her mother date or show affection toward a man, and she'd never supported Bernadette in any of her relationships, always giving her boyfriends a serious side-eye. So when her mother objected to Walter and told Bernadette that he was a snake who couldn't be trusted, that warning went unheeded.

Bernadette loved that Walter was equally determined to have her—but what she hadn't realized was that his dogged pursuit was for vastly different reasons than her desire to be with him—and he'd played his hand like a professional croupier, dealing out deceit coated-lies. He'd wooed her with candlelit dinners at upscale restaurants, taken her for long, romantic walks in the park, and surprised her at home and at her job with weekly bouquets of softly hued flowers accompanied by sweet notes that read "Just Because" and "You Mean So Much to Me." Walter had even cooked gourmet meals for her in his marble-tiled, stainless steel cook's kitchen, replete with signature cocktails on his sprawling lanai and ending with hours of beautiful lovemaking.

Walter was always on time, always answered his cell phone when Bernadette called, always treated her with respect, and always did exactly what he said he was going to do. Bernadette had known that men like Walter were like unicorns, especially in the dog-eat-dog dating pool of eligible men in Washington, DC. Looking for a good man who was straight, employed, and single with no attachments or serious baggage was the equivalent to mining for gold; the prospect of striking the mark was extremely slim.

"I feel like I need to pinch you, and myself," Bernadette had said to Walter, "to make sure you, and this, is real. This seems too good to be true, which my mother says it is. And I guess a part of me believes her because no one has ever treated me like this."

Walter paused for a quiet moment, then looked directly into Bernadette's eyes. "Bernie, I understand where your mother is coming from because she loves you and she's just being protective like any parent would. I can't speak for the men who came before me, but I can assure you that I don't want any to come after me. I want to be your one and only, because you're my one and only. I love you, Bernadette."

Tears formed in Bernadette's eyes. "I love you too, Walter."

Statistics had told Bernadette that as a single, middle-aged African American woman with a college degree, making a mid-six-figure salary, living in an upper-middle-class neighborhood in the heart of the nation's capital, her meeting and marrying an African American man of equal standing was a long shot. She counted herself lucky to have a man like Walter in hot pursuit of her affections, professing his love for her. She thought he was a dream come true, and after a three-month-long whirlwind romance, Walter proposed with a flawless, brilliant cut, four-carat Tiffany ring. Bernadette enthusiastically said yes and within days she picked out a date and began interviewing caterers and florists for what she envisioned was going to be a wedding to rival all weddings.

"Bernie, I don't trust him," Bernadette's mother had said, when against Bernadette's better judgment, she'd asked her mother to accompany her as she tried on wedding dresses.

"Mom, please. For once can't you just be happy for me, or at least don't discourage me? I've finally found someone who loves me, and I love him."

Her mother shook her head. "I love you too much to lie to you, baby. You're my only child, and I wouldn't tell you anything untrue or that I thought would hurt you. I'm trying to help you," she'd said as she'd assisted Bernadette out of the ivory-colored sheath wedding dress she'd just tried on.

"I thought this was going to be a great mother/daughter moment for us, and that it would help you get over your bitterness so you'd find a way to be happy for me. If I'd known you were going to act this way I would have never asked you to come."

Her mother snickered. "Is that what you think? You think I'm not happy for you because I'm bitter?"

"You've never gotten over what my father did to you, and you've let your anger and resentment rule your life. But, Mom, as much as I love you, I can't allow you to poison my relationship with Walter or cast a shadow over the happiness I feel when I'm with him."

Bernadette's mother reached out, took her hand, and gave it a gentle squeeze. "Oh, honey, you don't have a clue. Yes, I might be bitter, but don't mistake my shortcomings as a reason for why I think your relationship with Walter isn't going to last. Trust me, time will prove me right."

Bernadette's mother/daughter dress-shopping excursion came to an abrupt halt, as did their daily phone calls. Bernadette vowed to surround herself only with people who were supportive of her relationship with, and impending marriage to, Walter.

With more determination than ever, Bernadette continued her wedding plans. She knew that Walter's custom-built, seven-thousand-square-foot home would be the perfect setting to celebrate what would be the beginning of their fairy-tale life together. His home sat on several acres of land in Prince George's County, close to a beautiful man-made lake, and Bernadette couldn't wait to host a lavish outdoor wedding befitting the power couple that she and Walter had become. She couldn't imagine being any happier than she was today because although at her age she had ruled out the possibility of having children, her dream of growing old with someone was finally within reach. But one month after Walter had proposed, Bernadette's happily-ever-after came to an end with breakneck speed.

Walter's work schedule had been hectic ever since they'd met, which made the fact that he always found a way to make himself available to her even more special in Bernadette's eyes. But after he'd proposed, his long hours kicked into overdrive.

"I'm working hard so you won't have to," he told Bernadette one evening over steak, lobster tails, and vintage wine.

She'd been so touched by his dedication to their relationship and the loving care he consistently showed for her that she wanted to do something special to show her appreciation for his thoughtfulness.

Wednesdays were Walter's work from home days, so Bernadette decided to surprise him with lunch from Panera Bread, which was the spot of their first lunch date. She slipped inside Walter's house unnoticed through a side entrance near his garage. She planned to set up their romantic feast of delicious sandwiches, savory soup, and tasty pastries in his bedroom and then cap off the meal with an afternoon tryst. She smiled with anticipation because she knew Walter would be pleasantly caught off guard and thrilled about spending time with her.

Bernadette didn't think Walter was home because she hadn't seen his luxury sedan when she'd peeped into his garage, so she was startled when she heard his voice booming from the direction of his home office. But instead of sounding his usual calm, confident, and polished self, his voice had taken on a hard edge, filled with the frustration and desperation of someone about to lose control. Bernadette was shocked and momentarily couldn't believe what she was hearing.

"Uh-huh, yeah . . . I understand," Walter said to the person on the other end. "I'm tellin' you, just give me a little time and I'll get you your hundred grand in another month or two after I lock up this trick I'm about to marry."

Bernadette covered her mouth in disbelief as she continued to listen to her real-life nightmare unfold.

Walter smirked on his end. "Yeah, man, the one you saw me with last month . . . yeah, she's gonna be my ticket to easy street, and once we make things legal I'll have access to everything she's got. And I'll need it, too, 'cause trying to pay for all these fancy restaurants and flowers is adding up."

Bernadette continued to listen to a story that sounded as if it was ripped from a novel. Walter went on to say that he didn't have the money to pay off his $100,000 gambling debt because every penny he made went to spousal support for three ex-wives and child support for seven children, not to mention the fact that his girlfriend on the side had just announced she was pregnant with his child.

Bernadette was rendered motionless and speechless in the middle of Walter's hallway, tightly gripping her Panera Bread to-go bag. But slowly, she summoned the strength to put one foot in front of the other and make her way into Walter's office.

Walter kept talking on the phone, oblivious to the fact that Bernadette was standing in his doorway. "You son of a bitch!" Bernadette yelled.

Walter's eyes enlarged to the size of baseballs and his face looked as if he was staring at a ghost. "Baby, I can explain."

"My mother was right about you!" Bernadette threw the cup of fresh-squeezed lemonade she was holding and hit Walter square in his face, then she reached into the bag, pulled out a steaming hot container of broccoli-cheddar soup and drenched him in the creamy greenish-yellow liquid.

But in that instant, Bernadette realized she'd gone too far because Walter flew into a rage.

"Uuggghhh," Walter cried out. "You just burned me, you crazy bitch, and you ruined my brand-new shirt. I oughta kick your high siddity ass!"

But instead of feeling fearful of the man standing in front of her, whom she now viewed as a stranger, Bernadette gathered all the years of hurt and bad relationships she'd experienced into the moment. "You ought to kick my ass?!" Bernadette screamed back. Her voice was a mixture of controlled anger mixed with a touch of set-it-off. "I'm the one who should be kicking your ass!" Bernadette said, gritting her teeth. She lunged at Walter, and in one quick motion she picked up the stapler off his desk and launched it like a missile at his face, hitting him in his nose, causing blood to gush.

Walter grabbed his nose in pain, but Bernadette showed no mercy. She reached for the sharp metal letter opener and stabbed it into Walter's forearm. He cried out again and staggered backward as he pulled the office tool turned deadly weapon out of his bleeding flesh. "Bitch, I'm gonna kill your crazy ass!" Walter yelled.

"Dead men can't fight," Bernadette said as she lunged at him with full force. She didn't know where her strength came from—it could have been from pent-up hurt, feelings of abandonment from her father, bitterness from her mother, unrequited love from her past relationships, or a combination of them all. But one thing Bernadette did know was that her raw emotions led her to fight Walter like a man and beat him to a pulp. But she didn't come out unscathed. She suffered a fractured right hand and a nasty black eye.

"Press charges and put his butt behind bars," her mother told her later that evening. "If he tried to swindle you, I'm sure he's involved in all kinds of shadiness."

After what Bernadette had just lived through, all she wanted to do was put Walter and his deception behind her. In the days that followed her shocking discovery and violent breakup, Bernadette learned that Walter's luxury car had really been a rental from Prestige Foreign Cars, and the beautiful home he lived in was the property of one of his real estate clients who'd been living abroad for the last six months while Walter house-sat for him.

Bernadette shared a few details with her mother and poured her heart out only to her close cousin, whom she considered a sister. But she was much too devastated and embarrassed to reveal the full truth to the rest of her family and friends.

Over the next few weeks she retreated into the four walls of her luxurious Dupont Circle townhome and eventually told everyone that she'd realized that she and Walter had been incompatible. She knew that no one really believed her story, and she was grateful that not a soul had pushed her for the ugly details of their breakup, especially after Walter was arrested two months later for wire fraud.

Walter Pearson's deception had done more than embarrass Bernadette; he'd hurt her to her core, and she vowed to never allow herself to be deceived by another man, ever.

# Chapter 2

## TESS

*One Year Ago*

Tess's eyes darted from one end of the room to the other, trying to figure out the best way to cause Antwan maximum damage without landing herself in jail. "I'm gonna make that sorry, sneaky, low-down son of a bitch pay," Tess hissed. "His conniving ass is gonna learn that I'm the wrong bitch to fuck with."

Testimony Sinclair, or Tess—the name that everyone called her—was so mad she could barely see past the red rage flickering behind her big, brown doe eyes. Her boyfriend, Antwan, had been MIA for the last two days. He'd sent her a text message early yesterday morning saying he was under a tight deadline at work, but her intuition told her that he was up to something, and being the curious person she was, she knew she needed to get to the bottom of what was really going on with him. So this morning she'd risen early, something she rarely did, and driven over to Antwan's house. She'd parked her car across the street and waited to see what she might discover. Sure enough, thirty minutes later he had emerged, accompanied by a full-figured, Jill Scott–looking woman who was rocking a mile-high afro and a satisfied smile.

"I knew it!" Tess had screamed. She was about to swing her car door open, run across the street, and confront them, but a tiny voice inside her head cautioned her to stay put because if she didn't it would take a team of armed officers to break up what would ensue. But as she watched her boyfriend and his side chick drive away, a bigger, more forceful voice told her, "Girl, don't get mad, get even!"

Tess reached into her handbag and pulled out the bump key she'd made a few months ago that would unlock Antwan's door. After jiggling it around in the lock, she gently opened the door and let herself into his neatly kept house. Her eyes zeroed in on two empty glasses beside a bottle of wine on his coffee table. "That cheating mutherfucker," Tess said. She picked up the empty bottle of Chardonnay and then sent it crashing into large shards across Antwan's hardwood floors.

Tess knew she should leave because the little voice inside her head returned and told her that being in her boyfriend's house like this wasn't a good idea. But once again, the bigger voice pushed out its weaker opponent and said, "Girl, you're already in here, so you better make the most of it!"

Tess decided to once again listen to the dominant voice, and she headed back to Antwan's bedroom.

Once she was inside she was more pissed off than ever by what she found. Antwan was a near-OCD neat freak and always made up his bed as soon as he rose, no matter what. One time when she hadn't moved fast enough he'd tried to make up his bed with her still in it. But this morning, instead of finding his bed made with military style precision the way he usually kept it, it was a disheveled mess with sheets hanging off the edge. Tess shook her head and ran her hand over her thick mop of curly hair. She felt like striking a match and letting it land wherever it may because she was completely disgusted.

"This is the reason his sorry ass has been avoiding me for two days straight," she said aloud. "Deadline my ass! That bastard! I can't believe I fell for his bullshit again. But this is the last time."

Tess and Antwan Bolling had been dating two years, and in that time he'd repeatedly cheated on her with multiple women, sometimes juggling two women at a time in addition to Tess. One time he'd even cheated with his ex-girlfriend whom he'd broken up with shortly before he and Tess had met. Tess had forgiven him the first time because his "slip-up with the past," as he'd called it, had happened only a few weeks into his and Tess's relationship, and they hadn't made a solid commitment to each other. So Tess had brushed it off and decided that she and Antwan could start anew, as a committed couple this time around. She'd laid down the law and told him that she expected monogamy, and that if he couldn't deal, he needed to move along.

"Tess, I promise you. I'm going to be faithful to you and only you," Antwan had said.

"How can I believe you? How can I trust you?"

"My word is my bond, and I'm giving that to you, along with my heart."

Telling a man that she expected monogamy had been a big deal for Tess because Antwan was the only man she'd ever wanted to be faithful to. They had instantly clicked when she'd met him at her book signing two years ago. She'd been signing copies of her latest novel when a handsome man had caught her eye. His dreamy, hazel-colored eyes, deep dimples, and kinky coily twists of hair had grabbed her attention among the throng of readers who had come to Barnes & Noble to have their books signed that evening. After her event had ended, Tess had been on her way out of the store when she'd spotted Antwan standing near the door. He'd introduced himself and given her his number and the rest was a wrap.

They were both accomplished writers, she a popular *New York Times* best-selling author, he a highly respected award-winning newspaper journalist. They'd bonded over classic literature, good food, wild sex, and fine wine. No man had ever understood Tess in the way that Antwan had, and his compassion and kindness had made her fall hard for him. But despite his many good qualities, the one thing Tess had noticed early on in their relationship was Antwan's wandering eye. Every time they were out he'd stare at other women, and if they happened to be very attractive, his eyes would linger to the point of disrespect. Then there was the fact that his phone was always on vibrate or silent, and she'd suspected that was his way of trying to prevent her from detecting whether he was receiving phone calls, texts, or both.

There were other things that gave Tess pause as well, like the fact that Antwan was hesitant about making their relationship public. He'd said it was because his profession—being a Pulitzer Prize–winning columnist for the *Washington Post*'s Chicago bureau—and hers—being an international best-selling author with a legion of loyal readers—kept them both in the spotlight enough, and he didn't want his private life to become a public story.

"I want people to know that I'm in love!" Tess had said one night when they'd been out on the town and she'd wanted to post photos of the good time they were having on her Instagram and Facebook pages.

"Why does the world have to know?" Antwan had countered. "As long as the two of us know that we love each other, what difference does it make what others think?"

"It's not about what others think. Like I've said many times, I just want to share the love I feel."

Antwan was unyielding. "I don't want to share my life with the world."

"You post and share information on social media all the time."

"Only social or political commentary that's related to my column. I post about the news and world events, but my personal life is off-limits. You know that."

"Are you trying to keep me a secret?" Tess asked, trying not to frown.

Antwan wrapped her in his arms. "No, I just don't want to share my private life with the world, Tess. Can you respect that?"

Even though Tess didn't like or understand his reasoning, she'd acquiesced, mostly because Antwan repeatedly professed his love for her, that there was no one else, and that he'd learned his lesson about fidelity and would be faithful to her. But his promise had been short-lived when, nearly a year after she'd caught him cheating the first time, he'd fallen off the fidelity wagon again.

He'd tried to lie his way out of it, and he'd almost gotten away with his deceit until one of his friends had unknowingly given Tess the wrong answer to a trick question she'd asked, busting Antwan's bogus alibi. Once Tess confronted him, Antwan had finally admitted that he'd "slipped up" again, in what he'd called a moment of regressive weakness. "I only lied to protect your feelings," he'd told her. "I love you, Tess, and I would never do anything to intentionally hurt you. Blame it on my immaturity and shortcomings, not my heart."

Now, once again, Tess was standing face-to-face with Antwan's infidelity, staring pain squarely in the eyes. The reality hit her, and in that moment Tess knew this wouldn't be the last time her boyfriend cheated, but it would most certainly be the last time he cheated on *her.*

"I invested two years into this asshole!" Tess screamed, beginning to see bright red again. "I was faithful to him, and now look at this shit," she hissed as she stared down at the bra that his side chick had left behind. She sneered. "She's a young-minded bitch, because if she had to leave her damn underclothes behind as a calling card to me, what does that say about her?" But as soon as Tess said those words she knew that what she'd said about Antwan's side chick applied directly to her as well. After all, she'd gone through the trouble of having a bump key made several months ago, and today wasn't the first time she'd sneaked into Antwan's house to snoop around.

"What the hell's wrong with me?" Tess questioned out loud. "I'm successful. I'm smart. I have a great personality. And hell, I'm straight-up beautiful with a bangin'-ass body. So why would he cheat on me?"

It was a fact that Tess was successful, as was evidenced by her latest novel, which was still sitting at the top of the *New York Times* best sellers list, several months after its publication. Her magna cum laude degree from Winston-Salem State University confirmed that she was academically smart. Her vibrant personality was the reason that her friends and family called her the life of the party. And her smooth skin with near-perfect bone structure, along with her slim, well-toned body was a testament to the fact that she made men and women do a double take when she walked into the room.

"What's wrong with me?" Tess repeated softly. She breathed deeply as the loud voice inside her head told her: *Listen, sister, there ain't nothing wrong with you, except the fact that you're in love with a liar who's clearly not in love with you. This shit is about him and his problems. So stop feeling sorry for yourself. Remember, don't get mad, get even!*

Tess walked to the kitchen, opened the bottle of Hennessey sitting on the counter, and poured a glass. As she swallowed the smooth, brown liquid, her eyes landed on the butcher block knife set at the other end of the counter. She removed the kitchen sheers from the set and marched back to Antwan's bedroom, heading straight to his meticulously organized walk-in closet. One by one she removed his neatly hung clothes from the black, felt-lined hangers.

"Since he acts like half a man, I'm gonna make his wardrobe match who he is!" She cut one sleeve off every shirt, sweater, and jacket before moving on to his pants. She held up his neatly creased khakis and cut off one pant leg in four large snips, then she commenced to cutting off one leg of every pair of jeans, slacks, and shorts in sight. Next, she walked over to his dresser, opened his sock drawer, and cut off the toe section of every pair of socks that Antwan owned. She moved on to his underwear drawer and cut one leg off of each pair of boxer briefs and one sleeve off every immaculately folded T-shirt she could get her hands on. After she was satisfied that she'd destroyed his clothes she walked over to his master bathroom, opened the door to his linen closet, and cut every towel and washcloth in half. She would have tackled the sheets next, but her hand was beginning to cramp, so she decided to redirect her efforts on something less taxing.

"Hmmm, let's see what else can I fuck up," Tess said as she walked back out to the kitchen and poured herself another glass of Hennessey. She looked at his prized stainless steel Sub-Zero refrigerator and smiled. She reached over to his knife set, pulled out the serrated edge bread knife, and dragged it up and down the appliance's smooth surface until it looked as if it had been attacked by a wild animal. "That's good, if I do say so myself," Tess declared, admiring her handiwork. She pulled the door handle open, perused the shelves, and grabbed everything that was liquid or that she thought would aid her in her next phase of destruction. She poured milk, juice, and soda on his kitchen floor, cracked eggs on his couch, and smeared jelly, honey, and syrup onto his plush carpet covering his living room floor.

Tess proceeded to destroy pretty much anything she could get her hands on from Antwan's prized journalism awards that sat perched on his mahogany bookcase, to his collection of carefully curated prints hanging on the walls, to his two flat-screen TVs. She also broke every glass, plate, bowl, cup, and saucer in his cabinets. She wanted to work her way back to his guest bedroom and bathroom, but by now she was growing tired.

"I need to go home and decompress because this shit is exhausting," Tess said as she reached into Antwan's pantry, pulled out one of his reusable canvas grocery bags, and filled it with as many bottles of his wine and liquor as it would hold. "One thing I can say about that asshole is that he has good taste in alcohol."

Tess walked toward the door and looked out the living room window at the snow that had begun to fall. Her mind had been so focused on her troubles with Antwan, that she'd completely forgotten that the weather forecast had called for heavy snow that would bring more than a foot by nightfall. She wrapped herself up in her heavy wool coat and quietly closed the door behind her as she lugged her bag full of liquor to her car.

As Tess cautiously drove twenty miles below the speed limit across town and back to her house in the Gold Coast—arguably one of Chicago's most affluent neighborhoods—she felt as though she'd just completed the Ironman contest. She was physically tired and emotionally spent. Even though her gut had told her that Antwan was cheating on her again, she had held hope against hope, naïvely believing that he would eventually change his ways. She had thought he was the one; that he would be her forever man. She was in her late thirties, and for the first time in her life she wanted to get married, settle down, and even have a child or two, and she wanted to do that with Antwan. That was how much she loved him, but now, he'd turned her world upside down and dashed her dreams in the short span of a few hours.

Tess was almost home, and as she steered her car down her pristine street, her face went blank when she saw Antwan's number pop up on the screen of her car's Bluetooth system. Under any other circumstances she would have picked up right away, but right now she couldn't bring herself to speak with her lying, cheating boyfriend. The call went to her voice mail but he didn't leave a message.

When Tess entered her spacious home she kicked off her shoes, put away her bag full of alcohol, and went straight upstairs to her bedroom. She peeled out of her clothes, put on her oversized nightshirt, and crawled under her soft comforter. It was barely 9:00 a.m., and even though the day had just begun, Tess desperately wished it was over. Suddenly, it dawned on her that she'd almost forgotten about a very important call she needed to make. She reached into her handbag that she'd placed on the floor beside her bed and retrieved her cell phone.

Tess was about to dial the intended number when her phone rang. Her eyes shifted into long slits of anger when she saw Antwan's name appear. When he'd called while she'd been driving home she had felt sad, and too emotional to talk with him. But now she was seeing bright red again, just as she had back at his house. "The nerve of this mutherfucker! I ought to curse his ass out right now." Just as she was about to swipe her finger across her cell phone's screen to answer the call, she stopped in mid-motion.

"No, I'm not going to say a word to him. He'll know exactly where we stand when he walks through his door after he gets back home from wherever he and his whore were going so early this morning." Tess let his call roll over to her voice mail once again, and after a few seconds a loud beep signaled that unlike the first time he'd called, this time he left a message.

Tess dialed the number she'd been wanting and needing to call all morning. She propped herself up on her elbows, feeling content to let Antwan's message float into her voice mail box beside the other six missed calls and several text messages from friends and family, all wishing her Happy Birthday.

# Chapter 3

## ARIZONA

*Present Day*

Two years, two months, and two days had led to this moment. It was time. Arizona Mays and Chris Pendleton were about to break their vow of abstinence.

"Are you sure you want to do this?" Chris asked.

Arizona took a deep breath and nodded. "Yes, Chris, I'm sure. I've been thinking about this for a very long time and I'm ready. More than ready."

They kissed as they always did, but this time instead of keeping their midsections at a safe distance—so as not to awaken carnal desires—they moved in close, allowing their bodies to fold into one another. This kind of physical intimacy was routine for most couples, but it was unexplored territory for Arizona and Chris. They had each taken a vow of celibacy a few years before they'd met at their church's singles retreat. They had both survived bad relationships that had led them to ask God to send them a helpmate whom they would marry, and until that time they would remain chaste.

"In that case, let's do this right." Chris placed a gentle kiss onto

Arizona's forehead and took her hand into his as he rose from the couch. "My king-size bed is waiting for my queen," he said with a sexy smile.

Arizona lovingly smiled back and followed her fiancé into his bedroom. This was the only room in Chris's neatly organized three-bedroom ranch-style home that Arizona normally avoided, but tonight she gladly entered, allowing him to guide her to what she knew would be a memorable evening filled with intense pleasure and passion. She glanced over at the solid red comforter covering the bed and thought about the fact that she and Chris would soon be under his sheets.

Arizona's mind raced with anticipation, but in the midst of her thoughts she suddenly felt a stab of insecurity. It had been more than five years since any man had seen her naked, and now here she was, about to reveal every lump, bump, and imperfection that until this moment she'd not given much thought to. And even though she knew that Chris accepted her size 20 figure, anxiety and embarrassment clung to her like the extra pounds she'd become all too aware of.

"Baby, are you okay?" Chris asked with concern.

Arizona nodded and tried to paint on a smile. "Yes, I'm fine."

Chris looked deeply into her eyes. "Arizona, I know every inch of you and every expression you make, so I know when something's wrong. You're uneasy and you're having second thoughts."

"Chris, I want to make love to you . . ."

Chris placed a finger to her lips to silence her, then pulled her in close to his body. "Baby, I told you, we don't have to do this. We only have six more months until I'm your husband and you're my wife, and if you want to wait until then, we'll wait."

Arizona looked into her fiancé's piercing eyes and knew that he meant every word he'd just spoken. She was thankful for a man like Chris. Not only was he kind, honest, giving, loyal, and a good God-fearing man, he was fine looking. At six foot four inches tall, with muscles that could have belonged to a professional athlete, Chris's body was chiseled. His milk chocolate–colored skin was velvety smooth and his full lips gave his handsome face a sexy allure. A less confident woman would have been intimidated dating a man like Chris, but Arizona knew her worth. She was attractive, smart, loving, supportive, and caring, and she knew she would make a good and faithful wife. But she also knew her shortcomings, and she considered her weight to be close to the top of that list. She was disappointed in the fact that she'd let herself go after Solomon had been born. Late-night snacking, fast food meals on the go, and no structured exercise routine had contributed to seventy pounds that had made her once-svelte body a thing of the past.

"Chris, I love you and I've . . . we've been waiting for this moment for so long."

"And we can wait a little longer. I want you to be ready and comfortable. And besides," Chris said with a slight chuckle, "we did take a vow of celibacy, and then we upped the ante when we signed our premarital covenant as part of our counseling with Reverend Crestwood."

Arizona nodded in agreement. She knew that Chris was right and that the promise they'd made meant something. But she also knew that the sensation between her legs was like an itch that needed to be scratched, and that Chris could take care of that need. She looked into his eyes. "I'm going to be honest with you, Chris."

"Please do," he replied, staring back at Arizona.

Arizona took a step back away from Chris and looked down at the floor and then over to his bed. "I'm self-conscious about my weight."

"What?"

"I'm hesitant because of my weight . . . and the way my body looks."

Chris gave Arizona a puzzled look. "Baby, I'm not following you."

Arizona let out a hard sigh and moved her eyes back to his. "Do I have to spell it out? Don't you get it?"

"Yes and no."

"Chris, I'm overweight. My love handles have love handles. I have stretch marks, cellulite, and I have absolutely no muscle tone anywhere on my body." Arizona went on to tell him that she felt self-conscious about him seeing her naked, and that that was the real reason she didn't want to make love to him.

Chris reached out, put his long arm around Arizona's waist, and pulled her back in to him. "I want you to listen carefully to what I'm about to say."

Arizona nodded.

"When I met you, you were the size you are right now. When I fell in love with you, your size didn't change. When I asked you to marry me, I don't think your scale moved. And standing here, with you now, you've remained unchanged . . . right?"

Arizona nodded again.

"But there is one thing that has changed, and that's my love for you . . . it's grown. I love everything about you, Arizona Mays, and that includes your beautiful, voluptuous body. Looks are temporary, but what's in here," he pointed to her heart, "and in here," he pointed to her head, "is what matters to me. I love your caring heart and I appreciate your intelligence. You're a combination of beauty and brains."

Arizona smiled bashfully. "You're just saying that because you want to get laid."

"No doubt, I do," Chris said, causing them both to let out a small laugh. "But you know that what I just said is true."

Arizona felt like pinching herself to make sure this moment was real. She knew that Chris was a good man. A thoughtful man. A considerate man. And a complete gentleman. She couldn't believe how blessed she was to have a genuinely good man like Chris, and she said a quick prayer thanking God for sending her her Boaz. "Yes," Arizona replied. "I know what you said is true, Chris. And I love everything about you, too."

Arizona stood on the tips of her toes and kissed her fiancé deeply and passionately. "Let's do this."

22       TRICE HICKMAN

Arizona looked over at the alarm clock on Chris's nightstand. To her amazement the bright neon light read 10:30 p.m. Only one hour had passed since she and Chris had finished making love, but Arizona felt as though an entire day had come and gone. She glanced over at Chris, who was lying on his side, facing her with a peaceful, satisfied expression stretched across his face.

Arizona eased out of bed and walked across the room to Chris's large master bathroom. She turned on the light, shut the door, and sat on the edge of the bathtub. Panic rose up inside her body as she replayed her and Chris's lovemaking. She dropped her head into her hands and wanted to sob. "Is this my punishment for being disobedient and breaking our premarital covenant?" she whispered. She stood up and paced back and forth in quick steps. "This has got to be a bad dream, I mean, a really, really bad dream! Shit!"

As much as Arizona wanted to believe the last hour had been a dream, she knew it was bitter reality. She returned to the edge of the bathtub and held her legs tightly together. She shook her head. "How can this be?" she hissed. She stood, walked over to the vanity, and peered into the mirror, hoping the woman staring back at her had an explanation for what she'd just endured. Her thoughts were cut short when she heard the door crack open and saw Chris's head peep inside.

"Baby, are you okay?"

Arizona tried to paint on a smile. "Yes, I'm fine," she answered. She knew Chris would see the truth in her eyes, so she walked over to the water closet. "I have to use the bathroom really bad," she lied.

"Okay, don't take too long. I'm ready for round two," he said eagerly before closing the door behind him.

Arizona pulled the lid down on the commode, sat, and once again felt like sobbing. "Round two? Hell, I want round one!" she quietly hissed. Arizona had been anticipating a night of hot, passionate, unbridled lovemaking, and she'd thought that it would have been earth-shattering because of the two years of pent-up passion that had been simmering between them. Chris's kisses had always been sweet but short. His touch had always been soft but never lingering. And his embrace had always been caring but not heated. She'd thought it had been because he hadn't wanted to test the vow of celibacy they'd taken—a means of keeping temptation at bay. But now she knew that his actions were actually symptoms of an entirely different problem. She sat in stunned bewilderment as she replayed things in her mind.

After Chris had removed her clothes—save for her panties and bra—she'd slowly removed his. She'd been turned on with growing excitement as she'd taken inventory of his smooth, toned, dark brown skin and hard muscles that she couldn't wait to touch. She'd tossed his shirt and pants to the floor as they stood in front of each other with just one revealing layer to remove.

Without any words between them they walked over to the bed. Chris pulled back the comforter and Arizona turned off the light on the nightstand on her side of the bed. She'd glanced over at Chris and gave him a bashful smile. Although his words about her body and her size had comforted her, she'd still felt self-conscious and she'd appreciated his consideration by turning off the light on his nightstand as well.

Once they were under the covers their bodies had clung together like magnets, but right away, alarm bells rang in Arizona's head when their pelvises touched. Chris ground his lower body against hers, but all she could feel was his pelvic bone. "Where's the real bone?" she'd thought. She'd positioned herself directly under him but still couldn't feel the main muscle she'd been hoping would bring her pleasure.

"Are you ready, baby?" Chris had asked.

With anticipation and a little confusion, Arizona answered. "Yes."

He spread her legs with his knee and placed his midsection directly over hers. Slowly, he began to grind, but very quickly it turned into a flurry of torpedo like thrusts until he collapsed, gasping for breath on top of her.

"That was incredible . . . you . . . were . . . incre-di-ble," Chris panted, "and well worth the wait. I love you, Arizona."

Arizona stared up at him in disbelief. She blinked hard as Chris rolled off her, said a few words about how sorry he was that he hadn't lasted longer but that he'd make up for it the next time, then lay on his back and began to snore.

"What the hell just happened?" she whispered inside her head. Still confused and completely puzzled by what she'd just experienced, she leaned over to the nightstand and turned on the light because now she was eager to see and confirm what she feared. She moved over toward Chris and slowly pulled the comforter away from his body.

"Lord have mercy, sweet Jesus!" she whispered, then clasped her hand to her mouth. Now it was undeniably clear to her why she hadn't felt Chris penetrate her. His penis was not the size she'd expected at all. She'd heard stories about men who had a micropenis but never thought Chris would be one of them.

Arizona was snapped back into the present when her right leg tingled with numbness from sitting atop the hard commode for so long. She flushed the toilet for good measure and then walked to the sink and washed her hands. She'd imagined that her first time with Chris would be a magical experience, but instead it seemed more like a frighteningly bad dream. She looked into the mirror once again and shook her head. She knew what she needed to do was go back to the bedroom, tell Chris that she needed to go home, and then have a serious talk with God about what to do.

Arizona took a deep breath and walked out the door. She nearly lost her balance when she saw Chris lying propped on his elbow with the sheet pulled back on her side of the bed.

"Are you ready for round two?" he said with a wide, eager smile.

# Chapter 4

## BERNADETTE

*Present Day*

It was Friday, the start of the weekend, and Bernadette knew she should be thankful and happy on this day, not just because she was healthy and gainfully employed, lived in a beautiful home, drove a luxury vehicle, and had friends and family who loved her. She knew she should be thankful and happy because today marked another year of life. Today was her birthday, and she'd reached a milestone that quite a few of her friends, both from childhood and college, had not been blessed to see. Today Bernadette was fifty years old.

"A half century," she whispered to herself in half amazement and half disbelief. "Thank you, Jesus, for blessing me to make it this far, because Lord knows things could have gone in a different direction." Bernadette sat straight up in her bed and leaned back against her plush, tufted headboard. She pulled her comforter up to her shoulders to ward off the slight chill in the air. She inhaled a deep breath, trying to wrap her head around the enormity of the moment, and after it finally sank in, fear and worry soon followed.

"Wow, I'm really fifty," she said as she looked around her large bedroom and then over toward the empty space next to her. She stared at the untouched side of her 1600 thread count sheet covered bed, and frowned. Ever since her traumatic breakup with Walter five years ago, she'd sworn off relationships. She hadn't even gone out on a casual date since then. But six months ago, after moving to the small town of Bourbon, North Carolina, and with her milestone birthday looming, she'd begun to rethink many things in her life, including companionship.

Bernadette had worked hard over the last few years, pouring all her energy into accelerating her career, which had left little time for a personal life, and that had been perfectly fine with her because it had filled the void of not having a man in her life. The fast pace of the Washington, DC, political and social scene had kept her occupied and relatively content, or so she'd thought. But several months ago she received an offer she couldn't refuse; a lucrative six-figure salary along with an equally attractive bonus and exceptional perks and benefits package. The catch was that she had to move from the nation's capital where she'd been born and raised, to a small Southern town that carried the same name as a distilled alcoholic beverage.

"Where in the world is Bourbon?" she'd asked Hewitt Long, CEO of Trudent Health Systems, one of the largest hospital systems in the country. Hewitt Long had flown from North Carolina to DC to woo Bernadette into accepting the job.

"It's a nice little town nestled in the heart of eastern North Carolina," Hewitt had said. "Have you ever been to North Carolina?"

Bernadette nodded. "Yes, I visited once because my cousin graduated from Winston-Salem State University, an HBCU, which is an Historically Black College or University," she added, quickly giving Hewitt the meaning to explain the acronym, "that was located in Winston-Salem. I flew down there for her graduation. But that was years and years ago. Other than that visit I don't know much about the state, and certainly not Bourbon."

"Trust me, you'll love it there." Hewitt smiled. "Bourbon is close to beautiful beaches and historic landmarks. That part of the state is also known for good food and friendly folks who look out for each other. Best of all, it's home to one of the finest state-of-the-art hospitals in the region, and if you accept the position, which I sincerely hope you will, it will be a great new beginning for you."

When Bernadette had flown down to the small town for her final interview she hadn't been impressed. Although the hospital was state of the art, as Hewitt had said, the town, its energy, and its residents seemed way too slow for her taste. But the pay was great, and with the low cost of living in that area she figured she would only need to work five more years before she would be able to comfortably retire and live like a queen. So she packed up the only life she'd ever known in DC and headed down south.

Now, sitting in her bed, all alone, she suddenly realized that she'd created a very insular existence, and she didn't feel at all comfortable about the prospects of growing old all by herself. She didn't have a mate, children, or even a pet, all of which she thought she would have had at this stage of her life.

Bernadette was jarred from her thoughts when she heard her cell phone ring. Her mother had already called to wish her happy birthday, followed by her aunt Anna, and now the call that she'd been waiting for—and knew would come because it was a tradition—was now ringing.

"Happy birthday, cuzzo!" Tess screamed through the phone. "How does it feel to be half a century old?"

Bernadette chuckled and let out a sigh. "You really do have a way with words."

"What else would you expect from a writer?"

"Something a bit more expressive and slightly less abrasive."

Tess laughed through the phone. "I wouldn't be me if I was any other way. Besides, my charming personality brings excitement to your life, which you know you need."

Bernadette had to admit that Tess was right. Her cousin's wildly creative and free-spirited character was a stark contrast to Bernadette's button-up, play-by-the-rules personality. "Yes, I guess you're right, dear cousin. And by the way, happy birthday to you, too!" Bernadette said, trying to sound much more cheerful than the gloomy mood she was trying to keep at bay. "How does it feel to be the big 4-0?"

"Girl, stop!" Tess playfully scolded. "I'm not going to be forty for another ten years."

"How do you figure that? We were born on the same day, exactly ten years apart, which is one reason why I'll never forget your birthday or your age, even if you do," Bernadette said as she playfully laughed.

Bernadette had always considered Tess more like her sister than her cousin, and their blood bond transcended them into being best friends. Their mothers were sisters who were each other's best friend as well, and they talked on the phone every single day. Bernadette's mother, Rosa, was several years younger than her sister, Anna, who along with her husband had waited until later in life to have children. But even with their two daughters' significant age difference, the two sisters had made sure that their girls, who were each only children, had grown up to be just as close as Rosa and Anna had. They had been born at the same hospital, on the same day, at the same hour, exactly ten years apart, and their bond was unbreakable.

"Yeah, I know, and how could I forget? Our mothers remind us all the time," Tess said. "And for the record, if my mom tells me one more time about how people from her old neighborhood still use our birthdays to play the numbers to this day, I might just jump off a building."

Bernadette shook her head and chuckled. "Our mothers are definitely sisters because my mom does the same thing, and as a matter of fact she just reminded me of that this morning."

"I believe it because my mom did, too."

Bernadette pressed the button on her Keurig and watched the caffeinated brown liquid fill her cup. She looked out of her kitchen window and saw that clouds were beginning to form. "I'm not sure if I can get used to this North Carolina weather," she said as she stirred her coffee. "Just five minutes ago it was bright and sunny, and now it looks like it's going to snow, and that's the last thing I want on my birthday."

"Remember last year when it snowed on our birthday?" Tess asked.

"How could I forget? I thought I was gonna have to get bail money and a good lawyer that day."

"I know, right?"

"Whew, thank goodness I didn't," Bernadette said. They were referring to the terrible incident that happened when Tess found out that her boyfriend of two years, whom she'd thought was the one, had cheated on her. At the time, Bernadette could only chalk up her cousin's actions to a rage of fury. Tess had vandalized the man's home and then threatened to kill him when she had finally answered his happy birthday phone call later that evening.

Bernadette could still remember the hurt and pain she'd heard in Tess's voice as she'd recounted what she'd done and what had driven her to that point of rage. Bernadette had wanted to be the big-sister voice of reason, but she'd known there hadn't been much she could have said because just a few years prior to Tess's outburst, Bernadette had beaten her own ex-fiancé to a pulp after catching him in unscrupulous lies on top of deceit and fraud.

Tess sighed. "To this day I still don't understand why Antwan didn't have me arrested. I even threatened to kill his lyin' ass, but he didn't take the bait."

"Unlike that scumbag Walter, Antwan wasn't a bad person. He was just immature and misguided. The bottom line was that he simply wasn't ready to settle down."

"Then he should've told me that instead of stringing me along."

*In so many ways he did*, Bernadette thought, but didn't say. "I think he probably felt really guilty about what he did."

"You're giving him entirely too much credit," Tess huffed, "I think he didn't want folks in his business. You know how paranoid he was about keeping his private life under wraps."

"Yeah, that's true. But maybe he also felt remorseful."

"Last time I checked, the devil didn't have feelings of guilt or remorse."

Bernadette could hear the bitter hurt that still rested in Tess's voice, and every now and then whenever Antwan's name would come up in conversation, Tess would become emotional. Bernadette didn't want this to turn into a man-bashing party, so she decided to change the subject. "Tell me what kind of exciting plans you have for today. Celebrating twenty-five years of life is a milestone," she teased. "I know you're gonna party until the wee hours of the morning, so do tell."

"Actually, I'm not doing a thing."

"Come again?"

"I don't have any plans."

Bernadette shook her head. "Um, are you sure you're Testimony Sinclair? The beautiful, fun-loving life of the party who always does it big on her birthday doesn't have any plans?"

"I'm serious, Bernadette. It's as cold as Antarctica outside, I'm tired, and I have no desire to get dressed up and fight crazy crowds on a Friday night just to hang out with a bunch of people who're gonna get drunk, tell me how good I look to be so old, and then talk about me behind my back. I don't have the patience for bullshit anymore . . . especially seeing that I'm middle age and everything."

"Since when is twenty-five middle age?"

"Since someone very wise told me the truth about that 'forty is the new twenty-five' bullshit."

The two women burst into shared laughter again.

"I'm serious," Tess said, shifting her tone. "I don't know about you, Bernadette, but I've been doing a lot of thinking lately, about what I really want and what my future holds. Things are different, life is different, and I'm different. The things that used to satisfy me now make me nervous as hell. The truth is . . . I'm scared, Bernadette. I'm a forty-year-old woman with no man, no children, a big lonely house, and an empty bed."

Bernadette let out a loud sigh. "Tess, you're also a *New York Times* best-selling author with thousands of adoring readers across the country and overseas. You live in a beautiful house that is completely paid for, you're healthy and in your right mind, and to top it all off, you're gorgeous. Concentrate on that!"

Even though Bernadette had just rattled off her cousin's glowing good points—which were completely true—she fully understood and deeply felt every word that Tess had said because they were things that Bernadette thought about her own life. She took a small sip of her coffee and looked out the window at the dark clouds covering the sky. "Tess, can I confess something to you?"

"Of course."

"I've been thinking the same thing. Ever since I moved here to Bourbon, I've been looking at life differently, and for the first time in a very long time I want companionship. I want a man."

The line was silent.

"Are you there?" Bernadette asked.

"I'm here," Tess answered. "I'm just thinking about what you said, and, cuzzo, I'm here to tell you that there's nothing wrong with that."

"I thought that my career and material success could ease some of the loneliness that I feel. But it doesn't."

"I completely understand. I go out on dates and when I need a sexual release there are a few guys I can call. But I don't have a man, I mean a real man, and honestly, I'd like one, too."

Bernadette nodded. "Right now I'd give up my next paycheck if I thought it would get me a good man."

"Whoa, whoa, whoa! Girl, there ain't that much dick in the world!" Tess scoffed.

"I'm not talking about just any ol' guy, I'm talking about a man. Someone who's honest, kind, thoughtful, respectful, mature, and has his life together."

"That's a very, and I mean very, tall order."

"Why do you think I'm still single?" Bernadette left her kitchen, strolled down her long hallway to her spacious walk-in closet, and searched for a pair of leggings. She wanted to get in an early morning workout, and because it was cold outside, she'd decided to work out in her home gym downstairs in her basement. "But like I said," she continued, "ever since I moved here to Bourbon, I've been thinking about what it would be like to be in a loving relationship with a real man. I don't know if it's because of the fact that I'm in a new town with new people and I just want someone to spend time with, or if it's my age kicking in? I'm not sure. But what I do know is that I'm tired of coming home to a big, empty house with no one here to fill up the space but me and my thoughts."

"Same here," Tess agreed. "It's probably a combination of both, Bernadette. Honestly, it's tiring having to shoulder everything by yourself and walk through this world alone. Antwan did me wrong for sure, but it wasn't all bad. There were times that were great and nearly blissful. I still remember how safe, loved, and at ease I used to feel at the thought that I knew that no matter what had gone on throughout the course of my day, I had someone I could lean on and I didn't have to go through all the bullshit alone."

"That's what I'm talking about," Bernadette responded as she slipped out of her bathrobe and nightgown and into her workout top and bottom. She looked at her body in the mirror and felt proud of the fact that at fifty years old she had the shape and tone of a woman who was much younger. "Even though I know that all the sweet things Walter did had been a lie, the feeling I used to have was incredible. I want that feeling again, only this time I want it to be real . . . and lasting."

The line was silent as Bernadette and Tess both reflected on the truths they had each shared. Finally, Tess broke the quiet. "I told you my plans for today, so how about you? Are you going to do the usual?"

Bernadette always celebrated her birthday by treating herself to a delicious meal at a five-star restaurant. There was a time when eating alone didn't bother Bernadette, even on special days like this. But just like many things, this was something she no longer found appealing. However, since she didn't have better options, she decided she might as well have a good meal in her attempt to curb her other hunger.

"Yes," Bernadette responded. "I'm going to have my annual birthday dinner and then come home and cuddle up with my pillow. Somehow it just doesn't sound as satisfying as it used to."

"If I'd been thinking, I should've booked a flight to come there and we could celebrate together," Tess offered. "We haven't done that in ages."

"That would've been nice. I miss you, Tess."

"I miss you too, cuzzo. I'm in my writing cave right now—which is another good reason for me to stay in tonight—but as soon as I finish this book I'm working on, I'm gonna take a flight down there so I can see what kind of *Green Acres* situation you're living in."

Bernadette laughed. "Actually, and I know you'll be surprised to hear this, but Bourbon isn't that bad." She startled herself with her words. "I kind of like it here."

"Get outta here."

"I'm serious. I didn't ever think I'd enjoy living in a town like this, but I do. The cost of living is low, the people are friendly, the neighborhoods and streets are safe and clean. Girl, people down here are so polite it's scary. They speak and wave even if they don't know you!"

"That's called Southern hospitality."

Bernadette nodded on the other end as she pulled her leggings over her thighs. "I'm still trying to get used to strangers speaking and grinning at me."

"Isn't it crazy? I remember for that brief period of time when I lived in North Carolina during my college days, I constantly gave folks the serious side-eye because every time I walked down the street I met someone new. I thought it was a setup."

"Me too! One day I was like, do they have a decoy waiting behind the building to jump me and take my money?"

The two sister-cousins enjoyed a good laugh as they continued to talk about the surprising virtues of the South.

A half hour later Bernadette was breathing at a steady pace as she jogged on her treadmill. Her thoughts were racing just as fast as her feet were moving, still digesting the revealing conversation she'd had with Tess. Bernadette didn't want to feel sorry for herself, because as she'd reminded herself that morning, she had a lot to be thankful for. But at the same time she couldn't help but feel the very human emotion of longing that until now she had been able to push to a quiet place in her mind and out of her heart.

After Bernadette's workout, she took a long, relaxing shower, changed into a cozy pink chenille lounge set, and curled up on her couch with a cup of tea and one of Tess's books that she enjoyed rereading because it was one of her favorites. As she prepared to get lost in the pages a strange sensation overtook her. She couldn't explain why, but for some reason she had a feeling that she was headed for a life-changing experience. Normally, an unexplained feeling like this would have worried Bernadette because she was so cautious and pragmatic. But instead, she felt calm, and she welcomed the new experience.

"I'm ready for whatever's ahead," Bernadette whispered.

# Chapter 5

## TESS

"Just a minute," Tess yelled from down the hall. She was on her way to the door to retrieve her pizza from the delivery guy. She looked through the peephole and then opened the door to feel the rush of cold air whip around her slim body. "That was quick," she said, "and not a moment too soon because I'm starving."

"Oh my goodness!" the excited young man shouted. "You're Tess Sinclair, the author! My mother reads all your books . . . that's how I recognized you."

Tess was always startled whenever someone knew who she was, especially if the person happened to be a man, because the overwhelming majority of her readers were women. But ever since she'd sold the movie rights to one of her novels last year and had appeared on *Good Morning America* alongside actress Gabrielle Union, who'd been cast to play the lead role, she'd been "almost famous," as she liked to call it. "You'll have to thank your mother for me. I appreciate her support." Tess reached out to take the pizza, which she'd already paid for when she placed the order, but the delivery guy continued to hold on to the large, square box.

"My mom's not going to believe that I delivered a pizza to Tess Sinclair." He grinned.

Tess nodded and smiled. "Yep, that's me. And again, please tell her I said thanks a million for her support."

"There must be a lot of other famous people in this neighborhood, being that it's so fancy and all."

"Um, can I have my pizza now? It's getting kind of cold standing in this doorway."

"Oh, my bad. Sorry about that, Ms. Sinclair."

The young man still didn't let go of the box, and Tess's patience was beginning to wear thin. "I really need to get back to work. I already paid online and I included your tip." Tess took the pizza box out of the delivery guy's hand, stepped back, and was about to close the door when the young man stopped her with a request.

"Ms. Sinclair, can I take a picture with you? I want to send it to my mom and let her know that I met her favorite author!"

Tess had hoped the young man wouldn't ask her to take a picture with him because she had no intention of engaging in the simple exercise. She'd taken that position not because her face was bare of makeup, or because her wild curls were fighting to maintain their shape in her three-day-old bun, or because she was wearing a misshapen, oversized sweatshirt that was still nursing a stain from the spaghetti she'd spilled on it yesterday. She didn't want to take a picture with the young man because she knew that immediately after he snapped the photo it would make its rounds on social media before he reached his car parked in her long driveway, and Tess didn't want that to happen on today of all days.

Today was her birthday, and instead of celebrating in some grand fashion, the world would see that the renowned Tess Sinclair was spending her special day holed up in her house with an extra-large veggie thin crust from Sophia's Pizzeria. *How pathetic am I?* Tess thought to herself.

She once again quickly explained to the delivery guy that she was in a rush to get back to work, but that she would see to it that extra money would be added on to his tip. That seemed to satisfy the guy, and within a few seconds he was gone.

"It's a shame, but everything comes down to the dollar," Tess said.

She walked into her gourmet cook's kitchen that she'd never pre-pared a single meal in, and put two slices of pizza on a plastic dispos-able plate. "What kind of wine do I want?" she questioned aloud, wishing the silence in her house could somehow answer her. The re-ality of her thoughts made Tess pause and drew her back to the con-versation she'd had with her cousin that morning.

Even though they were ten years apart in age, they shared many things in common. Both were educated, highly successful, independent single women with no children. And after Tess's conversation with Bernadette, she'd learned that they were both at a crossroads in their lives when it came to their romantic relationships.

Tess walked over to the butler's pantry off the kitchen and dining room and selected a vintage red wine. She reached into the cabinet above and retrieved the largest wineglass she could find. "I need an Olivia Pope–size drink tonight." Tess sighed, referencing the fictional character who she wished could magically appear and handle her fledgling love life the way Olivia had handled her clients on the once wildly popular TV drama *Scandal*.

Tess balanced the pizza, wineglass, and unopened bottle in her arms and carefully negotiated each step up the grand staircase leading to her home office. "Back to the writing cave," she said, trying to muster up the desire, focus, and energy to write. She placed her food and drink on the small table in the corner that she'd designated as her eating section of the room. Because working on a novel required hours upon hours, days upon days, and months upon months of quiet, uninterrupted time, Tess had outfitted her office to comfortably ac-commodate the endless hours she spent in the space. She had one sec-tion set up with a desk, chair, computer, and lamps for writing. Another section was outfitted with a soft and luxurious sofa bed, plush pillows, and cozy throws so she could lie down and relax when she grew tired. And the section she was sitting in now was designated for meals and was equipped with a dinette set, a mini fridge, microwave, and an armoire turned snack station.

Tess was under deadline for her next novel, which as of that week was past due. In the fifteen years since she had written her first *New York Times* best seller, Tess had never missed a deadline, nor had she had any trouble cranking out her signature drama-filled mystery novels that had made her a small fortune and a household name with readers. But lately, nothing had seemed as it used to be in Tess's life. Her desire to go out and party had dwindled and her focus on writing had waned.

"What the hell's wrong with me?" Tess said as she took a huge bite of her pizza. Sauce dripped onto her sweatshirt, landing in the same spot where she'd spilled spaghetti yesterday. She looked down at the mess and shook her head. Whenever she was holed up in her writing cave trying to meet a deadline, it wasn't uncommon for her to sport sweats, mismatched socks, and messy hair. But not the same clothes two days in a row. "I need to pull it together," Tess said with determination. She poured herself a glass of wine and took a sip. "I need to refocus my mind before I start back writing. Maybe I just need to clear my head with some mindless stimulation."

Tess picked up her phone and decided to scroll through her Instagram feed while she ate her pizza and sipped her wine. She landed on Shartell Brown's page—her favorite online gossip columnist turned detective agency owner turned online gossip columnist again—when something caught her eye. Tess squinted and then clicked on the picture in question, and sure enough, it was her ex-boyfriend, Antwan Bolling. "What the fuck?!" Tess yelled out in disbelief as she peered closer. Antwan was standing in front of an elaborately decorated floral backdrop, holding hands with a tall beauty in a wedding dress.

Tess dropped her pizza onto her plate as her mind raced. She tried to zoom in on the picture because she'd left her reading glasses on her desk and couldn't see the image clearly. She walked over to her desk, slid her stylish reading glasses on her face, and logged onto her desktop computer so she could see the images in their full glory on her twenty-seven-inch monitor. Once she'd logged on, she went back to Shartell's page, located the photo, and gasped. Shartell's caption read:

> *@TheRealShartellBrown* . . . *After a six-month whirlwind romance, Pulitzer Prize Winning Journalist @AntwanBollingTheWriter and his beautiful new bride, celebrity makeup artist @MarieJettMy BlackIsBeautiful, wed in a lavish ceremony at the Ritz-Carlton, Buckhead. #blacklove #powercouple #relationshipgoals #thebollings #theywinning*

Tess cupped her mouth with one hand and shook her head from side to side. Antwan had been allergic to monogamy and was the most commitment-phobic person she'd ever dated. "I don't want to rush into anything too soon," he'd told Tess on countless occasions. Now, not only had he rushed in, he'd plunged headfirst.

"How can this be?" Tess asked herself. "I gave that man two good years of my life, but he couldn't stay faithful and didn't want to even think about marriage, and now he's sweepin' bitches off their feet in whirlwind romances?!" Tess was fuming with anger. She'd spent considerable time and energy trying to cultivate a meaningful relationship with Antwan, and now it seemed that he'd changed into a completely different person, and sadly, to the benefit of another woman. "I can't believe this!" Tess hissed aloud. But a little voice of reason inside Tess's head said, *Staying with him after he repeatedly cheated on and disrespected you was a choice that you made. He only did what you continually accepted and allowed him to do.*

Tess knew that the painful truth sounding off inside her head was valid. But right now she didn't give a flying flip about validity or rational thinking because an emotional voice whispered to her, *Girl, you need to do some investigating and find out how this happened and where you went wrong!* Tess had been so hurt and angry after their breakup that she'd blocked Antwan from all her social media accounts, and up until this moment she'd refused the temptation of trolling his. But now she was curious and she wanted to know what had been going on in his life to cause such a drastic change. Tess clicked on the hyperlink for Antwan's name and was taken to his page.

"That bastard!" Tess hissed. Antwan's profile picture was an image of him and his new bride, and it had apparently been taken last month during the Christmas holidays. The two were smiling, hugged up, looking disgustingly happy while wearing matching red cable knit sweaters and red and white Santa Claus hats. Tess clicked through photo after photo of the giddy couple posing inside what she knew to be Antwan's home, dining with friends, attending black tie events, and enjoying random fun around the city. But the coup de grace that literally made Tess stop breathing was a photo of the couple with Antwan's family, along with people who appeared to be his new wife's family, gathered around the two as Antwan knelt on one knee and proposed. Antwan's hashtags read #myhappilyeverafter #wifeymaterial #myforever.

"Un-freakin-believable!" Tess was incredulous. She'd had to practically bribe Antwan with tickets to a Washington Wizards basketball game in order to nudge him into going home with her to DC, to visit and meet her parents. She looked at the date of the post, which added insult upon injury. "That son of a bitch!" Tess screamed. "How could he?"

The date at the bottom of Antwan's post was a mere three months ago. "They only dated for six months, and he proposed three months ago, so that means he put a ring on her finger just a few months after we broke up!" Tess's anger had now risen to the state of fury. She'd given Antwan her heart, and in all that time he'd never been faithful, had never posted one single picture of the two of them on any of his social media pages—claiming he didn't want to share his private life with the world—but now he was spreading his personal business by posting and professing his love for another woman for the world to see.

Tess knew she shouldn't do it, but she couldn't resist clicking on @MarieJettMyBlackIsBeautiful's page. Tess formed her mouth into a scowl when she saw that the woman's profile picture was of her and

Antwan toasting with champagne-filled crystal flutes as the lights of the Eiffel Tower sparkled in the background. Paris was the place that Tess had told Antwan she'd wanted to go for her dream vacation. "I want to sip good wine, eat pastries, and walk the cobblestone streets of Paris," she'd told him several times, hoping he'd get the hint and surprise her with a romantic trip. She'd wanted to go so badly that one time she'd told him she would pay for the trip.

They never went.

Tess had felt a stab of betrayal when she'd seen Shartell Brown's post, but now she felt the jagged knife dig in and twist at her heart when she realized that the bride's wedding post, which read *Introducing the New Mrs. Bolling*, was dated today. "He married that bitch on my birthday! What kind of sick, revenge-type shit is that?" Tess pounded her fist on her desk as the painful memory flooded back to her from a year ago when she'd caught him cheating on her, on her birthday. Now he'd committed the ultimate betrayal by giving another woman the gift that Tess had wanted, and once again, he'd caused her pain on what was supposed to be her special day.

Her sadness and anger fueled her curiosity to see more photos. It was like the old cliché when people said they couldn't look away from a train wreck. Tess knew that scrolling through Marie's pictures would only further upset her, but she couldn't help herself. She read and looked through post after post of one happy photo after the other that mimicked Antwan's page, but Marie's page contained even more photos than Antwan's. As Tess dissected each picture, she had to admit that Marie Jett was stunningly gorgeous. She was an ex-model turned makeup expert and beauty influencer with an Instagram following of over half a million people. Her slender facial features, large afro, expressive brown eyes, long legs, thick hips, and overflowing cleavage made her the type of woman whom men wanted to be with and whom women wanted to be like. Tess wished she could trade places with the statuesque beauty.

After a few minutes, Tess had to make herself stop looking at the reminder of what could have been. She sat back in her chair and

rubbed her temples, which had begun to throb. She couldn't understand what she'd done wrong. She'd been faithful to Antwan. She'd
shown him love. She'd been thoughtful, attentive, and kind. She'd
been understanding and supportive of his deadlines and career. "I was
a damn good girlfriend to that low-life bastard . . . most of the time."
There were a few occasions when she'd cursed him out and had
"showed her ass," as her mother used to say, whenever she became
angry. But those times hadn't been many and had always been a result
of the lies she'd caught him in.

"He never wanted a commitment, never wanted to be faithful,
and the mutherfucker damn sure didn't want to get married. But here
he is, sharing his private life with the world and his last name with
some other heifer. What did I do wrong?" Tess asked aloud, as if
someone could give her the magic answer. Just then the answer came
to Tess as if it had been laid at her feet. She hadn't done anything
wrong, and even if she'd been the epitome of the perfect girlfriend
during their relationship, Antwan still wouldn't have been faithful to
her or asked her to marry him. She realized that the hard truth was
that Antwan did indeed want a commitment, he wanted to be faithful, and he wanted to share his private life with the world. He wanted
all those things, he just didn't want them with her.

# Chapter 6

## ARIZONA

From the time Arizona had been old enough to stand on her feet and bat her lashes, she'd had an insatiable appetite for and attraction to men, and unfortunately, her modus operandi was "the more inappropriate the better." She had developed an affinity for bad boys during her elementary school days. When she'd been in second grade, sweet and quiet little Sam Davis slipped her a piece of paper that read "Will you be my girlfriend?" with two spaces that had been left blank to indicate her response of yes or no. Arizona had swished her long ponytails to the side, smiled, and written NO in large letters with her #2 pencil. She sashayed over to Sam's desk, handed him what would be the first of many rejections for the awkward little boy, said, "I like Bobby Ray, and he's gonna be my boyfriend!" and then strutted her little feet back to her desk.

Bobby Ray Johnson was Arizona's oldest brother's best friend and also happened to be the neighborhood hoodlum. He'd been much older than Arizona and had barely known she'd existed outside of being his best friend's pesky, fast-tail little sister.

"This right here is some bullshit!" Bobby Ray had said when he'd been arrested for stealing from the neighborhood corner store. Arizona had thought he was bold and cuter than any boy she'd ever laid

eyes on. That had been the beginning of the end for Arizona's judgment when it came to men.

As Arizona grew into a teenager and then matured into a young
woman, her predilection for bad boys, danger, and trouble only grew.
She loved the swagger and excitement that the combination brought
in their wake. And in true Bonnie and Clyde fashion, she'd been the
typical ride-or-die chick who had perfectly complemented her men,
the majority of whom had either been fresh from prison or quickly
on their way there. She'd been a heavy drinking, club-hopping, foul-
mouthed young woman who'd only cared about having a good time
lying on her back with a man or partying until they turned the lights
on at the club.

Just as much as Arizona had loved bad boys, they'd loved her right
back. She'd been chunky as a child and thick as a teenager and had
grown into a voluptuously full-figured woman—attributes that were
greatly admired by the good ol' country boys in Bourbon. Arizona
was a Southern belle with spice. Her mother put considerable time
into trying to groom her into conducting herself like a lady, but Arizona's natural proclivity was anything but. She loved flaunting her
breasts in tight tank tops and corsets, and she squeezed her round hips
and thick thighs into miniskirts and stretch pants, which drove the
men in the clubs wild. Her womanly body and her pretty face gar-
nered Arizona attention, and she'd loved every minute of it.

But much to her parents' consternation, Arizona's reputation had
been well known around the Bottoms, the section of town in Bourbon, where her family had resided for more than five generations. Just
like Arizona, the Bottoms was equal parts gentility and roughness, and
even though Arizona had been constantly in trouble, she'd been surrounded by loving family, friends, and church members who'd been
in her corner whenever she'd needed them. When she'd gotten arrested for underage drinking, family and friends had been there to
catch her. When she'd wrecked both her parents' cars the summer
she'd gotten her driver's license, they'd been there to catch her. When
she'd blown a full academic scholarship at a four-year university be-

cause she'd partied her way to straight Fs, they'd been there to catch her. And when she'd gotten pregnant but hadn't had a clue as to who the father was because it had been a draw between three different men, she'd had love, support, and understanding to catch her.

Not knowing who'd gotten her pregnant had been one of the worst feelings of Arizona's life, but it had also signaled a momentous turning point that changed her. She'd known that it was a damning indictment about the reckless, out-of-control kind of life she'd been living, and she'd known that she didn't want her unborn child to end up the same way. Just as she'd loved bad boys from the moment she could stand on her two feet, the moment she'd learned she was pregnant, Arizona vowed to make a change.

Today, Arizona was a completely different woman. She was mature, stable, reliable, and responsible—and her five-year-old son, Solomon, was the reason she was the woman she'd grown into.

There was no doubt that Arizona was a very different person, and she'd changed in many ways, most notably, her choice in men. Chris Pendleton was proof of that. He was educated, gainfully employed, conscientious, well-respected, and levelheaded, and most of all, he was a kindhearted Christian man whom Arizona had prayed into her life. Chris was everything Arizona had asked God for, and up until last night, she'd thought God had delivered in spades. But now, as she looked into the mirror and applied her makeup—in preparation of treating herself to a celebratory dinner—she couldn't help but think about last night and the colossal disappointment it had been. She shook her head and sighed. "That's a huge shortcoming," she said as she slid the nude-colored glossy liquid across her full lips. "I still can't believe it. What am I gonna do?" she questioned out loud.

Today was Arizona's birthday, her thirtieth, to be exact, and she'd been excited about celebrating it for the last few months, and because this year her special day fell on the weekend, she planned to enjoy every minute of it. Today was her It's All About Me day, something she hadn't experienced since Solomon had been born. She had nowhere to be and her parents were keeping her son the entire weekend, which she'd been reluctant about at first, but she'd eventually warmed to the idea when her mother had explained the benefits.

"I know you don't want to be apart from your baby boy for so long," her mother had said, "but take it from me, Arizona, raising children only gets more challenging as they grow, so take advantage of this time while you can."

Arizona had thought about her mother's sage advice, which was always on point. This was an opportunity for her to do simple things like walk around the house naked if she wanted to, cook or not cook a meal, or lie in bed until noon, which she'd done today. This part of her birthday was what she'd dreamed it would be. But when her mind drifted back to last night, she was reminded that one of the most important bonds she'd been looking forward to with Chris had been a huge disappointment.

Arizona bristled as she swept the almond-hued finishing powder over her face to set her flawless makeup. She was a very attractive woman, and once she "beat her face" she knew her good looks were taken straight to gorgeous. She smiled in the mirror at herself, but then frowned as her mind went back to Chris and his small penis. She wanted to cry.

"Why, Lord, why?" Arizona said as she looked up at the ceiling. "I know you've put me through some tests, and I've overcome them all, but this right here . . ." Arizona took a deep breath, pounded her fist on the bathroom countertop. "This is just downright cruel."

Arizona's mind flashed back to the moment last night when she'd first realized that Chris's manhood was micro. He'd been on top of her, moaning and grinding hard in a steady rhythm. But all Arizona had felt was Chris's pelvic bone bumping and rubbing against hers. She'd initially thought that he'd purposely positioned himself that way so he could make a big and memorable impact when he finally did enter her. After a few minutes of the hard movements, he'd shifted his weight, positioned himself in the middle of her thighs, and thrust hard.

"Oh, baby! Oh, baby," Chris had panted.

Arizona's face had gone blank because she hadn't been able to figure out what was going on. He was moving between her legs, simulating something similar to intercourse, but there was no feeling inside her other than the throbbing sensation of needing to have her itch scratched.

"Baby, you feel so good! *Oh, Oh, Oooh.*" Chris had breathed heavy as he'd continued to simulate sex.

Panic had grown inside Arizona as she'd begun to awaken to the realization of what was happening. She'd opened her eyes and looked into Chris's face. His forehead had been creased with a thick bead of sweat, his teeth had been gritted as if he'd clenched down on food, and his eyes had been closed in deep, concentrated ecstasy as he'd continued to make in-and-out thrusting motions. Then suddenly, Chris's movements had sped up to a jackhammer frenzy before he'd yelled out with carnal satisfaction.

*"That was incredible . . . you . . . were . . . icre-di-ble,"* Chris had shouted before lowering his full weight upon Arizona's chest. He'd breathed and panted as if he'd just chopped down a tree.

Arizona's mind had been dizzy with confusion and horror. *Did he just come?* she'd thought to herself. *No, he couldn't have . . . could he?* But the larger question that remained, which she'd regretfully already known the answer to, was where was his penis? Arizona had known the only explanation had to be that he'd been so small that it had been unrecognizable to her vagina.

"Baby, I love you, and I'm sorry," Chris had gently whispered.

His words had jarred Arizona out of her fog of shock and questions and back into the horrible moment. "What did you say?"

"I said I love you and I'm sorry," Chris had continued. "I know for our first time you were expecting our lovemaking to last much longer, and so was I. But you felt so good, baby, and this felt so right that I got caught up in the moment, and before I knew it I gave in too soon. But I promise you, I'll make it last the next time."

Arizona's eyes had shrunk with worry as she had tried to envision
what a next time with Chris would be like. She'd taken a deep breath
and fixed her eyes on the alarm clock sitting on the nightstand. Four
minutes. Four short but infinite minutes. That's how long Chris's and
her mystery lovemaking session had lasted. From the time they'd
crawled under the covers until he'd collapsed on top of her chest.

Arizona had taken another deep breath and turned on her side in
order to face Chris and have a very difficult but honest conversation
with her fiancé. Yet as she'd opened her mouth, he had, too, and out
came the unmistakable sound of snoring.

*I can't believe this man just fell asleep on me!* Arizona had shouted in
her head. She had been dazed and livid at the same time. Still not
wanting to believe what she knew was true, she'd pulled back the
comforter to take a look at what Chris was working with.

*Oh no! Oh no!* she'd repeated in her head. She had known that
after men ejaculated, their penises shrank, but it would require a man
to have a semblance of a penis in the first place, and as Arizona stared
at Chris's genital area, the only thing visible had made her want to cry.
There was little, if anything there.

Arizona had known she had to get up and clear her head, so she'd
gone to the bathroom for some space. She'd sat on the commode and
thought things over so long that her leg had gone to sleep. When
she'd heard the door crack and Chris asked her if she was okay, she
had decided she needed to come back out. As soon as she'd crawled
into the bed Chris's eyes had opened, his lips had formed a smile, and
he'd said he was ready for round two. And as he'd promised, the second time had indeed lasted longer. Exactly one minute longer . . . on
the dot. And unfortunately, Arizona had experienced the same dis-
pleasure as she had the first time.

Arizona's mind was brought back to the present when she heard
the buzzing of her cell phone. "Chris," she sighed. She startled herself
because for the first time since she'd started dating Chris, she wasn't
excited about seeing his name and number appear on her phone's

screen. She closed her eyes, took a deep breath, and answered his call. "Hey, babe."

"Happy birthday to my beautiful, gorgeous, awesome, fantastic, fabulously luscious bride-to-be!" Chris sang into the phone.

"Thank you, babe." Arizona forced a smile into her voice. "How's your day going? Is work busy?"

Chris was the general manager at the St. Hamilton, Bourbon's only upscale boutique hotel. He'd started working in the hospitality industry when he was a college student at North Carolina Central University, and then had transferred to Morehouse College, both of which had been worlds away from his home in Queens, New York. Chris had applied himself at work just as he had in school, and had risen from being a bellman, to room service staff, on to being a front desk clerk, to working in sales, and then eventually securing a management position with Hilton Hotels upon graduating magna cum laude with a degree in business administration.

Chris's hard work ethic, professionalism, and honesty were just a few of the many qualities that Arizona loved about him. He'd been promoted to general manager six months ago, shortly after he'd proposed to Arizona, and in that time he'd made a tremendous turnaround in the hotel's function and the staff's satisfaction, which was all for the better. Lately, things had been super busy and Chris had been working long hours to keep up with all his projects and tasks.

"My day is going well," Chris replied. "Cold, but well, especially now that I'm talking to my beautiful birthday girl. I knew you were sleeping in this morning and that's why I held off on calling you until now. But I couldn't wait any longer. I had to hear the voice of the woman I love, and welcome you to the thirty-and-over club," Chris said.

Arizona could hear Chris's excitement through the phone. She wanted to feel the same enthusiasm, especially because it was her birthday, and the love of her life had called and was showering her with loving and adoring words. But she couldn't bring herself to a level of excitement that matched Chris's. "Thanks for welcoming me to the club. I feel good."

"You sure?" Chris asked. "You sound like you just woke up . . . Did I wake you?"

"No, I've been up. I guess I'm just a little tired."

"Oh . . ."

Arizona knew that Chris's next question was going to be, *I know you, Arizona, what's wrong?* so she beat him to it. "I've been doing some deep thinking, reflecting, and praying since I woke up," she offered, which was true.

"A milestone birthday will do that. I did the same thing when I turned thirty, two years ago before we started dating."

"So you know what I mean."

"Yes, I do," Chris affirmed.

"I'm glad you understand. I feel grateful and thankful to God for another year of life. But I'm also a little scared. I mean, I'm no longer twenty, and time is gonna rush even faster."

"And that's okay, baby. I got you. Whatever you feel, whatever you want, whatever you need, I'm here for you."

Arizona knew that Chris meant every word he'd just said, and as she walked over to her closet, fishing through the growing selection of clothes, courtesy of her fiancé, that were draped on pink plastic hangers she knew was part of the proof of his declaration. She'd always been a plus size woman, but after giving birth to Solomon, she'd gained more than fifty additional pounds that had taken up residence around her body and seemed to have no intention of moving any time soon. Her weight, combined with her tight budget as a single mother, had once left her wardrobe sparse. But ever since she'd started dating Chris, he'd made sure that she, and Solomon, had clothes, shoes, food, toiletries, and anything else they needed. Arizona felt a pinch of guilt as she ran her hand over a cashmere sweater that Chris had bought her a few months ago.

"I don't deserve you, Chris Pendleton."

"No such thing, Arizona Mays. You deserve more than me, but I promise you with everything I have inside me, I'm going to work my butt off to make sure that you're happy."

"Babe . . . why do you love me?" Arizona hadn't meant to blurt out the question, but she couldn't help but ask him because of the growing conflict she'd begun to feel deep in the pit of her stomach.

Chris chuckled on the other end. "Wow, you didn't lie when you said you've been thinking and reflecting."

"I told you . . . but seriously, why?"

Chris didn't hesitate with his answer. "Love is a mixture of feelings and actions. I feel deeply connected to you, Arizona. When we first met I was attracted to your beauty, your infectious smile, and your wit. Every time I looked at you I felt good inside. As I got to know you, and especially after we started dating, I was drawn to different things, like how loving and caring you are, how strong and hardworking, how thoughtful you are, how you sacrifice to take care of Solomon, and me, too. The actions you showed every day reinforced my love.

"Arizona," he continued, "it's hard to find what we have in each other. I prayed for you and you prayed for me, and on my end, God gave me what I asked for . . . actually, he gave me a lot more. That's why I know without any doubt that I love you."

The same pinch of guilt she'd felt just moments ago had come back and was growing into full-on pain. Arizona couldn't believe that she was letting something as little—literally speaking—as a small penis get in the way of her big blessing, which was a good man who loved her, and whom she loved. "You're an amazing man," Arizona said with sincerity. "Thank you for loving me, despite my flaws."

"That's what real life is all about."

Arizona had a mountain of thoughts flying through her mind and she needed time to digest her feelings. But just as he always did, Chris stepped in to save her, even if this time it was unintentional.

"Listen, baby, I've got to get back to work. But I hope you have a wonderful dinner tonight and I'll see you in the morning for breakfast."

Arizona and Chris said their goodbyes and she went back to her troubled thoughts. She knew she needed guidance on this matter, but the subject was so sensitive that she didn't know who she could turn to for direction as well as discretion. One thing that she'd learned from growing up in a small town was that everybody seemed to know their neighbor's business. Arizona looked up, closed her eyes, and took her worries to God.

# Chapter 7

## BERNADETTE

"I'd like to start with the smoked salmon crostini and a glass of Veuve Clicquot," Bernadette said to the attentive server. She'd asked to be seated in a quiet part of the Magnolia Room, the upscale, sophisticated restaurant that was only five minutes from her house in the exclusive Palisades section of town.

Bernadette had almost decided against treating herself to dinner tonight. But after an hour of volleying the thought back and forth through her mind, she'd decided to brave the cold and celebrate her birthday with a good meal, as she had done on so many birthdays in the past. But she'd known this birthday was different. A half century was a big deal, and even though this was the first birthday she could remember that she hadn't been at all thrilled about eating dinner alone, Bernadette had known that going out to enjoy a delicious meal would be a lot better than putting a frozen pizza in the oven while she watched old DVDs by herself.

Once she'd decided she was going out, next came the decision about what to wear, and because she'd only planned to be at the restaurant for an hour or less, she hadn't wanted to get dressed up. But then a thought had occurred to her. "This might be my lucky night," Bernadette had said to herself. "Who knows, I might meet someone, and if we hit it off, I want to look good." She paused and closed her eyes. "God, please let me meet someone tonight. Someone who's kind, and good, and above all, straight up and honest."

She walked into her large closet and glided her delicately manicured hands across the silk blouses, tailored jackets, slim pencil skirts, and men's inspired trousers, all hanging in neat, color-coded order. She knew she should probably wear a thick sweater because it was cold outside, but she wanted to look sophisticated with a touch of sexy, and a sweater wasn't going to cut it. "Hell, even if I don't meet a soul tonight, I want to look good for my own benefit," she'd said.

She'd decided on a fitted long-sleeve black and white silk blouse. She looked at herself in her floor-length mirror as she slid a black leather skirt over her small hips. "If I wasn't afraid that I'd end up with possible life-threatening complications I'd get butt injections," Bernadette said as she sized up her flat backside. "Oh well, it is what it is."

She accessorized her outfit with a dainty pair of gold hoop earrings and matching bracelet, then topped off her look with black suede stiletto boots. For the finishing touch, Bernadette picked up her bottle of Tiffany & Co. perfume and lightly spritzed each side of her neck before doing the same to her wrists. She swept the front of her shoulder length hair to one side and pinned the rest up into a neat chignon that rested at the nape of her neck. "Perfect," she said, giving herself a stamp of approval. Satisfied with her look, Bernadette wrapped her brown Alpaca cape around her body and braved the cold.

Now, sitting in the warmth of the restaurant, Bernadette wasn't so sure it had been a good idea to go out after all. She'd purposely decided to go early because she'd known that the later she waited on a Friday night, the more crowded it would be. But it was barely five o'clock and the place was packed.

"I'm dining alone, is there a section that's quiet and more secluded?" Bernadette had asked, looking around the main dining room that was big and opulent enough to host an elaborate wedding reception.

The bubbly hostess nodded. "Yes, we have a more intimate seating option," she said and then paused. "It's where we usually sit our couples. Is that okay with you?"

Bernadette didn't want to be a lone single woman surrounded by couples in love. "Do you have another section?"

"You can try the bar, but it's not as private."

So, to Bernadette's chagrin, she was seated in what she'd deemed Lover's Lane. If she'd had a date this would be the perfect spot. The room boasted low lighting, beautiful chandeliers, a fireplace on each side of the room, and beautiful fresh flowers and candles on each table. She looked around the romantic setting and wished God would answer the prayer she'd sent up before she'd stepped out.

"Would you like to order your entrée, ma'am?" the server asked Bernadette, pulling her mind back into the present.

"I think I'll need a little more time to look over the menu."

"No rush, ma'am. Take all the time you need," the attentive server responded. "In the meantime I'll bring out a selection of gourmet breads while you wait for your appetizer."

Bernadette smiled. "Thank you, and please bring out the Veuve when you can." Even though she wasn't sure about what she wanted to eat, she had no doubt that a glass of champagne was what she needed.

"Yes, ma'am. I'll make sure to get that out to you right away." He winked and quickly pranced away.

Bernadette continued to peruse the menu when she saw a familiar-looking woman heading her way behind the ultra-bubbly hostess. The attractive woman was tall and full-figured, with golden copper-colored skin that looked as if it had been kissed by the sun. The fact that she'd been able to achieve such radiance in the dead of winter impressed Bernadette. The woman strutted into the room wearing a cream-colored ribbed turtleneck, wide-legged herringbone trousers, and sleek stilettos that made her stand nearly six feet tall. She carried her tan-colored coat in the crook of one arm and what appeared to be a knock-off Berkin in the other.

Bernadette had a feeling of déjà vu, as if she'd already met the attractive woman, but she couldn't put her finger on where. In the six months since Bernadette had moved to Bourbon, she'd been consumed with work, so she hadn't gotten out much at all, and because it had been unseasonably cold outside over the last few months, that had further hindered her ability to explore her new surroundings. The hostess led the woman to the small table positioned directly beside Bernadette.

Now that the woman was in close range, Bernadette was even more sure that she knew her, but she still couldn't figure out the connection. As she discreetly inspected the plus-size beauty, it struck her that even though the woman was smiling, she didn't look happy, and it was as if she was trying to fool everyone around her into believing something that wasn't true. Bernadette recognized the expression all too well because it was one she wore nearly every day. She wondered why a woman like her was dining alone. Bernadette knew the same could be said for herself, but looking at the attractive lady, something told her that she definitely had a man. Then it suddenly occurred to Bernadette that the reason the woman looked unhappy was more than likely because her date had yet to arrive. Being stood up was also something that Bernadette was all too familiar with.

Once the woman was seated comfortably at her table, she looked around, and that's when she and Bernadette locked eyes. Bernadette could see that not only was the woman unhappy, she was also deep in thought according to the hard vertical line etched across her high forehead. Bernadette hoped the woman's date would get there within the next few minutes.

Bernadette was staring so hard that she knew it was obvious, so she decided to nip the awkwardness in the bud. "Hi." Bernadette nodded and smiled.

"Hi, how are you?" the attractive woman asked with a ring of familiarity.

"I'm well, and yourself?"

The woman nodded. "I'm blessed . . . and I'm ready to enjoy a good meal."

"Me too," Bernadette responded. "This is my first time here, is the food good?"

"It's my first time, too. But I've always heard great things about this place, and since it's the fanciest and the priciest restaurant in the whole county, it better be real good."

Bernadette smiled and nodded politely, noting that the woman spoke without a filter. "Well, that's nice to know."

"I've been wanting to come here for years, so I figured since today is my birthday it's a good reason to eat a delicious meal without having to cook it myself."

Bernadette lit up like a Christmas tree. "It's my birthday, too."

"Get outta here, are you serious?"

"Yes, I am. And let me say, happy birthday to you!"

"Right back at'cha," the woman said.

Bernadette smiled but didn't know what to say beyond that. She hoped the woman's dinner guest would arrive soon because the last thing she needed was to have to make polite but unsolicited conversation with a stranger. All she wanted to do was eat a fabulous dinner, have a good drink, and then go home and get a good night's sleep.

"Are you expecting company to help you celebrate?" the woman asked.

Bernadette knew that not only did the woman not have a filter, she was lacking subtlety as well. "No, I wanted a quiet evening, so I'm treating myself to dinner." She didn't ask the woman whether she was dining alone or not because Bernadette was sure she'd tell her.

The woman smiled wide and unknowingly obliged Bernadette's thoughts. "This is wild. I'm doing the same thing!"

Bernadette was surprised. The woman was young and very attractive and seemed to have an outgoing personality. Now Bernadette was curious about why a woman like her was flying solo on such an important day. And just like she'd known the woman would divulge whether she was dining alone, Bernadette was sure the woman would explain why she was there by herself. And as predicted, the woman answered the question that Bernadette didn't have to ask.

"I told my son, my fiancé, and the rest of my family and friends that the best birthday present they could give me was a day off from everything, including them."

Bernadette raised an eyebrow and smiled. "Wow. That's quite a request."

"Don't get me wrong," the woman said, shaking her head. "I love my family and my fiancé to pieces, but sometimes I get tired. I look out for everyone except myself, so I decided it was time that I had an It's All About Me day," she said with pride. "My parents are keeping my son, my fiancé is preparing for my birthday party tomorrow night. I'm having an early dinner and then I'm going to go home, soak in a hot tub of bubbles, drink a glass of wine, and relax. I haven't done that since before my son was born, which has been more than five years. I'm long overdue."

Now Bernadette understood the woman's statement, and she wished she'd had that same healthy respect for self-care when she was the woman's age. And truth be known, at the ripened age of fifty, Bernadette still didn't know how to say no, especially when it came to anything involving her professional career. "Good for you. That's a very healthy way to approach life."

"Thank you, Ms. Gibson."

Bernadette was startled when the woman called her by name. Looking familiar was one thing, but knowing Bernadette's name was another.

"You don't remember me, do you?" the woman asked with a chuckle.

"You look very familiar, but I can't remember where we've met. Obviously you know me, I just don't know from where."

"I work at Bourbon General in the payroll department. We met at the staff meeting last quarter when they announced you were the new VP. I shook your hand after the meeting and congratulated you."

"I knew I recognized you, and I should have remembered from where, especially being that you're a colleague. Please forgive my oversight."

The young woman smiled and waved her hand as if she was swatting the air. "No need to apologize. There were hundreds of people there, shaking your hand and welcoming you just like I did, so I didn't expect you to remember little ol' me."

"Well, it's good to meet you again." Bernadette leaned over and extended her hand for an introduction.

"Arizona Mays," the woman answered, "and it's good to meet you again as well, my fellow Aquarian." She gave Bernadette a genuine smile and a soft handshake.

Bernadette immediately noticed that Arizona's grip was more befitting someone much less commanding than she appeared to be. In Bernadette's high-power world of business, a firm handshake set the tone for what kind of person you were. Firmness equaled strength and success. Soft and gentle was akin to weakness and vulnerability, and Bernadette didn't have time for the latter. As she studied Arizona she wondered how much they had in common beyond the day they'd been born. "It's ironic that we share the same birthday," Bernadette said, "and that we chose to celebrate at the same restaurant, solo. What a coincidence."

"My mama says there's no such thing as irony, coincidence, or even luck. She says it's all God's way of remaining anonymous."

Just then the attentive server returned with a basket of gourmet bread for Bernadette, as well as a flute of bubbly champagne. "Thank you," Bernadette said.

"You're welcome, ma'am. Are you ready to order?" He smiled, turned slightly toward Arizona, and placed a basket of bread on her table as well. "I'll be with you in just a minute, ma'am," he said politely.

Bernadette shook her head and responded. "No, I'm afraid I'll need a few more minutes."

"Me too," Arizona said without being asked. "But what she's

drinking looks good." She eyed Bernadette's drink. "What kind of wine is that?"

"It's Veuve Clicquot," Bernadette answered. As soon as she said the words she knew by the blank stare on Arizona's face that the woman didn't have a clue, so she said, "I'm sorry, it's champagne."

"Oh . . ."

Bernadette looked at the server and smiled. "Please bring the lady a glass, on me."

Arizona shook her head. "No, you don't have to do that."

"I know I don't have to, but I want to."

"Well, thank you. That's very nice of you. I've never had Vuu . . . uh, whatchamacallit."

Bernadette chuckled. "There's a first time for everything." She smiled, but she noticed that Arizona didn't smile back.

"Yeah, I guess so."

The server spoke up. "A glass of champagne is on its way, ma'am. I'll be back shortly," he said before hurrying off.

Bernadette noticed that the woman looked as if she was in deep thought again and whatever was holding her attention couldn't be good. "Arizona, are you okay?"

"Actually, no, Ms. Gibson. I'm not."

"My name is Bernadette." She extended her hand to the chair in front of her. "Please, join me."

"Are you sure? I thought you said you wanted to have a quiet dinner by yourself."

"Initially, yes. I was going to have a solo celebration just like you. But where we differ is that I have me time every day of the week." Now Bernadette shared the same unhappy expression that Arizona wore on her face.

"Sounds like we could both use each other's company." Arizona rose from her seat, pulled out the chair at Bernadette's table, and sat down.

Just as she took her seat, the eager server came back with Arizona's glass of champagne. "Here you are, ma'am. I'll give you ladies time to look over your menus and I'll be back shortly."

"This came right on time," Arizona said. "I've never had champagne before."

Bernadette looked astonished. "Really?"

Arizona nodded. "I'm a down home country girl. I grew up on moonshine and Budweiser, and I've had plenty of both and everything in between. My fiancé, Chris, is gonna do a champagne toast for me tomorrow night, but I guess I'm beating him to the punch."

Bernadette could see that the mention of her fiancé made Arizona uneasy, and she wondered why. "Well, an evening of celebrating yourself is cause for champagne, in my opinion."

"Yes, out with my twenties and in with my thirties."

"You're a baby." Bernadette held her breath and braced herself for Arizona trying to guess her age, given her penchant for blunt pronouncements. But to Bernadette's surprise and relief, Arizona used good judgment and remained silent. She'd just proven that no matter how loose with the tongue a person could be, a woman's age was always off limits.

"Thank you, but I'm getting up there," Arizona said as she looked around the beautiful restaurant. "I never thought I'd make it to thirty because I was completely buck-wild back in the day, and I've been to more funerals of people I grew up with than I care to remember. But after my son was born, I turned my life around because for the first time I felt like I had something to live for. Then I met Chris, and he showed me that I was worthy of real love," she said, then paused. "I'm thankful."

Bernadette nodded. "That's beautiful."

"Thanks. How about you? What's your deal? I mean, I read your bio at work and everything, and I know you're a powerful VP from Washington, DC. You're highly educated, successful, and I heard you live right here in the Palisades. You got it goin' on, so why're you in this fancy restaurant celebrating by yourself?"

Bernadette knew it wouldn't take long for Arizona's in-your-face subtlety to reappear. But she couldn't refute a thing that Arizona had said. If it had been anyone else delivering that assessment and question, Bernadette would have had choice words for them. But in the very short amount of time that she'd been talking with Arizona, she could tell that the woman was kind, good, straight-up, and honest. She was what Bernadette had asked God to send her way, and the revelation nearly made her fall out of her seat, but she managed to maintain her composure. "That's a loaded question. How much time do you have?" Bernadette said jokingly.

"I don't have anywhere to be and no one to answer to, so I've got as long as you need."

Once again, Bernadette thought about her revelation. "Well, to my surprise . . . I'm going to answer your question. But first, let's toast." She raised her glass. "To God's way of remaining anonymous."

# Chapter 8

## ARIZONA

From the moment Arizona had met Bernadette Gibson six months ago during an all-staff meeting at Bourbon General Hospital, she'd respected the woman and had known that one day their paths would cross in a way that would help her, but Arizona had no idea that it would be she who would be in a position to help a woman as accomplished and successful as Bernadette.

As Arizona listened to Bernadette bare her soul over tender filet mignon and succulent lobster tails that had both gone mostly untouched, she was amazed that the woman who she'd thought had it all was longing for what Arizona had and was now on the fence about keeping. She knew this had to be a sign and an example of the fact that things could be worse than having a man who was sexually lacking. But she had to admit that even the thought of Chris's physical and sexual challenges filled her with worry and uneasiness. However, for now she would focus her attention on something that didn't wreck her nerves, and that was how she could help her newfound friend.

"I was talking to my cousin earlier this morning," Bernadette said, "whose birthday is also today, and I told her that I'm at a point in my life where I want more on a personal level." She paused, then sipped the last of the champagne in her glass. "I usually don't share my private life like this, and especially not with professional colleagues. But I get a good vibe from you, Arizona, and I feel like I can trust you. Plus, turning fifty frees you up from worrying about every little thing."

"First of all, you look at least five years younger than your age, and that's real talk."

"Thank you, and coming from you," Bernadette chuckled, "I know you mean it."

"Yes, I do." Arizona nodded and smiled. "And secondly, I put in my notice two weeks ago, and yesterday was officially my last day at Bourbon General, praise the Lord! So you truly don't have to worry about me. And besides, I was never one to get caught up in workplace gossip because too much foolishness can happen."

"Why did you leave Bourbon General?"

"I'm going to pursue my passion of being a full-time makeup artist."

"That explains why you look flawless. I was admiring your makeup when you walked in."

"I appreciate your compliment. I love anything to do with beauty, and fashion, too. But makeup is where I excel. I've been doing it on the side for as long as I can remember. Last year I did a wedding, the bride posted photos on her Instagram page of the makeup I did for her and her bridesmaids, and as they say, the rest is history. I've been rollin' ever since from referrals and word of mouth."

"Wow, Arizona! Congratulations, that's fantastic."

"Thanks. It's a blessing for sure. And I wouldn't be able to do it without God on one side and Chris on the other." Arizona felt choked up and conflicted every time she mentioned her fiancé's name. She knew that because of his love, support, and strong belief in her, she'd felt empowered with the courage to quit her job and pursue her dreams. Chris had even told her that she didn't have to worry about how she was going to pay her bills because once she took her leap of faith he would work two jobs if he had to in order to make sure that she and Solomon had everything they needed. He was a good man, for sure, but after last night she also knew he was a man with shortcomings, literally. And that was why she felt conflicted every time she thought of Chris or mentioned his name. Arizona was sure that Bernadette had noticed her expression because she was a smart and very observant woman.

"If things keep rollin' the way they're going," Arizona continued, "I'll be making more money running my own business than I did at Bourbon General."

"That's another cause for celebration. You should feel very proud."

"Yes, I do. And I appreciate that coming from you. Bernadette, you give me career goals."

Bernadette shook her head and gave, Arizona a half laugh, half frown. "My life looks good on paper, but when you read the fine print it's full of hidden clauses and stipulations. Trust issues are at the top of the list."

"After what you went through with that con artist, I can see why."

"And believe it or not, I glossed over the really, really despicable parts. I've had a string of heartache in my day, and I mean one after the other. But that relationship . . ." Bernadette shook her head. "He devastated me. I believed in him, in us, and it was all a big lie."

Arizona could see that even though Bernadette had said she'd been hurt by her ex five years ago, she spoke about him as if the wound was fresh. "Have you tried forgiving him?"

"Excuse me?"

"It's obvious that you're still carrying pain and anger from what he did to you. But, Bernadette, that was five years ago. As my mama would say, your anger toward him is blocking your blessings. And I know that's true 'cause I've been there and done that, and it's a road that leads to absolutely nowhere but a lonely dead end."

Bernadette let out a deep, long sigh and formed an expression that bordered on shock and confusion. "I'm sorry, but if you think

I'm gonna forgive that lowlife, you're out of your mind, Arizona. As a matter of fact, he's the one who should've sought my forgiveness a long time ago."

Arizona leaned in close. "I'm not tryin' to upset you, or play the holier than thou card, but the Good Book talks about forgiveness. If God can forgive us for all the messed-up stuff we do, how can we not forgive others?"

"You're kidding, right?"

"No, I'm tryin' to help you. I can tell you're a good person, Bernadette, but like all of us, you've probably made mistakes in your life."

"Of course I have."

"And you've been blessed in spite of your mistakes and short-comings, otherwise you wouldn't be as successful as you are. It's a fact that your ex did you wrong, but you also have the power to forgive him, which will help you forgive yourself."

"Arizona . . ."

"And basically, if God has forgiven and blessed you, he's also forgiven that low-down scum bag for what he did to you. If The Most High can forgive your ex, I know you can. And once you do you'll be free to move on."

"Do you ladies need anything?" the server asked. "Or would you like me to box up your entrées?"

Although the food was delicious, neither Arizona nor Bernadette had eaten much because they'd been so heavily vested in their conversation.

"I'd like mine boxed up to go," Bernadette answered and then looked at Arizona.

"Yes, so would I."

"Would you ladies care for dessert?"

Arizona and Bernadette both looked at each other before Arizona spoke up. "Well, since it's our birthday we should at least get some birthday cake."

"It's your birthday!" the attentive waiter said with excitement as if it was his birthday as well. "You must definitely order dessert." He reached for Bernadette's plate and then Arizona's. "I'll box this up and have our dessert selection tray sent out for you shortly."

Arizona could see that Bernadette's mood had shifted to an unhappy place and she felt bad for bringing her down, especially on a day when she should be celebrating. "Bernadette, I'm sorry if I offended you or made you feel unhappy. That wasn't what I was trying to do."

"What you said was absolutely right. I didn't want to hear it, though, but I know it's what I needed to be told." Bernadette let out a long sigh. "Being angry is exhausting, and quite frankly, I'm tired."

The two women were interrupted again when a server with a delectable dessert tray approached their table. The elegant silver and crystal tray held eight sweet treats to choose from. Bernadette chose the strawberry cheesecake and Arizona selected the Magnolia Room brown butter pecan pie.

"We didn't eat our food," Bernadette said, "so we better eat our dessert."

Arizona smiled. "I guess you're right. But truth be told, I don't need to eat anything, especially if I want to drop some weight. I need to get serious."

"You look fantastic," Bernadette said.

"Says the woman who's petite and has probably never had to diet a day in her life."

"All I'm saying is that you look great just as you are. You're a beautiful woman, Arizona."

"Well, thank you."

Bernadette paused. "Can I ask you something?"

"Sure."

"When are you getting married?"

Arizona shifted in her chair.

"The only reason I'm asking is because you've mentioned your fiancé several times, and you've talked about how wonderful and supportive he is, but you haven't mentioned the wedding. Have you set a date?"

Arizona exhaled. "Yes, we're getting married June sixteenth."

"That's less than six months from now."

"Uh-huh," Arizona answered in a flat tone.

"Excuse me for saying this, and feel free to tell me to mind my own business, but you don't seem happy about getting married. Is everything okay?"

Arizona hated when people asked obvious questions. She knew that Bernadette knew that she wasn't okay, otherwise she wouldn't have asked. But she also understood that Bernadette was trying to be polite and tactful, the latter of which Arizona knew she needed some skills training in. She hadn't planned on talking to anyone about what had happened last night, but because Bernadette had bared her soul, Arizona gave herself permission to do the same.

"No, everything's not okay," Arizona said. "What I'm about to share with you is strictly confidential, and if you breathe a word of this to anyone, so help me I'll break your legs."

Bernadette laughed, but then stopped when she saw that Arizona was serious. "Arizona, even though we've just met and we don't know each other that well, the one thing that I think we can both agree on is that we're smart women, and we know when we're being played, so I think you know that you don't have to worry about me telling anyone what we discuss at this table tonight."

She knew that Bernadette was right, and she also knew that she could trust her newfound friend to give her advice from a more mature perspective. Arizona looked around the intimate but crowded dining room. Even though she didn't know another soul in the room and the noise was at a decibel level that would make her voice get lost in the chatter around her, she still didn't feel comfortable talking about such an intimate matter in the company of others. But the more she thought about the burden she was carrying, the more urgent she felt about unloading it. She saw their server walk by and stopped him. "Is there any other place in this restaurant that's a little more private?"

The server tilted his head and thought for a moment. "We have a terrace area on the side of the restaurant that's completely empty because it's so cold outside. But we have a fireplace and heaters out there, which actually make it quite comfortable. Would you ladies like to go there?"

Arizona looked at Bernadette for the okay.

"I'm from DC, so I'm used to cold winters. I'm game if you are."

Ten minutes later, Arizona and Bernadette were sitting at a table for two, eating dessert by a cozy fire, with heaters on either side of them to combat the cold night air. They had even ordered another glass of champagne, and were surprised when their server came out with a full bottle, compliments of the house in honor of their birthdays and their first time dining at the Magnolia Room.

"I can't believe I'm at the Magnolia Room, eating outside in the doggone cold," Arizona said as she took a bite out of her dessert. "But it's not as cold as I thought it would be, and as the server said, 'it is quite comfortable,'" Arizona mimicked.

"Yes it's lovely out here."

"I have to thank you for introducing me to champagne because this stuff is so good!" Arizona raised her glass and clinked it against Bernadette's.

"I'm glad you like it."

"I love it. I didn't know what I was missin', but you best believe I'm on track now."

"Well, I don't know about your dessert, but this is the best cheesecake I've ever had in my life."

"This pecan pie is better than my mama's, but don't tell her I said that."

"Your secret is safe with me . . . and speaking of which, tell me what's going on with you and your fiancé."

Arizona took a long sip from her flute and then inhaled a large breath of cold air to give her strength for the story she was about to tell. "Once I start, I don't want you to ask any questions until I'm finished, 'cause I got to get all of this out."

"All right."

Arizona began by telling Bernadette about her sordid past that included smoking weed in high school, getting a DUI on her twenty-first birthday, and spending a night in jail six months later as a result of breaking probation, and then capped off her tale of debauchery with a quick account of the convicted felons she'd dated, and the wild and reckless times they'd had. Then she told Bernadette about the birth of her son, Solomon, and how having him had saved her life, and that meeting and falling in love with her fiancé, Chris, had brought nothing but love and joy to her from their first hello. She talked about the shared vow of celibacy that she and Chris had taken, and then finally, she ended with the disastrous details of the previous night.

By the time Arizona finished her story, their dessert plates were clean and the entire bottle of champagne was empty. The alcohol had loosened up both women, and what little tact Arizona possessed had left after her third glass of champagne.

"Chris is everything I could ever want in a husband, father, and helpmate," Arizona said, trying hard not to slur her words. "But he's not the lover I thought he was gonna be, not even close. I'm so confused I don't know what to do."

Bernadette nodded, reached across the table, and placed her hand atop Arizona's. "You're in one hell of a tough situation."

"Don't I know it! Some advice would be good right about now."

Bernadette leaned back. "When you say he's small . . . like, how small are we talking?"

"Almost nonexistent small, "she said in a low, sad voice.

"Oh, Jesus." Bernadette squinted her eyes and bit her lower lip as her forehead creased with what looked like astonishment and questions.

Arizona could see that Bernadette had something to say but most likely didn't know how to phrase it. One of the things that Arizona had noticed early on was that while Bernadette was direct, she was also diplomatic and skilled in her approach to saying things and asking questions. Even though she was feeling relaxed from the bubbly she'd consumed, she was still trying to maintain her dignified composure. But right now Arizona didn't give a care in the world about diplomacy or good manners. She needed help, so she gave Bernadette permission to speak freely.

"Listen," Arizona said, "I know you're a very tactful and professional person, and you're tryin' to be polite, but I want you to know that you can ask me any question you want, and you can say exactly what's on your mind. I have very thick skin and right now I need brutally honest advice."

Bernadette nodded. "Okay, when you two were having sex, could you feel him at all?"

"No, I couldn't. He was moving on top of me, grunting and thrusting in an in-and-out motion, but I didn't even know he was inside me. I thought we were dry humping."

"Good Lord!"

"That's what I said," Arizona said, completely slurring her words. "I've been with a lot of men in my day. But I never, ever, experienced anything like that."

"So all this time, for the past two years, you never had a clue that he was, um . . ."

"Deprived?" Arizona blurted out.

"Uh, I think there's a better term for it, but yes."

"Heck no! And that's what scares me, Bernadette." Arizona brought her hand to her head, rubbed her temples, and spoke with complete clarity. "If I'd known then what I know now, I probably wouldn't have even gone out with Chris at all. That sounds awful, right?"

"No, it sounds honest. And that's what you need to be with him."

Arizona let out a deep breath. "Maybe it can get better."

"Given what you experienced, deep down, do you truthfully believe that?" Bernadette asked.

The two women sat in silence for a moment before Bernadette spoke up. "On a scale of one to ten, with ten being the highest, how important is sex to you in a relationship?"

Arizona answered without hesitation. "A fifteen."

"You're in trouble."

"Tell me something I don't know."

"I'm no relationship expert by any stretch, and I've failed miserably at so many that I've lost count. But the one thing that I do know a whole lot about is sex."

Arizona perked up. "I'm all ears."

"If sex, and I mean good sex, is high on your list of must-haves but your mate can't bring it, you're going to be dissatisfied. And when you're dissatisfied, over a period of time it wears on you, and that wear and tear will erode the relationship. After that it's just a matter of time before you start seeking satisfaction in different ways or places."

Arizona knew that Bernadette was right because it was the very real possibility she'd been thinking about all last night and well into the wee hours of this morning. She couldn't get the image of Chris's tiny penis out of her mind, and every time she thought about it she had to shake her head and close her eyes. "It disturbed me so bad that I googled it."

Bernadette's eyes widened. "First of all, how do you even begin to google something like that? And second, what kind of advice did the Internet give you?"

"I typed in 'Medical Causes of Extremely Small Penis.'"

"Wow."

"And the first thing that popped up was Micropenis."

Bernadette shook her head. "Oh, my. I don't even know what to say, but I'm sure Google had plenty, so lay it on me . . . no pun intended."

"Well, according to *WebMD,* and I'm sayin' this from memory as best I can, 'the most common cause of micropenis is abnormal hy-po-tha-la-mic or pi-tu-i-tary function.'"

"Okay . . ."

"And that about describes what Chris is working with. My big, strong man has a micro dick," Arizona said, nearly in tears.

"Lord have mercy. I'm so sorry," Bernadette said, barely above a whisper.

"I know, I know." Arizona echoed. "I was so shocked I could hardly believe it. Chris is a six-foot-four, muscular, sexy, Hershey's milk chocolate brotha with a smile that'll make you weak in your knees. Bernadette, I just knew he was packin', and from the day I first met him I imagined he was probably hung like a horse. But it just goes to show you that the old sayin' is true, you can't judge a book by its cover."

"What did Chris say afterward, and what was his reaction? He's got to know that he's challenged in that area, and that he wasn't able to please you."

"That's the crazy part. I don't think he knows . . . he doesn't have a clue."

"Wait a minute. He doesn't know he's small, or he doesn't know that he wasn't able to please you, or both?"

"I believe he knows that his penis is small, I mean, there's no way around it. But he had an orgasm, and from the way he acted, he thinks I enjoyed it, too."

"How did he act?"

"Happy as a drunk in a vineyard. He even told me he couldn't wait until we did it again because the next time he was gonna try to last longer."

Bernadette looked baffled. "I don't get it. Did you fake it?"

"Heck no. I just laid there."

"Maybe I'm missing something, because this doesn't make any sense at all."

Just then the attentive server was back. "Are you ladies okay out here? Do you need anything?"

Arizona gave the young man a "leave us alone" stare, but Bernadette politely turned to him and said. "I think we're good, thank you."

"Okay, ladies, and just so you know, our dining room will be closing in thirty minutes."

Arizona looked at her watch. "It's almost midnight?"

"Yes, ma'am," the server said. "I guess time flies when you're in good company."

"You're absolutely right," Bernadette said. "But since you're closing soon, I guess we need to wrap things up. Can you bring the check?"

"Yes, ma'am, I'll be back in just a second."

Bernadette waited for the server to leave before she resumed their conversation. "We don't have much time, so I'll make it quick and to the point. One thing I just don't understand is, as bold, outspoken and blunt as you are, why didn't you say something to him?"

The server hadn't been joking when he said he would be back in a second because suddenly he reappeared. He placed a long black and gold leather case containing a bill in front of each woman. "I'll let you look over your bills and I'll be back in a second."

"No need," Bernadette said. "Wait just a minute." She opened her case and perused it, then reached for Arizona's and did the same as she fished inside her designer handbag for her wallet. Arizona was about to protest when Bernadette stopped her. "This is my birthday present to you."

"Bernadette, you really don't have to. You already treated me to my first ever glass of champagne, and that's more than enough."

"You can treat me next year," Bernadette said with a wink. She placed her American Express platinum card on top of the two cases. "We're wrapping up, so give us five minutes and I'll pick up my card and sign the receipt at the hostess stand on our way out."

The server nodded. "It was a pleasure serving you ladies tonight. I hope you had a great time celebrating your birthdays with us, and I hope you both come back soon."

Arizona and Bernadette thanked him and agreed that they would be back.

"Thanks again, Bernadette," Arizona said. "I appreciate everything." She attempted to pull her wool coat over her shoulders and nearly lost her balance. "Oh Lord. I think I might be a little bit tipsy."

"A little?" Bernadette chuckled. "I'm a little tipsy, but you're a little drunk."

"Whew, it's been a while since I drank this much alcohol. This champagne is no joke."

"If you don't mind, I'm going to call a car for us both." Bernadette reached into her handbag for her phone as she wrapped her alpaca cape around her slim shoulders.

"This is Bourbon, North Carolina, not Washington, DC. Ain't nobody gonna pick us up this time of night."

Bernadette tapped on her keys and smiled. "Our driver will be here in five minutes. Let's go up front so I can get my credit card and wait for our ride."

"Wow, I guess it pays to live on the rich side of town."

"No, it pays to have access to Bourbon General's private car service."

True to the car service driver's word, five minutes later Arizona and Bernadette climbed into the back seat of a luxury black sedan. Arizona rested her imposter designer bag on her lap. Even though tonight was the first time she'd spoken at length with Bernadette, she'd felt more comfortable and free talking with her than she did with some of her closest girlfriends whom she'd known for years. Bernadette was honest and smart, and Arizona knew she could learn a lot from the accomplished businesswoman.

As they drove out of the restaurant's parking lot, Arizona surveyed the beautiful houses with their immaculately landscaped yards, the vast offering of shops and stores that provided convenience for neighborhood residents, and the overall sense of elitism that came with the exclusive part of town. "It must be nice," she said aloud.

"What?"

"Livin' out here."

"It's okay, I guess. My neighbors are over the top friendly, but I guess it's just that Southern hospitality I still haven't gotten used to."

"You live out here?"

Bernadette nodded. "Yes, but I want to switch gears and revisit what you said about your dilemma with Chris. You're such a direct and confident woman who speaks her mind, and that's why it's puzzling to me that you didn't tell Chris how you felt after you two made love."

"Hmph, I asked myself the same thing, and you know what I came up with?"

"What?"

"I love the man. I love him so much that I don't want to hurt his feelings, Bernadette. I think it would crush him if I told him that he was horrible in bed, and I can't do that."

"I understand. But if you don't tell him it's going to eat away at you."

Arizona let out a loud sigh. They were now on her side of town, the Bottoms, which was a drastic difference from the luxury she'd just experienced in the Palisades. She looked at the builder grade houses, scattered corner stores, and working-class struggle that was embedded in the community she'd grown up in.

"Don't you agree?" Bernadette asked, pulling Arizona's mind back into the moment.

"Yes, you're right. I know I'm going to have to say something."

Just then the driver slowed his car in front of Arizona's house. It was after midnight, and even though she was tired from her long day and lack of sleep, she didn't want to get out of the car because once she did she knew she'd be stepping back into the reality of her dilemma with Chris. But Arizona was a realist and she knew she needed to deal with life as it came. Before she said good night to Bernadette, she invited her new friend to the party that Chris was throwing for her tomorrow night.

Thirty minutes later, Arizona was fresh out of the shower and comfortably snuggled under her thick, braided trim comforter. She took a deep breath of satisfaction as she thought about her day, its highs and lows, and how nothing had gone as she'd thought it would. When she'd awakened this morning she'd been stressed and worried well into the afternoon. But thanks to Bernadette, Arizona gained a sense of clarity and direction about the blessings she'd been granted, and the things she needed to do in order to achieve physical, mental, and emotional satisfaction and honesty in her relationship with Chris. She smiled, turned her light out on her bedside table, and thought about the words she would need to use tomorrow when she talked to Chris.

# Chapter 9

## TESS

"I hope they both fall over a damn cliff and then get eaten by a pack of hungry wolves," Tess grumbled. "That'll be the perfect ending to their island honeymoon."

Tess dragged herself down her long hallway and entered her home office. It was nearly noon, and she still felt groggy despite the twelve hours of slumber that two Ambien sleep-aid pills had helped her to achieve last night. She'd always suffered from insomnia, which actually served her well when she was under a deadline like she was now. But she didn't want to stay awake because being conscious would lead her to think about her failed relationships in the past and the troubling reality of what was shaping up to be a lonely future.

"Good afternoon, cave," Tess whispered. Her voice was somber and her mood was even worse. Normally when she walked into her writing cave a blanket of peace covered her body that sparked creative ideas, ignited her vivid imagination, and fueled her adventurous spirit. But not today. This afternoon, all those wonderful feelings had been replaced with an overwhelming sense of defeat that draped her from the top of her head to the bottom of her feet.

"I've got to put that bastard and his bitch out of my mind because they're interfering with my muse and fucking up my flow." Tess walked over to the window and looked out at the snow-covered sidewalk. It was bitterly cold, and as she placed the palm of her hand against the glass, she couldn't let go of the hard but true fact that she wished it was she who was lying on the beach beside Antwan, sipping a fruity drink while playing footsie with him as the Caribbean sun beat down on their skin.

"I need to pull it together," Tess huffed as she shuffled over to the box of pizza she'd left from the night before. She opened it up and looked at the lone slice with its congealed cheese and cold vegetables. "It's a damn shame when you order an extra-large pizza and you eat it all by yourself in less than twenty-four hours," she said as she bit into the hardened crust. She reached for the bottle of red wine beside it and pulled out the cork. "I need to get cracking on this manuscript. Focus, focus, focus," she told herself as she turned the bottle to her mouth and drained what was left of the Cabernet Sauvignon.

Tess finally made it over to her desk and sat in her chair where the magic happened, and where she hoped she would be able to cast her sour mood to a faraway place. She was already past her deadline to turn in her manuscript to her editor. This book was the sequel to her last best seller that she'd released last year, and her legion of loyal readers was anxiously waiting to see what would happen next to the characters she'd created. To say that she felt pressure was mild, but, she'd done it eleven times before, and she was hoping she could make it an even dozen. She booted up her computer, stretched her neck and shoulders, and then settled in for a long afternoon of writing.

Six hours later it was dark outside and frigidly cold, and Tess was exhausted. She stared at the screen of her twenty-seven-inch monitor and squinted at the single paragraph she'd written. "An entire day down the fucking drain," she said in a weary voice. She'd tried to get into the zone, the space where nothing mattered except her characters and the scenes they led her to write as she'd create an entirely new world from her imagination. But her creativity was on hold because the only thing she could think about was the fact that Antwan was someone else's husband.

She'd gone back to his Instagram page and then moved on to Facebook, where she'd spent hours reading posts and scrutinizing the happy pictures that the loving couple had tagged each other in. She tortured herself with the thought of what could have been if Antwan had chosen her, and she racked her brain with the question of why he hadn't.

"What's wrong with me?" Tess asked herself. "Where did I go wrong? I gave that bastard my love and he trampled all over it like it was nothing." Tess knew she had to break through the fog of her self-induced pity-party. She needed clarity, so she called Bernadette.

"Hey, cuzzo," Bernadette answered on the second ring. "I saw that it's only five degrees in Chicago and the windchill is negative ten."

"Yeah, that was the high earlier today. It's below zero now and the forecast is calling for the temperature to dip even lower."

"That's crazy. How in the world do you stand it?"

"That's a good question, and I've asked myself the same thing. I thought I'd get used to it after being here for more than ten years. But every year after the first snowfall I still feel like it's my first Chicago winter."

"That's why you need to come down South."

Tess laughed.

"I'm serious. It's the dead of winter here and even though it's cold, it's the South kind of cold, which isn't that bad. I'll take this thirty-degree temperature any day. As a matter of fact, I can't wait until spring because I'm sure it's going to be beautiful here."

"I bet it will."

"You okay? You don't sound like yourself."

"I'm fine. Just tired."

"I know you're under deadline with your book, but take the night off. You wrote all day and night on your birthday, so at the very least you should celebrate before the weekend ends, and knowing you, I have no doubt there's any shortage of men for you to chose from."

Tess wanted to laugh and cry at the same time. Bernadette was right, there were at least seven men she could call at the very moment who would drop what they were doing, bundle up, and brave the cold to come see her for a little late-night fun. The only problem was that none of those men meant anything to her, and she knew that beyond their shared connection of wanting good sex, she meant nothing to them either. The thought of being a forty-year-old booty call babe made Tess want to cry. But she sucked up her emotions and changed the subject. "So, what are you up to tonight?" she asked.

"I'm actually getting ready to get dressed and go out to a party."

"Really?" Tess was surprised that Bernadette was going out, and to a party at that.

Tess carefully listened to her cousin and noticed there was something different in Bernadette's tone. She couldn't put her finger on what it was, but there was definitely a lilt of excitement in her voice. Usually, the only thing that elicited that type of emotion from Bernadette was when she was talking about a business strategy, finances, or something related to work. Bernadette was a serial workaholic, and ever since she'd given up on love, she'd plunged full throttle into her career, and she had great success to show for her efforts. But Tess knew they hadn't remotely broached any discussion about Bernadette's job, so she wondered what had her cousin sounding like she'd just gotten a bonus on top of a raise. Now it was Tess's turn to ask, "Are you okay?"

"Yes . . . don't I sound okay?"

"You actually sound great. Like you're happy."

"I guess that's because . . ." Bernadette paused for a moment. "I guess I am."

"Oh, you must have scored a major deal at work. Don't tell me they're getting ready to make you CEO of the hospital."

"You know me very well, but actually, the way I feel right now has absolutely nothing to do with work."

"Okay, wait a minute. Have you found a friend with benefits?"

"Girl, please! My good mood has nothing to do with Bourbon General or a man, however, give me a couple years and I will be the top dog in charge, in and out of the boardroom," Bernadette said with confidence. "But tonight, I'm just happy because I'm alive and I'm free.

Now Tess definitely knew something was up with her cousin. She rose from her plush, velveteen tufted office chair and began pacing the floor. Bernadette had always been pragmatic, serious and focused. She wasn't the type who said things like, *I'm just happy because I'm alive and free.* Tess didn't even know what that statement meant, or what had caused Bernadette to say it.

Initially, Tess thought about the possibility that Bernadette had met someone last night when she'd gone to dinner to celebrate, and that was why she'd made the friends with benefits comment. But Tess had quickly dismissed the thought, not because Bernadette had denied it, but because she knew that even if her cousin had met a tall, educated, and handsome CEO type—which had always been her weakness—he'd have to have done a whole lot of work to bring Bernadette to this point of happiness.

Tess knew Bernadette's hard-shell coating all too well, and she knew there was no way a booty-call hookup was going to happen after just one night. Tess had a bad feeling in the pit of her stomach because she knew what could make Bernadette, or anyone for that matter, act the way she was now. She sucked in a deep breath and hoped she was wrong about what she was about to ask.

"Bernadette, are you using drugs?"

"Have you lost your mind? What would possess you to think or even ask me a ridiculous question like that?"

"Because you're either smoking, snorting, or swallowing something that's making you sound like a completely different person."

"You left out shooting up," Bernadette said sarcastically.

"I know you're terrified of needles."

"I should reach through this phone and choke you. It's a shame that you think the only way I can be happy is to use drugs. Do you really think I'm that pathetic?"

Tess had just come to the sad realization that her own life was pathetic, and she now felt bad for making her cousin feel the same way.

Unlike her, Bernadette had always walked a path so straight she didn't need a ruler. Bernadette colored inside the lines, and Tess knew she had to apologize. "I'm sorry, Bernadette. What I said was completely out of line. The only reason I thought that is because what you just said sounded very unlike you, almost like it was coming from a person who was pretending to be you."

"Apology accepted. And I admit that I probably sound different, and honestly, the feeling I have is still kind of foreign to me, so I can understand why you think something's going on with me."

"Tell me what happened, and why you're suddenly so happy and free?"

Tess listened intently as Bernadette told her about a woman she'd met while dining at the restaurant last night, whose birthday also happened to be yesterday as well. The woman's name was Arizona, and she and Bernadette had hit it off so well that they'd talked until the restaurant closed. Bernadette said that even though Arizona was young and had never lived outside Bourbon, she had a unique perspective that made her rethink many things in her life, and at the top of the list was her desire to have a relationship.

"I didn't get into bed until one a.m.," Bernadette said, "but when I did, I slept like a baby. I drifted off and when I woke up this morning I felt relaxed, free, and happy . . . you want to know why?"

"You found a new vibrator and it took the edge off?"

"The only reason why I'm not going to hang up on you is because that's not a far-fetched theory. But no, Miss Smarty Pants. I feel good because I forgave Walter."

Tess walked back to her comfortable office chair and sat down to regain her balance and rewind the words that Bernadette just said. Before she had a chance to ask the first of several questions swirling around in her head, Bernadette gave her the answers.

"I know you're wondering what in the hell brought this on, and it all started when Arizona asked a simple question that stunned me."

"Which was?"

"Had I forgiven Walter."

"Forgive him for what? That maggot should be the one asking for your forgiveness, not the other way around," Tess huffed in disgust.

"That's what I initially said. But Arizona looked at things from a different angle."

Tess smirked on her end of the phone. "Listen, I'm sure this Arizona woman is a lovely person, otherwise you wouldn't have spent your entire evening at dinner talking with her. But she's off her rocker. How could she even ask you that question after you explained what that dirty little rat-bastard did to you?"

"In her youthful wisdom she told me something that I've heard and read a million times from self-help gurus, but it didn't click until Arizona broke it down. She told me that if I didn't forgive Walter, there was no way I could go on to find happiness, and then she told me to pray about it and give it to God. Before I got into bed, I bent down on my knees and prayed, and I asked the Lord to change what was in my heart. I asked him to let happiness walk into my life, and then I climbed into my cozy bed and was asleep so fast that I don't even remember drifting off. When I woke up this morning, I felt better and less stressed than I have in years. I haven't completely let go of the anger I have for Walter's sorry behind, but I know that I'm on the road to getting there and, Tess, it feels good. I finally feel like I can be happy again."

Tess leaned back into her chair and digested Bernadette's words, the same words she'd heard from self-help gurus as well. She secretly envied Bernadette for her newfound clarity, but she hoped her cousin wouldn't try to sway her into forgiving Antwan because the wound he'd inflicted had reopened and the blood was still fresh.

"Right now as we speak," Bernadette continued, "I'm getting ready to slip into a cute outfit for Arizona's birthday party."

"I can't believe you're going out two nights in a row," Tess said. "I guess God did step in."

"Very funny."

"Thank you. I try."

"Arizona's fiancé is throwing a party for her at the hotel where he works and she invited me to go, so I'm going to get out and have a little fun. And who knows, I might just meet someone."

Tess didn't want to sound skeptical, especially because it was clear that Bernadette was excited about her shiny new outlook on life. But she also wanted to give her cousin a little dose of reality mixed with middle-age wisdom. "I hope you have a wonderful time tonight, cuzzo. But remember, if you haven't roller-skated in years and you quickly lace up and take off, you could be in for a quick fall. Take your time, go slow, and protect yourself. I've heard folks are crazy in small towns like Mayberry."

"It's Bourbon, and no, they're not," Bernadette said through laughter. "Just be happy for me, Tess. And by the way, you should try letting go of the pain you're holding on to from your relationship with Antwan."

The mention of her ex-lover's name sent a sharp pain to the pit of Tess's stomach. She wanted to let go, but right now she was in a tug-of-war with doing the mature thing and being as messy as a schoolgirl. Unlike Bernadette who had released anger in her sleep, Tess was plotting while wide awake. She'd thought about creating a fake profile on Instagram and then bombarding Antwan's posts with comments about his lying, cheating ways, filled with warnings for his new bride. And because his page was public, for what he'd once said was strictly for media purposes, she knew it would be easy to do.

"Tess, are you still there?" Bernadette asked, drawing Tess back into the present.

"Yes, like I said, I'm sleepy from a long night in the cave," she lied. "I know you need to start getting dressed for the party and I need to get back to my manuscript, so let's call it a night."

"Okay, cuzzo."

"Have a great time and remember, take it slow."

Bernadette laughed. "Yes, ma'am, I will."

"And call me tomorrow because you know I'll be waiting to hear how things go."

"You got it, and I hope you have a great writing night on what I know is going to be another best seller."

After Tess hung up the phone she logged onto her computer and went straight to Antwan's Instagram page. She knew she shouldn't do it, but her curiosity mixed with mild obsession drove her to see what her ex was up to. He had just posted a picture ten minutes ago of him and his wife having dinner for two in what looked to be a luxuriously decorated, five-star hotel suite. The soft glow from the light of dozens of candles filled the room with romance that was oozing through the computer screen. The happy couple had obviously gotten a waiter to snap a magazine-worthy picture of them sitting at a well-appointed table for two as they clinked their champagne flutes while they starred into each other's eyes. "This is some bullshit!" Tess grumbled.

But even as Tess spewed those words, she knew it wasn't true. She knew deep down that what Antwan and his new wife had was love. As a writer, she had the ability to use her vivid imagination, but she also possessed the uncanny knack for spotting what was real from what was made up to craft the perfect story. She'd become skilled at looking into people's eyes and knowing what was phony and what wasn't, and as she clicked back through pictures that the couple had taken earlier today, what she saw was happiness. Genuine happiness. And what Tess realized once again was the bitter fact that it wasn't that Antwan hadn't wanted to make his business public, or that he couldn't be faithful, it was that he hadn't wanted to and couldn't be those things with her.

# Chapter 10

## BERNADETTE

"New view, new you," Bernadette said to herself as she sat at her lighted vanity inside her spacious master bathroom. Ever since she'd opened her eyes that morning she'd been practicing how to speak, think, and act with a different outlook on her life. "I can choose happiness," she said as she reached for her MAC pressed powder. She dabbed the foundation with her fluffy makeup brush and stroked it onto her smooth, deep pecan-colored skin. "I can have happiness, because I deserve it."

Bernadette finished applying her makeup to the best of her ability, then topped off her look with her signature MAC Ruby Woo lipstick. She wished she could have enlisted Arizona's makeup expertise because the woman knew what she was doing. Bernadette wanted to enhance her plain features and she wished she could bring out her eyes, which she'd always thought were much too big for the slender shape of her face. She surveyed herself, turning from side to side, inspecting her amateur handiwork at different angles. She sighed. "I look okay, but I'm realistic and I know I need some help."

Bernadette was fifty years old and she still couldn't determine her best side profile. She envied women who possessed natural beauty and didn't need the aid of what one of her ex-boyfriends had called "war paint." But as Bernadette had just said, she was a realist, and she knew that the canvas she was working with required a little help if she wanted to have a fighting chance of being physically attractive.

But as much as she knew her overall looks were six on a scale of ten, she also knew that her skin was without a doubt in double digits. From the top of her head to the bottom of her feet, Bernadette's skin was a smooth, evenly pigmented deep brown color that was so rich it looked and felt like silk. She'd been blessed to have never suffered from pimples, blemishes, scars, stretch marks, or even the dreaded cellulite that most women battled with creams and pills.

Bernadette rose from her fur-lined sitting stool, walked over to her closet, and once again debated about what she should wear to Arizona's party tonight. When they'd talked earlier that morning, Arizona had told her, "Come dressed to impress and you might just catch a man."

"Dressed to impress is vague, Arizona," Bernadette had said, wanting more details. "What's the theme? Is there a certain color I should wear?"

"You overthink stuff. Just put on something nice . . . and make it sexy."

Nothing in Bernadette's entire wardrobe could be classified as sexy, so she came as close as she could with an off-the-shoulder little black dress that she'd purchased a few years ago but hadn't had the opportunity to wear. She pulled the designer garment off the wooden hanger and slipped it on. "Perfect," she said as she ran her fingers over the soft material. The jersey knit fabric hugged her body and showcased her flat stomach, another asset she was thankful for, especially at her age. Bernadette walked over to her floor-length mirror and turned to look at her flat backside that no amount of squats, lunges, or any other exercise had been able to inflate. "It is what it is."

Ten minutes later, Bernadette was driving her car up to the entrance of the St. Hamilton. The stately property's exterior reminded her of the richly appointed boutique hotels that she'd become accustomed to in DC. With its sculpted topiaries at either side of the massive brass and glass entrance doors, the St. Hamilton looked like a small palace.

After Bernadette stepped out of her car at the valet stand, she was greeted by two bellmen whose immaculate navy blue uniforms included tails and a top hat. Their crisp white gloves and cheerful smiles added an extra touch of regality and sophistication to an already impressive establishment. Bernadette was beginning to see that Bourbon had its own distinct style.

"Good evening, ma' am," one of the doormen said with a smile. "Are you here to check in or are you attending the Mays' party this evening?"

"I'm here for the party," Bernadette answered.

The doorman spoke into the mouthpiece that was attached to his headset. "The young lady about to come through the doors is here for the party. Please direct her to the ballroom." He tipped his hat to Bernadette. "I hope you have a wonderful evening."

Bernadette loved that Southern men were generous with compliments, because she considered being called a young lady a grand compliment. As she strode into the impeccably decorated lobby she was greeted by yet another welcoming gesture, this time from a woman who looked as bubbly as the hostess from the restaurant last night.

"Hello, ma'am, the Mays' celebration is upstairs in the Washington Ballroom. You'll need to go to the end of the hall, make a left, and take the elevator up to the fifth floor," the woman said with a wide smile. "I hope you enjoy your evening."

"Thank you." Bernadette returned the woman's smile. She was still adjusting to how friendly and well-mannered people were in the South. Growing up in the heart of Washington, DC, she'd become accustomed to the blunt, no-nonsense way of navigating through life. But being in Bourbon was an eye-opening experience, and as she was beginning to realize, it was a refreshing one.

As she ventured farther down the hallway, the faint smell of cologne and heavy footsteps caught her attention. With each step the smell got stronger, a combination of cedarwood and fresh greens, and the footsteps got closer, heavy but measured. She turned left at the end of the hallway as instructed, and so did the footsteps along with the masculine scent that smelled so good she wanted to see who it belonged to. Bernadette was glad that the elevator was just a few feet away so she could turn and see who was behind her. But before she could reach to press the button, a large hand pressed it for her. The elevator door immediately opened and she stepped inside. She stood perfectly still and watched as the tall, handsome man walked inside.

Bernadette felt her heart beat fast as she looked at the stranger standing to her left. He'd planted himself directly beside her and then turned so he could face her. "Good evening," he said in a deep, strong voice.

"Hi," was all Bernadette could think to say. She was the type of woman who rarely, if ever, was at a loss for words. She commanded boardrooms during business meetings and speaking engagements at national conferences, but the handsome stranger had left her tongue-tied and feeling school girl silly. She breathed in deeply and inhaled his sexy scent. Bernadette immediately pegged him for a pretty boy . . . a middle-aged pretty boy at that, which meant he was double trouble.

He pressed button number five and asked, "Which floor?"

Bernadette didn't want him to think that she was even slightly fazed by him, as she knew many women most likely were, so she concentrated and found her voice. "I'm going up to five as well."

He smiled, and despite her best efforts a warm feeling flooded her body. At six four, he was a full foot taller than she, and his impressive height was matched by his broad shoulders that filled out the width of his wool coat. His low cut, curly black hair had trace specks of gray, and his slight five o'clock shadow only added to his allure. Bernadette looked down at the man's shoes, which her discerning eye could tell were high-end, and then she slowly made her way back up to his face.

No one could dispute that the stranger was a fine specimen of a man. Not only did his tall, masculine frame look sexy, his smooth café au lait–colored skin and high cheekbones gave him a regal look. According to Bernadette's ranking scale for looks, he had to be a twenty out of ten.

"You're not from around here, are you?" the man asked.

"No, I'm not. How did you know?"

"Because I don't recognize you."

"Bourbon is a small town, but do you really think you know all ninety-five thousand residents who live here?" Bernadette had quickly recovered from her shock and awe stage and was back to her old self. She slightly smirked, knowing this man was used to being admired and saying whatever he pleased, especially to the ladies. A player, she thought to herself.

He nodded. "Just about, give or take a handful of folks."

"Do you work for the Census Bureau?"

"You got jokes. Give me your address and phone number so I can look through my files."

Bernadette hated to admit it, but his smile and quick wit made her want to laugh. But she knew that he was dead serious by the assured tone of his voice and the intense look in his eyes.

Before Bernadette knew it the bell dinged and the doors opened. She secretly wished the hotel had twenty floors instead of the mere five it took to reach the ballroom. She knew that once they stepped off the elevator and walked into the party, women would be swarming the handsome stranger who knew everyone in Bourbon.

"Ladies first." He extended his hand for Bernadette.

"Thank you."

He winked with a straight face. "It's my pleasure, pretty lady."

Bernadette didn't know if it was her imagination or wishful thinking, but the handsome stranger seemed to be flirting with her. Once they were off the elevator, the man leaned over and extended his hand for a greeting. "Please forgive me for not giving you a proper greeting. My name is Cooper Dennis, but my friends call me Coop."

Bernadette placed her small, delicate fingers inside his baseball mitt–size hand and gave him a firm shake. "Bernadette Gibson."

"You've got a mighty hard grip for such a little lady."

"You mean my firm handshake?" she corrected.

"No, I mean your grip. I might need an ice pack."

But standing next to the sexy, handsome stranger, Bernadette realized that her long-held theory about the meaning of one's handshake did not apply to him. His hands were soft, his touch was warm, and his grip was soft. But there was nothing weak or vulnerable about him. He was strong, bold, and fearless, and she could tell all that by the look in his eyes, which was so intense it sent a shudder through her body.

There was a coat check over to the right, and they both headed that way to relieve themselves of their winter outerwear.

"Let me help you with that," Coop said as he moved to help Bernadette slip out of her wrap. "Nice alpaca."

Bernadette blinked twice. Most women, let alone men, weren't familiar with the high-fiber material made from fleecing alpacas to fashion coats, hats, and gloves. "You have an excellent eye," Bernadette said.

"You have no idea." His fingers grazed the top of her slender shoulders and sent another shudder through her body.

Bernadette thought that everything about Coop was effortlessly sexy, and she knew that he knew it, too. But like his handshake, she could see that it was simply his natural way. His own brand of swagger. And in her eyes, that made him dangerous. She'd only dated one pretty boy in her life, and that had been thirty years ago during her college days. He'd been a popular campus hunk who had been one of the who's who on campus. She'd felt honored and was in disbelief that someone who was part of the in crowd and so good looking would want to date a regular, plain Jane, brainy wallflower like her.

Their whirlwind romance had ended after he'd turned in his near-perfect midterm paper, which he'd convinced Bernadette to write for him. The campus hunk received an A and Bernadette got a broken heart. It had been the first of many times that men had either used her, cheated on her, or both.

With their coats safely put away and claim tickets in their hands, Bernadette and Coop entered the crowded ballroom. The music was pumping, the dance floor was jumping, drinks were flowing, and people were celebrating like the ball was about to drop in Times Square. Bernadette surveyed the large ballroom and estimated that there had to be at least three hundred people who'd come out to celebrate Arizona's birthday. She also noticed that even though the room was filled with people, many of them stopped what they were doing when they saw Cooper Dennis standing beside her. It was almost as if a major celebrity had walked into the room.

"Coop! Coop! Hey, man!" and "What's up, Coop!" was all Bernadette heard.

A short, stout man hurriedly walked up to Coop and extended his hand for the classic soul brother dap. "Coop, whatchu know good, man!"

"Nothin' much. Just livin'."

"Livin' large, man."

"I get by," Coop said modestly.

"Com'on over and say hey to the fellas," the stout man said, acting as though Bernadette wasn't even standing there. "It's been a minute since anybody seen you outside the club, man."

Bernadette's lips formed a sarcastic smirk. He was a pretty playboy, just as she'd suspected. And what was worse was that he apparently hung out in the club so much that it was his main spot. Now his earlier statement made sense. It wasn't that he knew every person in Bourbon, it was that he knew nearly every woman in the town, and that was because he'd probably met them at the club, which also explained the lingering stares of nearly every female, young and old, within eyeshot. Bernadette didn't care how drop dead gorgeous Coop was, how sexy he was, how good he smelled, or how his very touch had made her shudder; she had no interest in him.

"Excuse me, Ms. Gibson," Coop said in a polite tone. "But this fool right here has no manners, and I apologize that he interrupted us getting to know each other."

The stout man's eyes grew large. "Oh, my bad." He looked at Bernadette and slightly bowed his head, showing a large bald spot in the middle of his scalp. "Please forgive my manners. I'm William Henry. It's a pleasure to meetchu."

Coop shook his head. "William Henry, I didn't mean for you to introduce yourself. I'm tryin' to get to know her."

William Henry looked as if he still didn't fully comprehend what the handsome player said, and by now Bernadette had had enough. She looked the sexy man in his eyes. "You know my name and I know yours, so there's not much more to discuss." Bernadette smiled. "Have a good night, gentlemen." And with that, she turned and walked away. She knew they both were probably watching her as she made her way across the room, so she added an extra sway to her narrow hips.

"Bernadette!" Arizona yelled. "I'm so glad you're here." Arizona trotted up to Bernadette and greeted her with a warm hug. "Thank you so, so much for coming."

Bernadette had thought that Arizona looked good last night, but tonight she was stunningly gorgeous and glammed up like she belonged on the set of a Vogue style shoot. Her rose gold–colored sequined dress glistened against her sun-kissed almond-colored skin and complemented her voluptuous hips. Bernadette saw that men were staring at Arizona's assets, but the birthday girl didn't acknowledge one single glance, and that was because it was probably a regular occurrence for Arizona. Women like her had that special "it" that drew men like a magnet.

"Thank you for inviting me," Bernadette yelled over the noise.

"I saved a place for you at my table, com'on."

Arizona took Bernadette by her hand and led her through the maze of people throughout the large ballroom until they reached an area that was roped off, allowing enough space for two tables of ten. Tall signs that said Reserved sat atop each table. Arizona introduced Bernadette to her parents, Myron and Carlotta Mays, two aunts on her mother's side, and a few of her cousins. Bernadette remembered Arizona telling her that her mother was slightly older than Bernadette, but that Mother Nature hadn't been kind to her as she'd aged. Bernadette had thought it was a harsh thing to say, especially about one's own mother, but what she was beginning to learn about her brutally blunt new friend was that despite the bite of her words, they were laced with honesty. Even though Carlotta was Bernadette's peer, the woman could have been mistaken for Arizona's grandmother.

Bernadette and Arizona settled in at the birthday girl's table that was decorated with flowers and balloons. A three-tier cake—representing each decade of Arizona's life—topped with a faux tube of lipstick and bottle of perfume, both fashioned from fondant, was displayed a few feet away. Bernadette was impressed with the scale of the event. Because Arizona's birthday party was so lavish, Bernadette could only imagine what her wedding was going to be like. Then she suddenly thought about Chris. She leaned over to Arizona. "Where is your fiancé?"

Arizona smiled. "He needed to take care of something at the front desk, but he should be back in a few minutes. Even though he's off the clock he's still workin', because you're always on call when you're general manager of a hotel."

"He's doing a great job because this hotel is fabulous and so is your party."

"Yes, Chris has been planning this for months."

"It looks like everyone he invited must've showed up. This crowd is huge."

Arizona looked around. "Yeah, and there's actually a few people from work here."

Bernadette looked around, knowing she wasn't familiar enough to recognize them. "Half of Bourbon is in here," she joked.

Arizona spoke above the music and chatter. "If you think this is something, it doesn't compare to what's planned for the wedding."

"Well, I want an invitation and a front row seat."

Bernadette swayed to the beat of the music and spotted Coop across the room. She looked away when she saw him staring back at her.

"I saw you and Coop walk in together," Arizona said with a wink. "And now he's staring you down like he's thirsty . . . I ain't never seen Coop look thirsty."

"You know him?"

"Girl, who don't know Coop? He's legendary."

"Oh really?"

Arizona nodded. "Coop is like a celebrity in Bourbon, everybody knows him and he knows everybody."

"That's what he told me on the elevator ride up. I'm sure he's quite the ladies' man."

"Yeah, but not like you think. Nearly every woman in this room except me would give her right arm and maybe even a leg to be with him. But Coop keeps pretty much to himself, and as far as I know he's single and likes it that way."

Bernadette was shocked. "He's not a player?"

"He used to be, back in his heyday, and from the stories I've heard he was somethin' else. But that was a long, long time ago, and as far back as I can remember he's been a big deal in Bourbon. He owns over half of the rental houses in the Bottoms, a couple Laundromats, two car washes, and Southern Comfort."

"You mean the jazz club?"

"Yep. Have you been?"

Now Bernadette knew why the clueless man who'd approached them had said he hadn't seen Coop outside the club. It was because he was the owner. Bernadette had seen the billboard for Southern Comfort every day on her way to work, and she'd heard advertisements for the club on the local radio station. She'd been wanting to go ever since she moved to Bourbon. A few months back she'd planned an evening there because she loved jazz and wanted to venture out and enjoy a relaxing night of good music and wine. But her demandingly long work hours at Bourbon General had drained her so much that by the time her days ended, all she wanted to do was crawl into bed so she could prepare for another grueling day.

Now, Bernadette had to admit that Coop had piqued her interest.

"He's one of the wealthiest men in town," Arizona said. "Black or white, and what separates Coop is that he's a self-made man. His daddy didn't hand down a business or money to him like most of the other rich men in Bourbon. No sir, Coop came out of prison with nothin' and built an empire."

"Prison?"

"Yep, a long time ago . . . for drugs."

"Oh . . ."

"But he's a changed man. Even my mama said so, and she don't play. She'll call a spade a spade with no problem."

Bernadette nodded. "So, you get it from your mama."

"I guess I do." The two women laughed and chitchatted, again bonding like old friends.

Bernadette looked over in Coop's direction and saw that he was still staring her way. His eyes were piercing, with a hint of mystery. The half-smile kissing his lips made her blush. She didn't want to lust after Coop, but she couldn't help herself. He oozed with sexiness and it made her feel warm inside. She wondered why out of all the women in the room, he'd zeroed in on her.

Bernadette knew she wasn't a bad-looking woman, but she also knew she wasn't what one would call attractive, either. She was average at best. Average face, average body, and average sex appeal. But despite her ordinary looks, Coop was still staring at her above all the women in the room, and it made Bernadette wonder what he had up his sleeve. She looked away so he wouldn't think she was interested, and her eyes went straight to another handsome man coming their way.

The man looked like a chocolate-covered Adonis, and as Arizona had told Bernadette, he'd come dressed to impress. He walked with the swagger and confidence of a professional athlete. He was Coop's height and his muscles bulged through the tailored shirt that was tucked neatly inside his precision creased pants. Bernadette watched him as the man zeroed in on Arizona, and when he made eye contact with her, he smiled as though he'd just been given good news.

"Here comes Chris," Arizona said.

Bernadette looked at Arizona and then back at Chris. Arizona had told her that Chris was a specimen to behold, and again, she'd been right on point with her words. As Bernadette looked at the Chippendale dancer look-alike, all she could think was that as tall, muscular, and handsome as he was, he had a micropenis. The contradiction of the two ideas was so great it was hard to wrap her brain around the situation.

Bernadette watched Chris as he slowly pulled out the chair next to Arizona and sat down. He leaned into her, draped his muscular arm around her shoulder, and kissed her so delicately and with so much tenderness there wasn't a doubt in Bernadette's mind that he adored his fiancée.

"Sorry about that, baby." Chris smiled and took Arizona's hand into his. "I had to take care of a guest complaint. But I told the staff not to call me for the rest of the night because I'm celebrating with my beautiful wife-to-be."

Bernadette loved the way Chris was completely giddy with love when he looked at Arizona. She hoped that someday a man would look at her with the same amount of love and desire.

"Oh, please excuse me," Chris said. "You must be Bernadette." He extended his hand and exchanged a firm grip with Bernadette. "Arizona told me about the great time you two had last night, and I think it's awesome that you share the same birthday. So happy birthday to you, too."

"Thank you, Chris, and it's good to meet you as well. You and Arizona make a beautiful couple."

"Thank you," they responded in unison.

"Speaking of couples," Arizona said to Chris. "Coop's been eyein' Bernadette all night."

Chris looked in Coop's direction and then turned toward Bernadette. "Looks like you have an admirer."

Bernadette shook her head. "I don't think so." She hadn't made the statement because she was trying to be modest or coy, she'd made it because she didn't believe a man like Coop would genuinely be interested in her. Despite a few misguided assumptions on her part, she'd pretty much figured out what kind of man Coop was. He was used to getting what and who he wanted, and on the rare occasion someone resisted his charms, he considered it a challenge to change their mind. Bernadette knew she was his challenge—not his desire— so she made herself turn away from his gaze.

"I think you're wrong," Arizona said. "Coop doesn't stare women down like he's doing with you."

"Maybe he just wants a challenge."

Arizona gave Bernadette a sly smile. "You can ask him yourself 'cause he's walkin' this way."

Sure enough, Coop was walking in their direction, looking straight into Bernadette's eyes. His stride was long and his pace was steady, just as it had been when he'd been walking behind her downstairs. He glided through the maze of people on the dance floor, and when he reached the roped area he stepped around it to get to Arizona's table. "Happy birthday, darlin'," Coop said with a big smile.

Arizona stood and gave Coop a hug. "Thanks, Coop. I'm glad you came."

"You know I wouldn't miss it. Your mama told me I better come, and when Carlotta Mays tells you to do somethin', you better do it."

Arizona nodded in agreement. "Ain't that the truth."

"Chris, you outdid yourself with this party," Coop said.

"Thanks, Coop. Anything for my baby."

Coop smiled. "You're a smart and very lucky man. How long until the big day?"

"With tomorrow being the first of February, that means we've got four months to go."

Coop turned to Arizona. "I can't believe Carlotta's little girl is all grown up and gettin' married. You sure you're ready for the long haul?" Coop let them know he was joking by nudging Chris, and the two men joined together in laughter.

Bernadette noticed that Arizona looked uncomfortable, shifting in her seat as she fiddled with the linen napkin on the table.

Chris reached for Arizona's hand and kissed it. "The Bible says, when a man finds a wife, he finds a good thing."

Bernadette wanted to tear up with emotion because she could see and hear in Chris's voice that he deeply loved Arizona. His eyes were fixed on hers with a type of devotion that said he was indeed in it for the long haul.

Arizona smiled and Bernadette saw the same uneasiness that she'd shown last night. She'd told Bernadette that Chris had made overnight accommodations for them in the executive suite on the sixth floor, which was considered the penthouse, and she was nervous that he'd want to have sex again. She'd also told Bernadette that she was dreading the thought of having to talk to Chris about the horrible sex they'd had two nights ago, and she'd hoped that he'd be too tired to even think about sex after a long day of work and party planning.

Chris looked at Arizona, expecting her to say that she, too, was in it for the long haul. But Arizona remained silent, and it cast an awkward silence over the table. Bernadette spoke up. "That's very sweet, Chris. You both are blessed."

"Amen," Coop chimed in and winked at Bernadette.

Just then a popular line dance song blared through the room.

"We all gotta get out on the dance floor," Arizona said. "Let's go." She motioned to her parents, aunts, and cousins to make their way to the dance floor. "You too, Bernadette."

"Oh, no, I'm going to sit this one out." Bernadette said firmly.

Coop gently took Bernadette's hand. "The birthday girl said let's go."

Before Bernadette could object any further, Coop was leading her to the dance floor where the line dance was in full swing. Coop gave her a wink. "All right, pretty lady. Let's see what you got."

Bernadette eased into the rhythm of the song, and soon, she and Coop were dancing in sync, smiling and enjoying the beat. Bernadette swayed her hips from side to side and was feeling happier than she had in a very long time. That's when everything went south, literally.

Bernadette turned to perform a spin move when her heel got caught on a divot in the dance floor that had been laid over the ornate carpet, which caused her to trip and start a quick descent toward the ground. But before she hit the hard floor, she felt a big, strong pair of hands swoop her back up onto her feet, placing her in a spot so she could rejoin the beat where she'd left off. They continued to dance to the music until they were both sweating. Bernadette could see that he was in good shape because Coop was dancing rigorously without so much as a hint of being tired or out of breath.

"All right, beautiful people. We gonna slow it down for a beat," the DJ said. "Here's a little old-school Luther for you."

Coop's eyes gazed upon Bernadette. There was something about this man that she liked, but she didn't want to show her hand. "I'm going to head back to my seat now," Bernadette said.

Coop laughed but didn't say a word. Instead, he put one foot in front of the other and followed Bernadette back toward Arizona's table. When they reached the velvet rope, Bernadette turned and faced Coop. "Thanks for picking me up before I fell on my face."

Coop gave her a sly smile. "As long as you're with me you don't have to worry about anything. I got you."

This was another uncharacteristic moment where Bernadette was at a loss for words. Even though what he'd just said sounded like a player move, she could see that Coop was serious, which made her even more confused. She didn't understand why this gorgeous hunk of a man whom she'd just met would want to be with and protect her.

"Bernadette, I want to ask you something," Coop said.

"Okay, what?"

"Can I get to know you?"

Two hours later Bernadette walked into her house, and a quick shower and thirty minutes later she was under her cozy sheets. She should have been tired, but she was wide awake. She couldn't get Coop off her mind. After he'd asked if he could get to know her, the

DJ switched up songs again, returning the music to a fast pace that got everyone back on the floor, including Bernadette and Coop. They danced song after song, and the only reason they stopped was because it was time for Arizona to cut her cake.

Chris made a touching, swoon-worthy speech, and Arizona tried to look as though nothing was wrong. Bernadette knew that Arizona was probably thinking that now that the party was winding down and her birthday celebration was coming to an end, the moment of truth would be facing her when she and Chris would have to retreat upstairs to the suite he'd reserved for them. Bernadette felt for her friend, but she had her own dilemma on her hands with Coop. She left earlier than she'd wanted to, hoping she could sneak away from Coop. But he'd clung to her like a layer of skin, and before she'd known it he was walking her down to the valet stand and had programmed her number into his phone before she'd driven away.

Just as Bernadette was about to turn off her bedside lamp her phone buzzed, alerting her that a text message was coming in. She reached for her phone on her nightstand and looked at the message. It was from Coop.

Coop: Hey pretty lady. Just checking to make sure you made it home safely.

Bernadette smiled because his message made her feel warm inside. He'd asked her to text him once she got home to let him know that she'd made it back safely. But she'd been so tired after settling in home that she'd forgotten. But apparently he hadn't.

Bernadette: Yes, I'm home. Thanks for checking on me.

Bernadette held her breath and pressed Send, and just a few seconds later her phone buzzed again.

Coop: Good. Sleep tight.

Bernadette: You too.

Bernadette didn't know what to make of all the emotions running through her body and her mind. She'd awakened that morning with a new feeling and attitude to match, and now it seemed as though her prayers were being answered in just one day. But before she got too sentimental she remembered that this was how things had started out with Walter. He'd aggressively pursued her, and their fairy-tale romance had seemed too good to be true. Eventually, she'd realized that it was, but not before it was too late.

As Bernadette drifted off to sleep she reminded herself that as optimistic as she wanted to be, she knew she had to proceed with great caution.

# Chapter 11

## ARIZONA

Arizona was sitting on the edge of the couch in the living room of the presidential suite that Chris had reserved for them so they could continue her birthday celebration. He'd given her the room key shortly before the party ended and told her to go upstairs and get comfortable while he took care of making sure all the equipment was out of the ballroom, the decorations were taken down, and Arizona's gifts were transported to her house where she could open them tomorrow.

Arizona kicked off her four-inch rose gold stilettos that perfectly matched the dazzling, form-fitting dress she'd worn tonight. She bent over and rubbed her sore feet. "Whew, what a night. I wish I could unscrew my feet from my ankles right about now." When she stood up her knees sounded as if someone had stepped on a yard of bubble wrap. "I gotta take some of this weight off my bones," she said as she hobbled across the floor. She knew losing weight would take pressure off her entire body and that she'd feel better, but right now the pressure of the night ahead superseded her concerns about her dress size.

She walked toward the back of the suite, entered the luxuriously decorated bedroom, and gasped. "This is why I love that man," Arizona whispered. All she could do was smile at the sight before her.

The nightstands flanking the king-size bed were adorned with two dozen blush-colored roses, beautifully arranged inside a simple but elegant crystal vase. In the center of the bed there was a heart that had been fashioned from hundreds of pink rose petals. This was one of the most romantic things that anyone had ever done for Arizona, and what made the gesture especially sweet was the fact that she knew Chris had arranged the petals all by himself instead of delegating the task to the housekeeping staff. She knew it was her fiancé's handiwork because the heart was lopsided from his large hands and special touch, and in her eyes, the minor imperfection made it perfect. She clasped her hands over her heart. "That's Chris, imperfect perfection."

Arizona's eyes wandered over to the luggage rack that held her overnight bag near the stately mahogany desk. She ran her fingers across the condensation covering the ice bucket and the bottle of Moscato that was tucked inside. There was a hearty fruit and cheese tray beside it, and a bowl of chocolate-covered strawberries was next in line.

"He thinks of everything. What's wrong with me?" Arizona questioned herself in an admonishing tone. "I have a good man who loves me, wants to marry me and take care of me, and here I am, debating whether I want to grab my overnight bag and head back home after the wonderful party he threw for me tonight, and this romantic setup he did all by himself. I need to keep my behind right where I am."

Arizona pulled her dress over her head, unhooked her bra, and breathed with unrestricted freedom for the first time all night. "Time for me to take a shower, get comfortable, and wait on my man to come up so we can celebrate all alone." She walked over to the luggage rack and opened her bag to retrieve her toiletries. She smiled and shook her head when she saw a gift inside that made her heart beat fast. Lying atop the jeans and sweater that she planned on wearing tomorrow was a Belk department store bag containing a silk and lace nightie along with a birthday card.

"Oh, Lord," Arizona said with a loving sigh. She opened the envelope and became misty-eyed by what she read. Chris had hand written a note off to the side. *I can't wait to make you my wife. I love you for life . . . Your husband-to-be, Chris.*

Arizona stared at the words on the card and then at the sexy negligée that Chris had bought her. She ran her hand across the delicate silk material that was etched with intricate lace. She knew it wasn't a coincidence that Chris had bought her lingerie for the very first time in their relationship after they'd made love for the first time two nights ago. This was his way of letting her know that he wanted more, and it made Arizona feel fidgety and uncomfortable. "This isn't how you're supposed to feel when you think about having sex with the man you love. What am I gonna do?"

Arizona knew that no matter how hard and awkward the conversation might be, she was going to have to confront the issue of Chris's anatomy and her concerns about it. The only problem was that she didn't know how she was going to do it without sounding brutally harsh, which she didn't want to do. Arizona knew that her blunt tongue and social graces left something to be desired, but she also knew that she needed to have a heart-to-heart, honest conversation with her fiancé to let him know how she felt. "I need to find the right words to say and the right tone to say it . . . but how?" Suddenly, a thought came to her.

Arizona walked over to the closet and removed one of the thick white terry-cloth bathrobes draped on the wooden hanger. She struggled to wrap it around her. There had been a time when she could have easily tied the robe around her body and still had a little room. But those days were a distant memory. "I can't think about weight right now because if I do it'll make my bad mood worse," she mumbled to herself. She walked over to the ice bucket and poured herself a glass of Moscato only to see that it wasn't Moscato, it was the same fancy champagne she'd had last night during dinner with Bernadette. "This is just what I need right now." Arizona filled her flute to the top and drank half the glass in two large swallows. She looked at the clock knowing it was late, but she dialed Bernadette's number and hoped her friend would pick up. Arizona nearly jumped when Bernadette answered on the second ring.

"I'm sorry to call you so late," Arizona said. "I know it's past one a.m. . . . . did I wake you?"

"No, I just got into bed, though. What's going on, are you okay?"

"I'm in the presidential suite, drinking champagne and waiting on Chris, and girl, he bought me some sexy lingerie, and I'm sure he's expecting me to put it to good use tonight."

"Well, that's just horrible. A handsome, respectful man who loves you, put you up in the best room in the entire hotel, and gave you champagne and gifts. I don't know what the world is coming too. How dare he."

"Bernadette, now isn't the time to be funny."

"But, Arizona, you do know how crazy you sound, don't you?"

"Uh, yeah, I know. But my situation is a little different from how things look on the surface. I'm scared he's gonna want to have sex again."

"You're going to have to talk to him because something like this needs to be ironed out before you two say your I dos."

"And see, that's the thing. I'm not so sure anymore."

"About what?"

"Marrying Chris."

There was a long pause on the other end. "Bernadette, are you still there?"

"I'm here. I just had to sit up in my bed to make sure I'm hearing you correctly because this is serious."

"I know it is. Why do you think I'm calling you in the middle of the night? I need to tell Chris how I really feel, and that I have doubts, but I don't know how to say it in a way that won't hurt his feelings, so I was hoping you could give me some advice because you're good with words."

Bernadette took a deep breath on the other end. "Before I give you advice I want to ask you something."

"Okay."

"Are you really prepared to end your relationship with Chris over sex, or are you feeling that way because you're frustrated and don't know what to do?"

Arizona thought for a moment, but she didn't have an answer. "Honestly, I don't know. Part of me knows that Chris is the man for me. He's a gentleman, thoughtful, and very respectful of my feelings, and I know that he loves me like nobody's business."

"Yes, I believe that, too."

"But I also know how I am. I like sex, plain and simple. And not just sex, good sex."

"Don't we all?"

"There you go again. Bernadette, please stop making jokes. I'm serious."

"And so am I. Do you know how many women would love to be in your situation right now? You have a good-looking, kindhearted, intelligent, hardworking man with a good job who loves you and your son. He supports your dreams and he absolutely adores you. I bet the single ladies at your party tonight would love to have a man with half of Chris's qualities."

"Do you think they'd still want him if they knew his penis was the size of my toe?"

Bernadette was quiet for a minute. "Some would and some wouldn't. I guess the question for you to answer is what is it that you truly want, and what's most important to you. Arizona, I want you to think long and hard about that question."

Arizona had emptied her champagne flute and was giving herself a refill. "That question has been the only thing on my mind since last night. I've thought about it and like I said before, I love Chris, but I also love sex. It's a miracle that I've been celibate for this long, and honestly, holding out wasn't all that hard because I thought Chris would be worth the wait. But now, I just don't know." Arizona paused and took a sip of her bubbly. She walked back to the bedroom, looked down at the rose petals on the bed, and then sat on the edge of the fluffy, down-filled comforter. "Would you want a man with small penis? And I'm talking infant size."

"No, I wouldn't. But I'd try to make it work."

Arizona felt sad and defeated as she spoke. "In order to make it work you've got to have a lil' somethin' to work with in the first place, and he has nothing," she nearly sobbed, "trust me."

Bernadette sighed. "You young girls are something else. Let an old lady school you."

"That's why I called you."

Bernadette chuckled. "I walked into that one."

"Huh?"

"Never mind." Bernadette cleared her throat. "There are other ways you can receive satisfaction and achieve orgasm that don't involve a penis. Your clitoris is the key to pleasure, period, and it doesn't require a big penis, or a penis at all, to stimulate it. He can grind on it, rub it, lick it, or use a toy to stimulate it, and if he does it right you won't even think about his penis. At the end of the day you want to be satisfied, so don't get all caught up in the travel route as long as you end up reaching your destination."

Arizona stood up, walked back over to the bottle of bubbly, and poured herself another glass, this time filling it only halfway. She walked back to the bedroom and sat in the plush high-back chair beside the bed and thought about what Bernadette had said. She knew her friend was right.

"The more I think about it," Bernadette said, "I'm not sure if you should have a serious talk with Chris about your disappointment with his size, because honestly, that's a hell of a tough conversation for anyone to have."

"What do you think I should do?"

"First of all, put the champagne down so you'll have your wits about you."

"How do you know I'm still drinking?"

"Because it's almost a requirement to drink champagne when

you're living life in a presidential suite," Bernadette said, without missing a beat. "My advice to you is to see what kind of moves Chris has. Explore how you two can bring each other pleasure without actual intercourse. Kiss, caress, fondle, tickle, and have fun getting to know each other's body. Trust me, if you can do that you'll have a fighting chance."

"You talk like you have a lot of experience with this type of thing."

"Kind of, but on the other end of the spectrum of what you're dealing with. Just because a man is well endowed it doesn't mean he knows what to do with it. It's just like business, you have to minimize your losses and maximize your profits. If his penis can't satisfy you, maybe his tongue can. If he's not a good kisser, maybe his touch gets you excited. You have to work together to find what's going to please you, and the same goes for him, although with men it's less complicated."

Arizona knew that Bernadette was right. She had to give it a try. Chris had been horrible the other night, but it had also been their first time being intimate, and she had hope that he might be better the second time around. "You're right," Arizona said. "I'm going to keep an open mind and look for other ways that we both can achieve pleasure."

"There you go."

Just then Arizona heard the door open in the front room. "I'm back in the bedroom," she called out, then whispered to Bernadette, "Chris is back, so I've got to hang up."

"Good luck, and let me know how it goes."

"You know I will." Arizona closed her eyes and said a quick prayer for the best.

When Chris walked into the bedroom he looked exhausted. Arizona knew that he'd been running errands all day and working all night in order to make her party a huge success, which it had been. Now Chris looked like all he was ready to do was go to sleep, and that prospect gave Arizona a little relief.

"You look beautiful, baby," Chris said in a tired voice. He walked over to where Arizona was sitting and gave her a kiss on her cheek before taking a seat on the bed. "You like the rose petals?"

Arizona smiled with a nod of her head. "Yes, baby. You did an amazing job of arranging them."

Chris returned her smile. "How did you know I did it?"

"Because I know you. The perfectly imperfect lopsided heart had Chris Pendleton written all over it." Arizona leaned over and handed Chris her glass of champagne. "I think you need this."

"Yes, it's been a long day and an even longer night."

"Yes, it has, and thank you for all that you did to make my birthday special. I really appreciate you, baby."

"You only turn thirty once." Chris smiled and exhaled. "Now that your birthday is in the record books, we can concentrate on the next big event, which is our wedding. Tomorrow is February, and June will be here before you know it."

"Yes, it will."

Chris guzzled down the champagne and then sat the glass on the nightstand. "Are you okay?"

"Yeah, I'm fine. Just tired." It was a half lie.

"Arizona, like I said yesterday and you just said a minute ago, I know you, you know me, and we both know when something's not right with one of us. Something's not right with you. I could sense it tonight at your party, but I didn't want to make too much of a big deal out of it. But you definitely had something on your mind and you still do. Talk to me, what's going on?"

They stared at each other in silence. Arizona could see that Chris was confused and she knew he had every reason to be. He'd thrown her a fantastic party, given her great gifts, and skillfully orchestrated a romantic evening that most women could only dream of. Yet here she was, feeling down and out as if she'd just been given an eviction notice. She knew she needed to explain herself, and despite the advice that Bernadette had given her, she felt she needed to be completely honest about her concerns surrounding the future of their sexual relationship. But before she could open her mouth, Chris cut her off.

"Is this about us making love the other night?"

Arizona looked down at the floor. "Yes."

"I know, and I've been feeling the same way. We broke our vow of celibacy, and instead of me taking responsibility and apologizing, I made matters worse by telling you that I'd make it last longer the next time. That was wrong of me, Arizona. I respect you and I love you, and I shouldn't have put you in that kind of situation. I know that's what you've been thinking about since last night, and when you came into this room and saw the lingerie along with the rose petals, it probably made you feel worse instead of better."

Arizona could see that Chris was disappointed because he felt as if he'd let her down. His sincerity and love for her touched her heart and aroused a carnal desire that made her want him. She stood up and took a few steps to where he was sitting on the edge of the bed. She cupped his face in the palms of her hands. "I love that you're such a good, honest, and decent man. And I love that you love me. But right now, what I need . . . what we need, is to get busy under these sheets."

"Wait, Arizona. Are you sure? I mean, it's not that I don't want to, because trust me, I do. But I didn't think you wanted to. Isn't that the reason you've been on edge since Thursday night?"

"Yes and no. But don't worry about that. Right now I want to seize this moment. We're in a beautiful suite with roses, champagne, and a big, soft bed. We need to use all of this in our favor."

"Like I said the other night, we don't have to do this."

"I know, Chris. You've already told me that."

"Yeah, and look what happened. You've been moping around ever since Thursday night, and that's not right. I don't want to compromise things any further."

"This is truly what I want." Arizona knew that now was the time to test out Bernadette's advice. If Chris could fulfill her and satisfy her tonight, they would be on a road to making their sex life an enjoyable one, and her worries would be a distant memory. "Don't say another word. Just be a man of action." Arizona dropped her robe and stood naked in front of him.

Arizona smiled when she saw Chris's eyes roam over her body with heated desire. He stood and enveloped her with his long arms and pulled her into his firm chest. She closed her eyes as his hands caressed her skin, rubbing up and down in a circular motion. But instead of feeling pleasure, Arizona's eyes flew open with discomfort because there was nothing about his touch that aroused her. He made circles on the cheek of her left hip with one hand, while performing the same motion, but in the opposite direction on her other. She closed her eyes again and tried to get into the rhythm of what he was doing, but an image from a scene in one of her favorite movies, *The Karate Kid*, popped into her mind. She likened Chris's movements to the lesson when Mr. Miyagi demonstrated the wax-on, wax-off technique to his young charge, Daniel-san. Arizona knew this was all wrong, and she knew she had to do something to salvage the moment.

"Here baby, right here." Arizona gently moved one of Chris's hands to the small of her back in order to break up the hard, rigid rubbing that was beginning to irritate her.

"I love it when you tell me what you like." Chris moaned and then whispered, "Do you like it, baby?"

Arizona blocked out his moans and his words because they only served to heighten her anxiety. She knew she had to focus her mind in order to get into a sexy mood. But no matter how hard she tried to focus on feeling pleasure from Chris's touch, it just wasn't there. She wanted him to gently caress her, but his touch felt as if he was brushing her skin with a pumice stone. The pit of her stomach churned, and she knew she needed to try a different strategy. "Let's get in bed," she said in a low, sexy voice.

"You don't have to tell me twice."

Within thirty seconds Chris was as naked as a newborn, proudly displaying his microscopic penis that was barely visible, buried by hair and balls. Arizona took a quick glance and felt the blood drain from her head. She knew she had to once again refocus her mind to a more positive place. She hoped for the best and slid under the hotel's crisp sheets.

*Find pleasure in other ways,* Arizona told herself as she tried to hold on to Bernadette's sage advice. She kissed Chris, starting slowly, because she wanted to take her time and ease into arousal. But Chris quickly increased the pace by darting his tongue in and out of her mouth with quick bursts. He jabbed the side of her jaw, teeth, lips and gums as if he was searching for food.

*What the hell is he doing?* Arizona thought with alarm. She cupped his face with both hands and stopped him. "Chris, baby, slow down. We have all night."

"Oh, okay, baby," he panted.

Arizona couldn't figure out why he was rushing, and out of breath, as if he'd just run a 5K race. Chris was in great shape and he worked out at the gym five days a week, so she knew he couldn't possibly be overexerted from a little grinding and kissing. But as he rubbed and moved on top of her, his breathing became more labored, and then suddenly, he stopped.

"Ooohhh," Chris moaned. "I'm sorry, baby . . . did you feel it?"

Arizona was completely confused. "Feel what?"

"I know last night I said I'd make it last longer, but I got so excited . . ."

"Chris, what are you talking about?"

"I came."

"Huh?" Arizona knew he couldn't possibly mean what she thought he was saying, so she asked for clarification. "You mean you had an orgasm?"

Chris couldn't even speak, all he did was nod and smile.

"How?" Arizona asked. She was in a state of bewilderment.

"You excite me so much that it's hard for me to hold back. Baby, you put it on me, and I know if it's like this now, it's only gonna get better and better. Like Denzel said, 'Mo betta makes it mo betta.' I can't wait to make you my wife. I love you, Arizona."

Arizona heard what Chris was saying but she still couldn't believe what had come out of his mouth, and she didn't even want to think about what had come out of him. But a second later she was forced to deal with it when a rush of warm, sticky liquid slid down her thigh as Chris rolled off her and laid his head back on the fluffy pillow that he'd propped up against the headboard. Arizona pinched her eyes shut with frustration. She'd hoped that she could slowly ease her way into the delicate conversation that she knew they needed to have, but this pitiful excuse for lovemaking didn't even qualify as sex in her mind. Arizona didn't care if Chris's feelings or ego got hurt, bruised, or battered beyond recognition. She had things to say, and she wasn't going to let another second go by without telling Chris exactly how she felt. "We really, and I mean really, need to talk," she said in a frustrated tone.

Arizona stared at Chris and shook her head. His shallow breathing mixed with the slow rise and fall of his chest let her know that he was getting ready to fall asleep, so she gave his broad shoulder a hard nudge. "Chris, I said we need to talk. And I mean right now!"

"Baby, I'm so tired I can't think straight, and I . . . I'm not up for talking right . . ." And with that, Chris was sound asleep.

She nudged him again. "No, wake up. We need to talk, Chris."

When he started snoring, Arizona knew he was sound asleep, and no matter what she tried, he'd be out until the sun came up. "I can't even believe this," she whispered aloud. Arizona sat up in bed and knew that this was the beginning of the end.

# Chapter 12

## TESS

Tess sipped from the colorfully decorated disposable coffee cup that was filled to the brim with a piping-hot dose of Ethiopian roast. She was sitting on her living room couch, looking out her large window at the bright white snow covering her street. It was Sunday morning, and she realized that other than going down the street to get coffee from Joe's Café a few minutes ago, she hadn't been out of the house since last Sunday morning, when she'd gone there to get the same coffee she was drinking right now. She felt as if so much, yet so little, had happened in her life from then to now. She was nowhere near finishing her book; however, she'd closed another chapter of her life with the news of Antwan's happily-ever-after. She looked at the clock. It was ten in the morning where Bernadette lived, and Tess knew her cousin had probably been up since the sun rose, so she decided to call.

"Good Sunday morning, cuz!" Bernadette said, sounding cheerful and full of energy.

"You need to either tone it down several notches or transfer some of that happiness crap my way."

"Aren't we the ray of sunshine this morning," Bernadette chirped.

"Bernadette, please don't start with the sarcasm. I really can't take it today."

"First of all, you're the one who called me, so don't get mad if I answer my phone in a good mood. And secondly, Tess, what's wrong with you?"

"I'm tired, that's all."

"No, that's not it. As a matter of fact, I've noticed over the last few months you've been snippy and moody almost all the time, and it's only getting worse. I know you're under stress to finish your book, but I've never seen you like this, and frankly, I'm beginning to worry about you. Talk to me and tell me what's really going on?"

Tess rubbed her left temple and let out a loud sigh. "I'm sorry for the way I just came at you; I apologize. Like I said, I'm tired, and I have been for a while." She paused and tried to put a smile in her voice that wasn't in her heart. "Tell me all about last night. Did you have fun? Did you meet a fine Southern gentleman?"

"I had a good time, but before I go into any of that I want to know what's really going on with you. I heard what you said but I know there's more to it than that. Something's wrong and I want you to level with me."

Tess set her cup on her glass coffee table. "It's so stupid, and I feel silly for even trippin' about it."

"Testimony Sinclair, you better tell me what's going on right now!"

Tess could hear the urgent concern in Bernadette's voice, and it made her want to break down and cry. Bernadette was the protective big sister that Tess had always been able to count on through highs and lows, and right now she needed her cousin's strength to lean on. She took a deep breath, settled back into her couch, and proceeded to tell Bernadette about Antwan and his new bride.

She confessed that over the last two days she'd been on social media day and night trolling through pictures and posts of the happy couple. That morning she'd discovered that the newlyweds were still living it up and celebrating a joyous honeymoon that they'd chronicled for the world to see. The two had been featured on wedding sites like *Munaluchi*, *Weddings OnPoint*, *Black Bride*, and *The Knot*. And an hour ago, Tess had just read an online article titled "Black Love &

Beauty" on *Essence.com*, where the new Mrs. Bolling was a contribut-
ing beauty editor.

"Tess, I'm so sorry to hear this," Bernadette said.

"Thanks," Tess said in a low voice. "I've been so closed off for the
last few months that I didn't even know he was dating anyone. I
blocked him and most of his friends and the people we knew as a
couple because it was too painful to rehash and relive it all." Tess
sighed. "You wouldn't believe the kind of stares, questions, and downright crazy comments I received from people once they found out
that we'd broken up. But I guess I shouldn't have dropped completely
off the radar like I did because this really blindsided me. I'm still in
shock."

"I understand, cuz. Even though my relationship with Walter
ended the way it did, it still took time for me to get over him, and
honestly, it was harder getting over what he did to me than actually
getting over my feelings for him."

Tess was shocked by Bernadette's admission. "Wow, I didn't know
that."

"Neither did I until I started doing a lot of reflecting. I loved the
idea of what I thought Walter and I had. But with you and Antwan,
it's just the opposite of what I experienced. I think it's been harder for
you to get over your feelings for him than it was the things he actually did. Tess, you loved that man, and I think a part of you still does.
That's why you're so emotional about his marriage. If you didn't care
you wouldn't be stalking his Instagram and other social media pages."

Tess had to take a moment to think about what Bernadette had
just said. She hated to admit it, but she knew Bernadette was right.
She'd never resolved her feelings for Antwan, and now the pain was
staring her in the face all over again. Tess picked up her half-empty
coffee cup and walked into the kitchen. She knew she needed to eat,
take a shower, and get back into a normal routine, but she still felt
stuck.

"Have you eaten anything this morning?" Bernadette asked.

"Yes, a delicious cup of coffee."

"You need to take care of yourself, Tess. You're upset, vulnerable, sleep deprived, and in need of food. That's not good."

"I really don't feel like eating or sleeping. I just want to sulk."

"It's okay to feel hurt, and lonely, and sad, but you can't live in that space. Antwan has gone on with his life, and now you've got to move forward with yours."

Tess filled her stainless steel teakettle with distilled spring water and placed it on her chef's grade, six-burner stove in preparation for making a cup of chamomile tea to calm her nerves after her caffeine rush. "I thought about calling him."

"Please tell me you didn't."

"I said I thought about it, but I didn't actually do it. I'm not crazy."

"Thank goodness."

"But I might create a fake account and post something horrendous about him, like, 'I wonder if Antwan gave his new bride the herpes virus he's been carrying around for two years as a wedding gift?' "

Bernadette drew in a sharp breath of air on the other end. "Don't even play around about stuff like that. What's wrong with you?"

Tess scooped a heaping mound of natural brown sugar into her teacup. "It's dastardly, I know. But I would love to see him squirm."

"It's not true, is it?"

"Of course not. I just want to fuck with him."

"You've got problems, and you need to stop this right now, Tess. I know you talk a lot of junk and you've done some crazy things in your day, but this is going way too far. You need to pull yourself out of this funk and get it together."

Tess poured hot water over her tea bag and let it steep. She inhaled the fragrant chamomile as she stirred the sugar that she'd already placed in her cup. "I know you're right, Bernadette. I need to let go of the past, accept the situation for what it is, and move on with my life. But the truth is, and I know this is gonna sound bad . . . but I don't want to move on. I want to brood, and pout, and sulk, and troll his triflin' ass on social media. I want to plot all kinds of devious shit in my mind that I can do to hurt him. I've even hoped and prayed that he'd catch his new wife in bed with another man, that way he could feel the same kind of pain that he put me through."

Bernadette let out a long, hard sigh. "You're right. It does sound bad. But you know the pity party you're having won't change your situation, right?"

"Yeah, I know, but it'll definitely make me feel better."

Bernadette sucked her teeth. "No, it won't. And any temporary victory you might feel will fade away after you sit back and see that regardless of whatever you say or do to that man, at the end of the day he chose someone else and he's moved on with his life. Cuz, you need to do the same."

Tess took small sips of the steaming-hot tea and closed her eyes as the warm liquid eased down her throat. "Didn't I just tell you that I don't want to do the rational thing?"

"Stop acting like an irresponsible twentysomething with no common sense. This is serious, Tess, and the more you talk like this, the more worried I'm getting about you."

Instead of feeling better talking to Bernadette, Tess was beginning to feel worse. "Thanks for listening to me, cuz, but I gotta go."

"And do what?"

"Um, in case you haven't been listening to me, I have a book to write."

"I've been listening for the last hour, and from what you've told me you've barely written a paragraph in the last few days. And I'd be willing to bet my next paycheck that as soon as we get off the phone you're going to go back online and resume cyberstalking Antwan. Am I right?"

"Maybe."

There was a short pause on the phone before Bernadette spoke up. "Come to Bourbon."

"What?"

"You clearly need to get out of Chicago so you can thaw out and clear your mind. You're sitting around in that gigantic house all by yourself, and if left to your own devices you'll end up doing something that you'll regret later. So rather than get yourself into trouble by what you might write online, come here and finish writing your book."

"Are you serious?"

"Of course I am. I wouldn't offer if I wasn't."

Tess took a moment to think about Bernadette's offer. She knew that her cousin was right about what would happen if she was left to her own devices. She also knew that she needed to step outside the insular life she'd created over the last year or so, otherwise things would go from bad to worse. Bourbon hadn't been on her list of places she'd wanted to visit, but standing in her lonely kitchen on a freezing Sunday morning, the small town sounded downright exciting. "How long can I stay?"

"As long as you want." Bernadette cleared her throat. "I'm lyin', you can stay until you finish your book or heal your heart, whichever comes first."

"I love your honesty."

"Thank you. So what's it gonna be?"

"How soon can I come?"

"Whenever you can book a flight out here you'll have a room waiting for you."

"Is tomorrow too early?"

"Tomorrow is perfect! Tess, I can't wait to see you."

Tess was truly thankful, and this was the first time in a long time that she actually felt hopeful about something. "Okay, I'm going to look at flights after we hang up, and I'll let you know as soon as I book something."

"Okay, sounds good." Bernadette smiled on the other end of the phone. "I haven't seen you in forever, but don't worry, I won't be in your way when it comes to your writing. I know you need uninterrupted time, and with my crazy long work hours you won't even know I'm here."

"Yes, but I want to hang out and catch up with you before I se-quester myself from the world so I can finish this book."

"You got it, cuz."

Tess and Bernadette talked a few more minutes before they ended their call. Tess was thankful that she had a wonderful cousin and sister-friend like Bernadette who was always there for her. She finished drinking her tea and then headed upstairs to her writing cave. She sat at her desk and logged onto her computer. She was about to pull up rates on *Priceline.com*, but before she did that she moseyed over to Antwan's Instagram page to check out what he was up to since the last time she'd logged in a couple hours ago.

# Chapter 13

## BERNADETTE

Monday had always been Bernadette's least favorite day of the week because aside from being an abrupt end to the weekend—which she relished because of her intensely long work weeks—the day usually brought on an onslaught of unresolved problems lingering from the previous week. But this Monday was very different, and in fact, she was looking forward to today, and specifically, she was looking forward to lunchtime because she would be dining with Coop.

Bernadette and Coop had talked for four hours yesterday afternoon and then again for nearly an hour before she'd fallen asleep last night. When he'd texted her two nights ago to make sure she'd gotten home safely from Arizona's birthday party, she'd thought it had been a nice, gentlemanly gesture, and when he'd called yesterday there was no denying that they had incredible chemistry. She and Coop had talked with the ease of old friends and the excitement of new lovers, which had stirred a mixture of exhilaration, anxiety, intrigue, and anticipation in Bernadette. They hadn't flirted or hinted at anything other than general getting-to-know-you conversation, but the information and depth of sincerity with which they'd shared had been full and meaningful. She liked the fact that Coop was straight up, honest, and mature with no pretense or posturing to make himself seem like a big deal, even though Bernadette knew that he was indeed a very big deal in Bourbon, as was evidenced by his celebrity status at Arizona's party.

Coop had asked Bernadette to dinner last night, but she'd been hesitant because she'd had to finish two reports that were due first thing in the morning. But she also wanted to see Coop right away, and because Tess was set to arrive in town that same evening, Bernadette decided to meet him for a late lunch that afternoon.

Bernadette had asked her administrative assistant to clear her afternoon schedule so she would have plenty of time with Coop before going home to meet Tess after her cousin picked up her rental car from the airport. Bernadette's heart beat fast with anticipation as she drove up to Sue's Brown Bag, a soul food restaurant located in the heart of the Bottoms. Bernadette had only been on this side of town once, and that had been three nights ago when she'd called the car service to make sure she and Arizona arrived home safely after drinks at the Magnolia Room.

As Bernadette looked up and down the street it struck her how familiar, yet utterly different, the Bottoms was from where she'd grown up in southeast Washington, DC. Much like her old neighborhood, the Bottoms was sprinkled with men hanging out on the corner—even in the cold—mom-and-pop convenience stores filling each block, and old buildings that were in need of repair due to years of wear and tear. But the difference between the Bottoms and her old neighborhood was that the streets here looked clean, as though the proprietors of each business had swept them with a broom and then told the passersby to keep them clean. And even though the buildings looked old and in need of a fresh coat of paint and pressure washing, there was no broken glass from violent incidents or metal bars on doors or windows to deter burglars.

As Bernadette walked up to Sue's Brown Bag, she noticed a disheveled-looking man leaning against a pole directly in front of the restaurant. She eyed him carefully because his body language indicated that he wanted to approach her. She hoped he wasn't going start cat-calling or ask her for money. She made quick steps and was nearly at the front door when the man stood straight and looked her in the eyes.

"Good afternoon, ma'am. You're lookin' mighty lovely today." He smiled, revealing missing teeth on both his upper and lower gums.

Bernadette didn't normally smile or make small talk with strangers, especially disheveled men on the street. But when she returned his stare, something in his eyes made her know he was harmless, so she responded by saying, "I hope you're having a good day."

"Yes, ma'am. I'm above ground, so I can't complain one bit."

"Amen to that."

"Enjoy your meal, ma'am."

"Thank you," Bernadette said with a smile. She knew if this had been DC, the entire exchange would have gone down differently and might have ended with a possible 9-1-1 call to report harassment. But in Bourbon, even the guys hanging out on the corner were respectful, which made her fondness for the city grow even more.

Bernadette opened the door to the restaurant and was surprised to see that the façade belied what was inside. She'd expected the interior to look like a typical sandwich shop in the hood, a bit run down and in need of repair. But as she looked up at the modern pendant lights that were outfitted with Edison bulbs, and the leather-upholstered chairs neatly tucked under what she could see were custom-made wood tables that sat atop pristine hardwood floors, she smiled, thinking that this place echoed what she thought about Coop—it wasn't what it seemed, it was something better.

As Bernadette inhaled the scent of food that smelled so good it made her stomach rumble, she realized that not only was this place a full-fledged restaurant instead of a simple sandwich shop, it had sophisticated appeal while managing to feel as down home as sweet potato pie. Just as she was about to check her phone for the time, she looked across the room and saw Coop sitting at a booth in the back, staring at her with his signature, debonair smile. She didn't want to seem overly excited, but she was, and she was sure that Coop could tell because his smile turned into a sly grin.

Bernadette was five minutes early, and she'd hoped to arrive before Coop so she would have time to slip into the ladies' room and adjust her hair and makeup, because she wanted to look her best. But there was no time for that now, so she put one foot in front of the other and walked toward Coop's booth, aware that he was studying her from head to toe. Bernadette had always been self-conscious about her very average appearance, but she was also wise enough to know that maximizing the average could result in exceptional, which she had tried to achieve today. Her thick black hair was pulled back into a neat chignon, her barely there makeup was subtle, her stylish heels highlighted the curve of her toned calves, and her gray wool coat was fitted to her petite frame as if it was made especially for her. She widened her smile as she approached the booth where Coop was still grinning.

Coop stood and greeted her with a hug before helping to remove her coat. Bernadette settled into her side of the comfortable, leather-covered booth. "Good afternoon," she said, "I hope you haven't been waiting too long?"

Coop glanced at his classic Cartier tank watch, noting the time. "Not too long. But I must admit that I've been looking forward to lunch ever since breakfast."

"If the smell coming from the kitchen is any indication of how the food tastes, I can see why."

"Yes, the food here is great, but I've been looking forward to lunch because it meant I'd get to see you again."

Bernadette knew from their previous conversations that Coop's straightforward way shouldn't startle or surprise her, but it did, and it also made her feel special. She blushed. "Thank you. That's very kind of you, Coop."

"I'm an honest man, Bernadette. I know we just met and you're still feeling me out, which you should. But the one thing I can tell you right now is that I'mma always be honest with you. I don't play games and if it's comin' outta my mouth, you can believe it's true."

"That's good to know. I appreciate honesty."

"And so do I."

Bernadette was excited, but she was also beginning to feel surprisingly nervous. It was one thing to talk on the phone for hours, free from Coop's intensely hypnotic eyes staring into hers and observing her body language, but it was another to sit across from him, under his watchful gaze in real time. Now she was face-to-face with the first man whom she'd been interested in in years, and it made her palms sweat. She was relieved when the server came to their booth to take their order.

"Good afternoon, ma'am," the server said as she placed two menus on the table. She turned to Coop. "Hey, Coop. Good to see you."

Coop nodded to the young woman. "How ya' doin', Sandy?"

"My bunions hurt like crazy and I got a painful corn growin' on my left pinkie toe. But other than that, I guess I'm aw'right."

Bernadette couldn't believe that the woman, who looked to be in her mid to late twenties, was talking about bunions and corns right before asking customers what they wanted to eat. Even though the woman knew Coop, Bernadette thought her relaxed attitude was a bit much. She tried to hide her shock and discomfort by narrowing her eyes on the menu in front of her, but she knew that Coop had already zeroed in on her shift.

Coop shook his head. "Sandy, you can't talk like that in front of customers."

Sandy looked at Bernadette and then back at Coop. "Oh, my bad. I apologize. You know I get carried away sometimes. It's been a long day and these feet is howlin' like a dog in heat."

Bernadette smiled because she didn't have words.

"Sandy, we don't need to know about your feet or dogs in heat," Coop said with the gentle ease of a father trying his best to be patient with his clueless but well-intentioned child. "This is Ms. Bernadette Gibson, and it's her first time eating at this fine establishment, so if you can get us started with our drink order I'd appreciate it."

Sandy nodded. "Yes, sir, Coop . . . can I start y'all off with water, tea, or somethin' a lil' stronger to get you through the afternoon?" she said in Bernadette's direction.

Bernadette couldn't help but shake her head. "I'll have water, please."

Coop leaned back against the plush leather that lined the booth. "I'll have an Arnold Palmer."

"All righty, I'll be back with your drinks in a minute."

Once Sandy was out of earshot, Coop spoke up. "She's a good kid, just a little rough around the edges and needs some training. But she'll get there."

"You must come here often."

"Uh yeah, I do. How'd you know?" he said with a laugh.

"Lucky guess, I guess."

"You're a smart woman, Bernadette."

She smiled. "Thanks."

"My nephew owns the place, and I promised my sister before she passed away a few years ago that I'd look after him. I come to support him and make sure things are goin' all right."

"Is your late sister the Sue of Sue's Brown Bag?"

"You're right again. It's my nephew's way of paying honor to her. It makes me proud every time I walk through the door."

Bernadette saw a flash of sadness in Coop's eyes. It was clear that he was emotional at the thought of his late sister and what she'd apparently meant to him. Coop cleared his throat as Sandy approached the table with their drinks.

"Y'all ready to order, or do you need more time?" Sandy asked.

"I'm so sorry." Bernadette nodded her head and looked down at her unopened menu. "I've been talking since I sat down and haven't even looked over anything." She opened the colorfully designed menu and was overwhelmed—in a good way—by so many delectable-sounding

Southern creations. She looked at Coop for direction. "I trust your judgment. What do you recommend?" Bernadette could see by the surprised but happy look on Coop's face that he appreciated her comment.

"The fried green tomatoes is a great appetizer. We can start with that while you look over the menu, if you like?"

"Sounds like a great choice to me."

"Aw'righty, I'll get y'all's appetizer started," Sandy said before slowly hobbling back to the kitchen.

"So, how's your day been goin'?" Coop asked.

"It's been a usual, busy Monday. But all in all, I can't complain. How about you? How's your day been so far?"

"Mondays are pretty light for me because of my line of business, which is good because it gives me time to plan for the week ahead. I hope you can come to the club this weekend and check it out."

"Like I said the other night, I've wanted to go ever since I moved here, but things have been really hectic with trying to adjust to a new job, new city, new home, and everything in between. But now that I've been personally invited, by the owner no less, I have an incentive to go."

"I still can't believe last weekend was your first time going out since you moved here six months ago."

"I know. That's pretty pathetic, right?"

"Not pathetic, just surprising. But I'm glad you're gonna take me up on my offer."

Bernadette and Coop talked straight through their appetizer of fried green tomatoes that was so good it made Bernadette hum. Then they moved on to crispy, golden-brown fried chicken, perfectly seasoned collard greens, and smack-your-mouth macaroni and cheese that made Bernadette pat her feet against the floor with each bite. "Coop, this food is out-of-this-world good! And the mac and cheese should have a place in the food hall of fame."

"My nephew'll be happy to hear that you enjoyed his cookin'."

"Wait, your nephew owns this restaurant and he's the cook?"

"Yep. He's a talented young man."

"Wow, that's impressive. I know how difficult the restaurant business is, so the fact that he can run this place so well and also cook the food is phenomenal."

"He got his bachelor's degree in business from Howard University, and after that he went to Johnson and Wales and got a culinary degree, which is his true passion. It took him a while to settle into where he is now, and it ain't been easy, but I'm proud of him."

Sandy hobbled back over to the table. "You didn't like the food, ma'am," she asked, looking down at Bernadette's half-eaten meal.

"I was just raving about how good it is, but it's a lot more than I can eat in one setting, so this will be lunch or maybe dinner tomorrow night."

Sandy smiled. "You a petite lil' thing, so I can see why you couldn't finish your plate. I wish I could say the same." Sandy rubbed her large hands over the expanse of her equally large stomach. "I know you full, but do you want to take some dessert home with you?"

"Even though I have a treacherous sweet tooth, I'm so stuffed I can't even think about dessert."

Coop spoke up. "Get her a piece of pound cake to go."

"Comin' right up," Sandy said with a light chuckle.

Bernadette looked at her watch. "I need to get going if I want to get home in time to greet my cousin."

After Coop paid their bill, he walked Bernadette out to her car. It was cold and the wind was whipping through the air like karate chops delivering blows. It was only a little after five o'clock, but it was already dark outside, which made it feel even colder. She wanted Coop to wrap his strong arms around her and keep her warm, but she quickly dismissed the thought. "Thanks again for lunch, Coop. I really appreciate it and I'll definitely be back."

"It was my pleasure, and I'm hoping you will. I'm not sure how long your cousin's gonna be in town, but bring her on by."

"She'll be here for at least a few weeks, so yes, I'll definitely bring her by."

Bernadette pressed the unlock button on her key fob and as soon as the mechanism clicked, Coop opened her door.

"Thank you, Coop. Again, I really enjoyed lunch."

She was about to get into her car when Coop gently pulled her in close for a warm hug. "And again, it was my pleasure." He gave her a little squeeze and then let go.

Even through their heavy wool coats, Bernadette loved the way Coop's body felt against hers. She knew that if he could make her thighs tremble through several layers of clothes, she stood no chance of resisting him if she ever felt his bare skin pressed against hers. Bernadette couldn't believe she was having the thoughts that were swimming through her mind right now, and she knew she needed to get into her car and drive away before she stood on her tiptoes and took things to another level, right there on the sidewalk, in the middle of the street. "Enjoy the rest of your evening, Coop."

As Bernadette drove away, she looked through her rearview mirror and could see that Coop was still standing in place, watching her until she turned onto the next street. She felt warm inside and a happy smile curved at the corners of her lips. She was about to turn up the volume on her radio when her car's Bluetooth alerted her of an incoming call. It was Tess.

"Hey, cuz!" Bernadette practically sang into the phone.

"Hey, Bernadette! I'm here, in the dirty South," Tess said through laughter.

"You're crazy. Exactly where are you?"

"At the airport. I landed a few minutes ago, but they just announced that our bags are delayed and won't be here for another hour."

"Oh, no."

"Yeah, that's exactly what I said. But since it'll take a while I'm going to pick up my rental car and then circle back to baggage claim. Hopefully my bags will be here by then."

"Okay, I'm on my way home now, so just come on and I'll see you when you get there."

"Okay, and Bernadette . . ."

"Yes?"

"I'm so glad I'm here and I can't thank you enough for inviting me to stay with you. This means more to me than you know."

"You're welcome, Tess. I can't wait to see you."

After Bernadette hung up the phone she stopped by Trader Joe's near her house and picked up a fresh bouquet of flowers and a bottle of wine to welcome her cousin. She was excited about seeing Tess and she hoped this visit would be healing. Bernadette knew that her cousin was emotionally beaten down and was in need of love and support, just as she'd been five years ago when Tess had flown to DC to nurse Bernadette's broken heart after Walter's deception.

Once she arrived home, Bernadette put her delicious leftovers into her refrigerator, clipped the flowers and arranged them in a decorative vase, and chilled the wine and sat out two glasses from her collection of Waterford crystal. She was getting more excited by the minute about seeing her cousin and she'd even taken the rare step of clearing her calendar for the first part of tomorrow morning because she knew that she and Tess would most likely talk into the wee hours of the morning, catching up on life.

Buzz, buzz, buzz. A call was coming through on Bernadette's phone. "Tess is probably lost, even with GPS," Bernadette said to herself. She looked at the caller ID and was surprised to see that it was Coop. "Hello," Bernadette said, trying to control the smile in her voice. "I thought you were my cousin."

"She hasn't arrived yet?"

"No, her luggage was delayed so she's running late."

"Good, I mean, not that her luggage was delayed, but I'm glad I called before she got there. I just wanted to tell you again how much I enjoyed your company, and I realized that I let you get away without asking you out on a proper date."

"A proper date?"

"Yes. Dinner and a movie, or whatever you want to do. I'd really like to take you out, Bernadette."

Bernadette bit her bottom lip. Coop had once again made her feel as giddy as a schoolgirl. "Dinner and a movie sound good."

"Just tell me when and I'll make it happen."

"Hmmm, that's going to be tricky. The weekend is better for me, but I know that's your busiest time, with the club."

"If you say the weekend is best for you, then it's best for me, too. I'll call you later so we can work out the details."

Bernadette didn't want to admit it but she liked Coop, a lot, and she wanted to explore the possibilities of romance after her five-year drought. She'd already embraced forgiveness and now she was ready to embrace love, but a part of her was still admittedly cautious. She still wasn't sure that she could trust her judgment, and that reality scared her. Then a thought came to Bernadette. Although Tess had a spotty track record when it came to her own love life, she'd always been able to peg Bernadette's on the dot. And truth be told, if she'd listened to Tess about Walter from the very beginning, she would have saved herself time and heartache. She knew she had to introduce Tess to Coop before she went any further with him. For now, she'd go out with Coop this weekend, just the two of them.

# *Chapter 14*

## ARIZONA

"No, Chris. Like I told you last night, I need some time to think about things." Arizona rubbed her temple with one hand and turned her steering wheel with the other. She was on her way to pick up Solomon from after-school care and she didn't want him to see her upset when she got there. She was frustrated with Chris, and they'd only been talking a few minutes. "I have to get my mind straight before I pick up Solomon, then I have to go home, make dinner, get him down for the night, then work on the color palette for a client, make some changes to my business plan, and pray that I fall asleep before the sun comes up."

"I can come over and help you, Arizona," Chris responded, nearly pleading with her. "I can cook and take care of Solomon while you work."

"I don't think that's a good idea."

"Why not?"

Arizona replaced her words with a loud sigh.

"Baby, I know you're upset with me, but we need to talk. The only way we're going to work out issues before they become problems is to talk about them."

"Please stop saying I'm upset with you. I already told you that I'm not."

"Your actions don't support your words."

Chris's rational tone and logical thinking had always been one of the things that Arizona found very appealing and downright sexy about her future husband. But now, his pragmatism irritated her no end. She wanted to hang up the phone, but she knew that would be rude, so she tried to remain calm in order to deliver what she had to say. "Trust and believe, you would know if I was upset. So just take it from me, I'm not."

"Then explain why you're giving me the cold shoulder?"

Arizona let out another loud sigh.

"Okay, I know that ever since we made love last Thursday night you've been acting differently, and like I said before, I take full responsibility for that." Chris paused and then cleared his throat. "I came too quickly the first time, and the second time . . . well, you excited me so much, and I was already tired from a long day, and . . . well, I'm sorry. You felt so good that I got caught up in the moment. But I promise I'll make it up to you, baby. We've got a lifetime ahead of us."

And therein was the problem. No matter how much Arizona loved Chris, she couldn't imagine a lifetime of unfulfilling sex with a man who possessed a nonexistent penis and no sensual moves to speak of. She knew she needed to be blunt with Chris and tell him that not only was she turned off by his micro-size penis, but neither his touch, his kiss, nor his caress turned her on. She'd tried to take Bernadette's advice, but she could see that she and Chris were not physically compatible in any way.

She'd thought that after his disappointing performance Saturday night, he'd surely known he hadn't satisfied her and that she was unhappy and concerned. But when they'd awoken the next morning, he'd kissed her, jabbing his tongue around her mouth like a rookie, and told her that he was sorry he'd fallen asleep and that he'd do better the next time. Arizona had been so shocked and disappointed that all she could do was deliver a puzzled look that Chris had either ignored or misread, given that his response had been to order room service because he'd said she looked hungry. He'd proceeded to order them breakfast entrées complete with coffee, juice, muffins, fruit, and mimosas.

Arizona had watched her fiancé with an odd mixture of shock and deep gratitude. She'd been in shock because he was literally oblivious to his sexual and physical shortcomings. But she'd felt a deep well of gratitude because when Chris had ordered their food, he'd made sure to tell them to scramble her eggs hard, cook her bacon to a firm crisp, and put a slight burn on the edge of her pancakes, just the way she liked them. From their first date, Chris listened to, watched for, and anticipated Arizona's needs. His love was evident in his kind words and actions, and as she'd listened to him place her order, she'd heard care, patience, and devotion in his voice, and it was all because he loved her, which made her heart fill with thanks. In that moment, Arizona had known that she needed to give it another try.

Once again, she remembered Bernadette's advice about finding other ways to achieve pleasure with Chris. After he'd hung up the phone she'd sauntered over to him with a mischievous look in her eyes. She took the receiver from his hand and put the hotel phone back on its cradle. She straddled him on the edge of the bed. "Let's pick up where we left off last night."

They fell back onto the bed and Arizona rested her body atop Chris as she thrust her pelvis against his in a grinding motion. But he was quickly becoming overly excited, so she slowed things down because she didn't want him to have another premature orgasm. She wanted to see what Chris could do between her legs that didn't require his penis, so she moved his fingers to the spot between her legs that should have been wet but wasn't, and she prayed that Chris's touch would generate some heat. But instead of feeling excited, Arizona became frustrated.

"Chris, you're rubbing me too hard," she said.

"Oh, I'm sorry, baby." He panted, changing his rhythm and touch. "How about now, do you like this?"

"It actually hurts worse."

"I want you to feel pleasure, not pain." Chris slowed his hands to a turtle's crawl. "How does that feel?"

Arizona couldn't believe that Chris's large, soft, well-groomed hands had the same effect as sandpaper against wood. *What the hell?* She screamed inside her head. She wanted to tell him that it felt like her vagina was being slowly attacked by a wild animal. She was dismayed that her loving and attentive fiancé was so inept when it came to sexually pleasing her. He knew exactly how she liked her food, but he didn't have a clue about how she wanted to be touched, kissed, or caressed.

Luckily, room service knocked on the door and saved her from what could have been another catastrophe. And even though she'd completely lost her appetite for the breakfast that Chris had so thoughtfully ordered, she was grateful for the distraction of food. She tried to eat a forkful of eggs that were cooked exactly the way she liked them. But when she placed them into her mouth they tasted like fluffy plastic. Suddenly, the very thought of food made her queasy. And as she thought about it, she hadn't had much of an appetite since last Thursday, when they'd broken their vow of abstinence and ventured down a path that now had her second-guessing their pending walk down the aisle. Before last Friday she couldn't have imagined anything that would have made her rethink her decision to marry Chris. But now calling off the wedding was a very real possibility.

"Arizona, did you hear what I said?"

Chris's voice jarred Arizona back into the present. "Yes, I did. I just have so much on my mind that I can barely focus or think straight. But what I do know is that I need a little time to decompress."

"I understand, but I thought it would be nice to see you so we can decompress together, especially since I'm leaving Wednesday and I'll be gone for two weeks."

Arizona had almost forgotten that in two days Chris would be going to Washington, DC, to help out at one of the St. Hamilton's sister properties, filling in until their new general manager was in place. In the past, whenever Chris was about to go out of town for business they always spent as much time together as they could before he left. Even though she didn't want him to come over tonight, she also didn't want him to travel without first seeing him off.

Arizona regrouped her thoughts and put a smile into her voice. "I'm almost at Solomon's school. Once I pick him up I'm going to start dinner and you can come over in another hour or two."

"Okay. I love you, Arizona."

"I love you, too, Chris."

Arizona pushed the button on her car's Bluetooth system to end the call and let out a deep sigh filled with frustration and lots of troubling questions. As she turned onto the street that led to Bourbon Preparatory School, she focused on her son, and how excited he was going to be to see Chris tonight, and, how disappointed he would be that the man whom he called dad would be gone for the next two weeks.

Chris was the only father that Solomon had ever known, and as far as the well-behaved five-year-old was concerned, Chris was his daddy, period. If a day went by where Chris didn't come over to Arizona's house, she didn't bring Solomon to his, or they didn't speak by phone, Solomon would tell Arizona, "Mommy, I miss Dad. Am I gonna see him tomorrow?"

Arizona knew it would crush Solomon if Chris disappeared from their lives. She remembered the huge smile on Solomon's face when she and Chris had told him that they were going to get married. Arizona had taken delight in the fact that her son was excited about his role as ring bearer in their wedding and that he'd started practicing by walking around the house carrying a pillow from the sofa to replicate the real thing. Arizona knew that Solomon was looking forward to having a father in the home on a permanent basis, and he was extra excited when he'd learned that they'd be living in Chris's house after the wedding.

Arizona's thoughts became more and more complicated as she navigated her car toward the after-school pickup line. She smiled when she saw her handsome little boy standing outside with one of his teachers, patiently waiting for Arizona to pick him up. Once he got into the car Arizona glanced back at him in her rearview mirror as Solomon buckled himself in. She couldn't get over how much he was growing.

Even though Solomon was only five, people often mistook him for a child several years older because not only did he look more physically mature, he carried himself at a more advanced level than was expected for someone his age. When Solomon was three, and upon his Head Start teacher's urging, Arizona had agreed to have him tested for an academically gifted program. No one had been surprised that Solomon's IQ was already at a first grade level, essentially placing him in line with kids who were twice his age. Now he was in third grade and was outpacing everyone in his class, in and out of school.

"Mom, is Dad coming over tonight?" Solomon asked.

"My day was fine, and how was yours?" Arizona replied. She was determined to instill manners in her son.

"Sorry, Mom, how was your day?"

"Long but good now that I'm officially working for myself. How was your day?"

"It was good . . . is Dad coming over?"

Arizona smiled. "Yes, Solomon, your father's coming over tonight after I make dinner and get things settled around the house."

"Yaayyyy! How much longer until you and Dad get married?"

"Four months."

"That's a long time."

"That's not a long time, Solomon. As you get older you'll under-stand how fast days and months can pass by. Trust me. It seems like just yesterday I was changing your diapers and now look at you." Arizona took another quick glance at her son in her rearview mirror. "You're getting so big."

"I'm the tallest person in the entire third grade. I'm even as tall as some of the fourth graders."

"You get your height from me."

"No, I get my height from Dad. He's really tall."

Arizona remained silent as she crossed the train tracks, headed on her way back home. She wanted to tell Solomon that he was partially right. Chris was indeed tall. But Solomon's biological father's identity had been a mystery.

"Why can't you and Dad get married now?" Solomon asked.

"What?"

"Why do you have to wait?"

"Because I'm not ready," Arizona blurted out before she could censor herself. "What I mean is that your dad and I need time because weddings take a lot of planning."

"I can help you. I've been practicing how to carry the ring and I'm ready."

Arizona laughed. "It's not that simple, baby." She knew she needed to change the subject before she said something she'd regret. She was about to ask him about school when she turned onto her street and saw Chris's SUV parked out front. *What's he doing here this early?* Arizona asked in her mind.

"Dad's here!" Solomon shouted.

Arizona had barely put her car in park before Solomon unbuckled his seat belt, grabbed his overstuffed book bag, and raced toward the house. "Slow down and wipe your feet before you go inside," she called out to him.

Arizona was frustrated because she had specifically asked Chris to come over after she'd had time to cook dinner and get settled in. She'd had a busy day trying to schedule appointments, sketch new color palettes, arrange and organize her makeup collection, which consisted of well over five hundred products, and then work on adjusting her business plan that she needed to finalize soon. Throw in the stress she'd felt about her and Chris's relationship, and Arizona was reaching her breaking point. She took a deep breath and prayed she wouldn't say something that she couldn't take back.

When Arizona walked through her front door she was touched by what she saw across the room. Chris was standing at her dining room table, unpacking a take-out bag from Olive Garden.

"Can I have a breadstick?" Solomon asked. "I'm hungry."

Chris shook his head. "Not yet, big man. You need to wash your hands and help me finish setting the table while your mom gets settled in."

Arizona dropped her handbag on the couch and walked over to Chris. "How did you find time to stop by Olive Garden and then beat me home?"

Chris smiled. "I had already called the order in before I called you. Now go and get settled while Solomon and I set the table."

After a satisfying meal of spaghetti, salad, and breadsticks, Chris helped Solomon with his homework and then made sure he was bathed and in bed by eight thirty. Initially, Arizona had been against Chris coming over tonight because as she'd told him earlier, she'd wanted time to decompress and think about things. But as she sat at her work desk that was neatly situated in her small bedroom, she knew that if Chris hadn't come over there was no way she'd be working on her business plan like she was now.

Arizona felt guilty and shallow for the thoughts she'd been having. Here she was, able to work on her business plan to advance her dreams because the man who loved her unconditionally was helping her to make it happen. Chris was kind, loyal, and supportive, and he accepted all parts of her. Arizona knew she needed to do the same for Chris. She knew that sex was only one aspect of their relationship, and that other things were just as, if not more important, like honesty, trust, dependability, and love. Chris demonstrated all these things.

A knock on her bedroom door drew Arizona away from her thoughts.

"Can I come in?" Chris asked.

"You better."

Chris walked in and took a seat on the edge of Arizona's bed that was just a few feet from where she was sitting at her desk. "Solomon's out for the count. And is it me, or does he grow an inch every week?"

Arizona laughed. "I was just saying that on our drive home. I can't believe how big he's getting."

"Our baby isn't a baby anymore."

Arizona nodded. "Thank you, Chris."

"For what?"

"For being you. Being kind and thoughtful and incredibly good to Solomon and me. There's a lot of men out here who don't take care of their own child, let alone someone else's. But that's exactly what you're doing, and I know it's from your heart. I appreciate that more than you know."

Chris smiled. "Baby, you and Solomon are all that matter to me, and as far as I'm concerned he's my son from day one."

Arizona rose from her chair and sat next to Chris. "I apologize for acting distant for the last few days."

"I know you're disappointed in me . . ."

"Shhhh." Arizona pressed her fingers against Chris's lips to quiet him. "Let me explain." She rose from her bed, closed her bedroom door, and then returned to where Chris was sitting. "Yes, I've been disappointed because of a few things. For one, we broke our vow of abstinence, which I didn't think we'd do. But I'm actually glad that we did because now we can deal with this before we get married."

"There's not much to deal with, baby. I told you, I'm gonna do better because the more we make love, the stronger my stamina will be and I'll last longer."

This was Arizona's opportunity to let Chris know that stamina was the least of her concerns. She didn't care if he only lasted two minutes, as long as they were two good, satisfying, toe-curling, sweat-your-hair-out minutes. But she couldn't bring herself to say what was really on her mind because she knew it would hurt Chris's feelings.

She didn't want to utter anything less than encouraging words to such a kind, sweet and thoughtful man. He'd thrown her a birthday party fit for a queen, he'd paid off all her credit cards so that she could start her business virtually debt-free, and he'd just taken care of dinner, cleaned the kitchen, and put Solomon to bed in order to relieve her stress. No, she wasn't going to tell her fiancé anything that would hurt him.

So once again, Arizona decided to take Bernadette's advice and explore different ways of reaching sexual satisfaction with Chris. She leaned into him and delivered a delicate kiss to his lips. It was the same kind of kiss they'd shared a thousand times before, but this time instead of cutting it short as they usually did, she decided to step it up a notch, hoping it would lead to better results than Saturday night. And to her delight, Chris returned her gentle kiss, but suddenly in a flash his moves went right back to the way he'd handled her Saturday night—and it was all wrong.

Arizona tried to hold back her frustration, but not only was Chris's kiss unappealing, his sandpaper hands were at it again. She knew she needed to move him in another direction, toward something that would bring her pleasure. She stood, unzipped her jeans, and slid them down the length of her legs. She could see Chris's eyes light up and she smiled. "Take my panties off," she said.

"Gladly." Chris obeyed.

Arizona could see that he was becoming overly excited again so she stepped away and seductively delivered another command. "Take off your clothes and then pull back the comforter and turn down the sheets."

"Baby, you're turning me on. I love it when you take control."

Chris eagerly did as Arizona instructed and followed her second round of commands as she removed her sweater and bra. She was praying that he would continue to follow her directives, and most importantly, that he'd be good at what she was about to ask him to do next.

Slowly, Arizona eased her body onto her soft, cotton sheets, spread her legs wide, and looked into Chris's eyes. "Are you ready to eat dessert?"

"Oh, yeah, baby!"

Chris practically dove onto the bed, and within a matter of a few seconds his head was buried between Arizona's legs. She gasped and had to inhale deeply in order to catch her breath because she was so overwhelmed. She felt a numbing buzz between her thighs. *What in the hell is he doing?* Now Arizona was completely fed up. "Chris!"

He looked up, startled. "What's wrong?"

"Everything." Arizona closed her eyes and bit her tongue. She was tempted to unleash her dissatisfaction, but she stopped herself. She knew that if she said what was on her mind, in this moment, that her harsh words would leave a mark that she couldn't remove. And as Bernadette had told her, once you say it you can't take it back. So she inhaled another deep breath and spoke as gently as she could. "Baby, take your time. We don't have to rush."

Chris nodded, seeming to understand, and to make sure he did, she reiterated her point by telling him exactly how she wanted him to perform oral sex. Step by step, as if giving classroom instructions. Arizona verbally guided him through a tutorial of her vagina. She told him how to lick it, kiss it, and massage it with the amount of pressure and rhythm she liked. When she was confident that he'd listened and was ready, she closed her eyes, threw her head back, and waited to receive pleasure.

Two minutes later, which to Arizona felt like two hours, she was staring up at the ceiling in stunned silence. She didn't have a clue as to what Chris was doing, but whatever it was, she was certain oral sex wasn't a part of it. She'd been with quite a few men in her day, who'd all had different techniques and skill levels, but she'd never, ever, experienced anyone who was as bad in bed as Chris. When she'd told him to eat dessert, he'd taken it literally, because he was gnawing on her labia to the point that it was now numb, as if he'd given her a shot of Novocain. She let out another deep breath—this time out of utter defeat—and then closed her eyes. She started thinking about the emails she needed to send and respond to tomorrow, the errands she needed to run, and the business book she needed to check out of the library. Her mundane thoughts were interrupted when she heard a load groan. *Oh, no! This can't be happening . . . again!* Arizona thought.

"Uuuggghhhh, baby," Chris moaned. He panted and slowly lifted his head, resting it against her thigh.

Arizona moved her leg, causing Chris's head to fall against the mattress. "I'm so confused right now. I'm the one who should be coming, not you!" she nearly hissed.

"Arizona, I'm so sorry, baby."

"I'm tired of hearing you say that, Chris."

Chris propped himself on one elbow and slowly sat up, looking into Arizona's eyes. "Baby, you tasted so good, and I was caught up."

"Chris, I've tried to be patient and understanding, but now I have to let you know how I really feel." Arizona sat up and gathered the sheets to cover her chest.

"I know you're disappointed, but . . ."

"I'm not disappointed. I'm concerned and worried, Chris. I'm thinking to myself, is this gonna be our future? I'm telling you right now, I can't deal with this. I just can't." Arizona was about to unleash about Chris's small penis, elementary-level skills, and cluelessness about lovemaking, but she stopped herself. Even though she was at her breaking point, she was aware enough to know that her words, however truthful, were going to come out brutally cruel, and again, she wouldn't be able to take them back. So instead of going off, she leaned back against the headboard and looked up at the ceiling.

Uncomfortable silence fell over the room. Arizona was determined not to say another word because she wanted to hear what Chris had to say. She wanted him to explain what was really going on with him. A micropenis was one thing, but not having any other sexual skills, or self-control, was a potentially disastrous deal breaker in her book. Arizona shifted in her body in an attempt to spur Chris into some type of action. She not only wanted, but she needed him to say something. Anything. But to her dismay, he remained silent. She looked over at him and her heart sank. Chris had fallen asleep.

She wanted to kick Chris into consciousness so she could continue the conversation they should have had last Thursday night. She nudged him. "Chris, wake up!"

Chris yawned and then turned on his side. "Good night, Arizona. I love you, baby."

"We need to talk, so wake up!" she demanded.

No matter how much she wanted to talk, Arizona knew it wasn't going to happen tonight. She rose from bed, walked over to her chest of drawers, and pulled out a long, flannel nightgown. She turned around and looked at Chris's naked body, which was turned away from her. Arizona roamed her eyes over her fiancé's tight behind, broad, perfectly sculpted back, and overall muscular physique. He looked like a model straight out of *Men's Health* magazine, and Arizona was sad that his lovemaking skills didn't match his aesthetic. She was so frustrated that she didn't want to sleep in the same bed with him, but she also didn't want to sleep on her uncomfortable living room sofa.

Arizona was tired and she needed to rest her mind, so she quietly slid back into bed, positioning herself as far away from Chris as she could without falling off the edge. She closed her eyes and made up her mind. When the sun rose she was going to let Chris know that she wanted to call off their engagement.

# *Chapter 15*

## TESS

Tess's day had started off with an obscenely early flight out of O'Hare. She was a night owl, not a morning person, so getting up at 3:00 a.m. in order to make her 6:00 flight was a herculean task wrapped around a heroic effort. But Tess was determined to get to Bourbon as soon as she could because she knew if she stayed in Chicago a minute longer, something bad was going to happen.

She'd arrived at the airport in plenty of time, only to find that her flight had been delayed without warning. Then when she'd landed in North Carolina, she was told that there had been a mix-up with the baggage, so she had to wait an hour until it arrived on another flight. When she went to pick up the Mercedes-Benz rental car that she'd reserved, she was informed that the only car available was a Honda Civic. By the time she finally got her car and her luggage, she still had a two-and-a-half-hour drive from the Raleigh-Durham airport in the state capital to the quaint town of Bourbon, tucked quietly in the eastern part of the state. Needless to say, she was tired, slightly cranky, and ravenous by the time she reached Bernadette's house.

When Tess reached the Palisades neighborhood where Bernadette lived, she was impressed but wasn't surprised that her cousin was residing in the high-dollar district. The entire area screamed status and exclusivity, and Bernadette's street yelled it. When Tess steered her car into Bernadette's semicircular driveway, even though it was dark, outside she could see the grandeur of the home with its impressive masonry work, architectural angles, and ample square footage. Bernadette had greeted her at the door with a warm hug and a chilled bottle of wine, making her feel as if she was truly home. And the icing on the cake was that Bernadette had a soul food feast of fried chicken, macaroni and cheese, collard greens, and cornbread ready for her, compliments of her leftovers from an earlier meal.

A hot shower, delicious meal, and a short time later, Tess finally felt relaxed for the first time in what seemed like months. She also felt as if she was reading a romance novel as she listened to her cousin talk about the handsome, impossibly sexy man she'd met last weekend and had lunch with earlier today. She'd always looked up to Bernadette because her cousin was smart, ambitious, practical, and funny in her own intellectually dry-wit kind of way. And most importantly, Tess knew that Bernadette truly loved her, which was the reason Tess was stretched across the opposite end of the leather sectional sofa where she and Bernadette were talking and sipping alcohol-spiked hot chocolate.

"You sound like you're really into this guy," Tess said to Bernadette after she took a long, soothing sip of her spiked drink.

"I can't believe I'm admitting this, but honestly, I kind of am," Bernadette responded with a schoolgirl grin.

"And you've only known him since Saturday, which was two days ago, right?"

"That's what the calendar says."

Tess sucked her teeth. "You know what I'm getting at, don't you?"

"I sure do. That's why I said I can't believe I'm admitting that I'm into him . . . because that doesn't happen often. I'm just as surprised, and maybe more so than you."

"Wow, I'm trying to take it all in because I haven't heard you breathe a word about a man in so long that I've lost track. But now, you're practically singing the man's name."

"I am not."

"You are, too! I wish you could step outside your body and listen to yourself, 'Coop this and Coop that.' The pitch and tone in your voice changes when you say his name."

Bernadette gave Tess a serious look. "There's something very special about him."

"Uh-huh."

"No, I'm serious, Tess. You know I don't say things unless I mean it. I'm admittedly a hard critic, and I'm skeptical of practically everything. But with Coop, he's different."

Tess rolled her eyes. "What makes him so different?"

Bernadette set her now-lukewarm cocoa on the coffee table and leaned forward in Tess's direction. "Cuz, what's really going on with you?"

"What do you mean?"

"You sound cynical and bitchy. I know you're going through a rough time trying to finish your book, and you still haven't fully resolved your feelings for Antwan, but something's got to give. I want to help you, which is why I invited you to stay with me for as long as you need to. But I need to know what's driving all this. What else is going on with you, Tess?"

Tess knew that everything Bernadette had just said was absolutely true. And not only was she cynical and bitchy, she was sad, hurt, and unsure, and for the first time in her life, she felt inadequate. She was amazed that after being in her cousin's presence for only a few hours, Bernadette had uncovered the complicated root that led to emotions and truths that Tess had been trying to keep buried for the last six months. But now, Bernadette had unearthed Tess's true struggle, put it out in the open, and was forcing her to deal with it.

"Tess, you can tell me anything and you know I won't judge you." Bernadette said with gentleness. "Now what's really going on?"

Tess nodded and whispered, "It's so hard . . ."

"Talk to me, cuz."

A lone tear fell from Tess's right eye. "I might not ever be able to have kids."

"What? I don't understand?"

"Fibroids and endometriosis."

Bernadette let out a deep breath. "Oh, no, Tess. I didn't know you have fibroids, but I do know that it affects a high percentage of black women. Isn't it painful?"

"Very."

"And endometriosis, I've heard about it, but I'm not that familiar with it."

Tess shook her head. "Fibroids are a bitch, but endometriosis is a mutherfucker, and I've got a terrible case of it. Basically, it's a condition where tissue that normally lines the uterus grows outside the womb and causes severe pain, and in some cases infertility. The scarring and pain from it is unreal and downright debilitating."

"My goodness. When were you diagnosed?"

"During my mid-thirties."

Bernadette's face was covered in concern and alarm. "Tess, I can't believe this. Why didn't you tell me before now?"

"Because at the time you'd been going through all kinds of shit after your breakup with that bastard Walter, and I didn't want to worry you."

"Did you tell your mom?"

"No, because I knew she'd get right on the phone with your mom, and then you'd end up knowing anyway. So I just went through everything by myself."

"Listen, you're my family and I love you. I'll always be here for you no matter what. You could've still come to me, Tess."

"In retrospect I guess you're right," Tess said, then took a big gulp of her drink. "I'd started having really bad periods to the point that it was a struggle for me to function through a full day of writing. Once my OB-GYN told me what was wrong I changed my diet, underwent Lupron shots to shrink the fibroids, and tried every kind of holistic medicine concoction I could get my hands on. But none of it worked. My doctor told me that my fertility was literally hanging in

the balance, so about a year before I met Antwan, I had a myomec-
tomy."

"A what?"

"It's a surgery to remove fibroids. I had one the size of a grape-
fruit, and when you have large fibroids it makes it extremely difficult
to conceive and carry to full term. I wasn't in a relationship at the
time, but I knew I wanted to have a baby one day, so I scheduled the
surgery. It wasn't until they'd opened me up on the operating table
that they discovered the endometriosis, which was covering nearly
my entire abdominal wall."

"Oh, Tess," Bernadette said with gentleness. "I'm so sorry you
went through all that alone."

"It was a mess for sure. Well, fast-forward to about six months ago,
the bleeding and pain came back again in full force, and I immediately
knew what it was." Tess lowered her head. "I'm back at square one, and
it's worse this time. My doctor said I have eight fibroids the size of apples and a few marble-size ones, which is why my clothing of choice
these days has largely consisted of oversized shirts and sweatpants."

"Wow, I had no idea you were dealing with all this."

"But that's not even the tip of the avalanche."

"What else is going on?"

"I have a lazy ovary."

Bernadette's eyes grew large. "A lazy ovary?" she repeated.

"I know, right?" Tess said as she shook her head. "The correct
term is premature ovarian failure, and it's exactly what it sounds like.
My old-ass eggs are in bad shape, and that, along with my other problems, is why my doctor strongly recommended that I have a hysterectomy. I didn't want to accept it, so I got three additional second
opinions, and they all said the same thing."

"When are you going to have the surgery? And don't worry, no
matter what the date, I will be there."

Tess guzzled down the remainder of her liquored-up hot chocolate, then placed her cup on the end table next to her. "I know it

might sound crazy, but I'm not ready to give up on the remote possibility of having a child. I'm a fiction writer, and in my world anything is possible."

"Yes, anything is possible but, cuz, it sounds like your condition is really bad. At this point the most important factor is your health. You can always adopt."

"I know but, Bernadette, I want to carry a baby inside of me. I want to experience the feeling of knowing that there's life inside my body."

"I hear you, but you may have to accept the fact, just like I have, that childbearing isn't in the cards for you."

Tess sighed. "I'm forty years old, never been married, and never been pregnant. But none of that's by choice. I've always wanted a husband, two or three kids, a dog, and . . . a family to call my own, you know?"

"You're preaching to the choir. Add ten years onto everything you just said and that's me."

The two cousins stared at each other in silent agreement and solidarity. Tess didn't realize how much hurt she'd been carrying until this moment. "Even if I didn't have a man, or a dog, I hung on to the hope that I still had the ability to get pregnant, but these damn fibroids, endometriosis, and a fucking lazy ovary is trying to rob me of that."

Tess wasn't a crier, and she hated that she could feel more tears forming in her eyes. "Damnit," she hissed. "All I've ever wanted is to be loved. I mean genuinely loved. A man might not do it, but I thought if I had a child I'd have a shot. It's crazy that I spent the better part of my adult life taking birth control pills and avoiding pregnancy at all costs because I was holding on to the idea of the husband and white picket fence in the burbs. But now that I want to get pregnant with or without all the accessories, I can't, and if by some miracle I'm able to conceive there's a strong chance that I won't carry to full term. Ain't that a bitch?"

"Life isn't fair, that's for sure. But, Tess, you need to make a decision about your health. How are you feeling now?"

"I'm fine, physically. But as you can see, I'm an emotional wreck."

Bernadette rose from her side of the couch and sat beside Tess. "I found a really good doctor here in Bourbon and I can give you her number if you'd like. It never hurts to have a fifth second opinion."

Tess tried to smile. "Thanks, cuz, but that's okay. I just need time to think and breathe."

"Everything is going to work out, Tess, it always does."

It was nearly three in the morning before Tess and Bernadette finally went to bed. Bernadette had given Tess a large bedroom upstairs, which was beautifully decorated in subtle earth tones. She was glad that Bernadette's master bedroom was downstairs because it gave her the privacy she needed to write, clear her mind, and heal.

She walked over to the large chest of drawers on the opposite side of the room and fished through the wicker basket that Bernadette had filled with apples, oranges, chips, water, and a few chocolate treats. Tess took a bottle of spring water because her flight and alcohol had left her dehydrated. Once she was snuggled under the soft sheets she stretched her arms and legs, feeling a new sense of comfort. She'd been in Bourbon for less than a day and she could already see that this visit was exactly what she needed.

Tess was relieved to have released the burden of her health and reproductive challenges that she'd been carrying for what felt like a lifetime, and she was sure that her anger, obsession, and stalker-like behavior toward Antwan was a direct result of the frustration and regret she felt about her own life. When she'd seen Antwan and his new bride, who looked to be at the peak of childbearing age, it had reminded her of what she didn't have and might never obtain—a husband and children. A family. A happily-ever-after. But for now she knew she needed to block those thoughts from her mind because she was tired from her long day, and she needed a good night's sleep.

As Tess lay in the plush comfort of the king-size bed, preparing herself for sleep, she allowed herself the comfort of knowing that she needed to put the past behind her and grab hold of hope because she knew if Bernadette's situation could turn around for the better, so could hers.

Tess's eyes fluttered as she slowly awoke to the sun's bright light that was fighting to enter her room through the tiny slits in the custom bamboo miniblinds hanging at the window. She reached for her phone that was sitting on the nightstand, and couldn't believe it was 10 a.m. She was a night owl by nature, rarely falling asleep until the wee hours of the morning, so rising early wasn't her thing. Because she only averaged a few hours of sleep each night, Tess usually felt fatigued and sometimes needed to take a nap on some days. But this morning was markedly different, and she could feel the shift deep within. She knew things had changed, not because she was in a new city and state, or because she was waking up in a bed that was not her own. This morning was different because she was in a place where she felt loved.

When Tess thought about how her cousin had graciously opened her home, had a delicious meal, albeit leftovers, waiting for her, and then had made her cocoa—which was her favorite thing to drink during winter months—and had taken the time to stay up late and talk with her, she couldn't help but smile.

Tess stretched her wiry arms, yawned, and then swung her long, lanky legs over the side of the large bed. She slipped her feet into the fuzzy, warm house slippers that Bernadette had let her borrow, than tied her thick, leopard-pattern terry-cloth robe around her body and walked downstairs.

Now that the sun was beaming through the large windows spread throughout Bernadette's four-thousand-square-foot house, Tess was able to take in the pure beauty and grandeur of the place her cousin now called home. Tess knew that Bernadette had always had a great sense of style when it came to home décor, but as she walked toward the kitchen and then through Bernadette's tastefully arranged living room she knew that if her cousin decided to exit corporate America, she could easily start a career in the interior design business.

Tess walked over toward the large set of windows in the dining room and touched the dupioni silk curtains that give the room an effortless sense of luxurious grace. Her fingers slid across the gray and white colored material that felt so good that Tess could envision herself wearing an outfit made of it. She started laughing because it conjured up the image of the iconic skit that Carol Burnett performed when she'd spoofed the movie *Gone with the Wind*, pretending to be Scarlett O'Hara, wearing a dress made of curtains. This was the first time that Tess had laughed in weeks, and she realized how good it felt. "Yep, things are on the upswing," she said aloud.

Once she entered the kitchen, Tess smiled again. Bernadette had left a note detailing where she could find various things in her large chef's kitchen, along with some of Tess's favorite hazelnut-flavored coffee. Tess was nearly in tears when she thought about the love and kindness that her cousin had showered upon her in less than twenty-four hours, and she was determined to not let it be in vain.

After she made her coffee and toasted a cinnamon raison bagel, Tess marched back upstairs with a clear mind and determination to have a great day, and more specifically, she wanted to make significant progress on her manuscript. She'd already missed her deadline and now she was in catch-up mode. She knew that her legions of faithful readers were more than ready for her next book, and she didn't want to disappoint them. She knew that she needed to do something special with the book she was writing, and she wanted it to be meaningful. "I need to channel all the bullshit I've experienced into something useful," she said as she removed her nightgown and stepped into the shower.

Twenty minutes later, warmly dressed and smelling fresh, Tess sat at the small desk in the room to begin writing. As she opened up her document and stared at the words on the screen, she suddenly felt an overwhelming avalanche of fear blanket her thoughts, realizing exactly what she was up against. Her manuscript was past due and she wasn't even a fourth of the way finished.

*Get your head back in the game, Tess*, the voice of reason said to her. *Focus your thoughts and energy into the things that are going right instead of concentrating on or even giving attention to the things that go wrong.*

Then the other voice, the one of indulgence, countered what she'd just heard by saying, *You've been through so much and you need to take some time for yourself. Take a break, relax, and get back to your writing tomorrow. In the meantime, you can go online and see what that scumbag, Antwan, is up to. It might even give you good writing material.*

Whenever Tess's calm voice appeared, her hot-tempered other side would flare up and challenge anything that seemed reasonable or had sound logic behind it. Sitting at her adopted desk in Bernadette's beautifully decorated guest bedroom, Tess knew that she was blessed to have this opportunity and she needed to make the most of it. Even though she was tempted to minimize her document and click the Instagram icon on her screen, she resisted. She closed her eyes, looked up toward the ceiling, and said a silent prayer.

Ten hours later it was eleven o'clock at night. Tess had only left her room once when she'd gone downstairs to forage for food. She'd made a turkey breast sandwich and grabbed a can of Planters almonds that she'd found in Bernadette's pantry. Then she returned to her room to settle in for a long stretch of writing. She'd texted Bernadette earlier that afternoon to let her know that she'd be sequestered in her room and not to worry about checking on her after work.

Tess rose from her desk and paced the floor; an exercise she'd performed several times throughout the day to prevent her legs from stiffening and to keep her blood circulating. She was pleased with her progress, despite her shaky start that morning. After she'd listened to her calm voice and settled into her writing mode, it had still felt slightly off. She knew that something had to change, and before she knew it, she'd hit Select All and Delete.

Tess felt in her creative and spiritual gut that she needed to write an entirely different story, one that would resonate with her and, hopefully, her readers. Until now, she'd never considered using her life for the material backdrop of her plotlines, but as with many things, her view was changing. She wanted to write a story about what she was going through, which was disappointment and heartache. But she also wanted to write about what was on the other side of those feelings, which was a solid and loving relationship built on trust and respect that could grow into something beautiful. Tess knew that if she desired those things, there was a host of other women who wanted it, too. In that moment she knew that she needed to write a story about love.

Initially, the thought of writing about love had made her laugh and cry at the same time. She was far from an expert on the subject, and in fact, she'd never had a truly successful relationship in her forty years. But as she thought about her current circumstances and the kind of story she wanted to write, she kept coming back to the word "love." She concluded that although she wasn't an expert on the emotion, she was an expert on hurt, pain, and bad decisions. She was an expert on regret, resentment, and revenge. She was an expert on dealing with infidelity, disrespect, and terrible breakups. Deep in Tess's soul, she knew that if she'd been able to survive all these things and still remain standing, she could write a story about the kind of love she hoped and wished for.

With a newfound determination, Tess sent an email to her editor, Mya Tyson, and outlined her new story proposal. She didn't know what the title was going to be, but she did know that it was going to be something great.

# Chapter 16

## BERNADETTE

Like most people, Bernadette looked forward to the weekend, mainly because her workweek spilled over into the days that were meant for rest and relaxation. But oftentimes her weekends stood as a two-day reminder of the fact that she'd be spending that time alone. But ever since her lunch date with Coop on Monday, she'd been looking forward to the weekend, and now that it was Friday, she was more than ready to enjoy herself.

She and Coop had talked every day that week. When Bernadette arose each morning she was greeted by a sweet text from Coop that simply read, *Good morning, beautiful. I hope you slept well.* From there, she would call him on her drive into work and they would share what they had on their calendars for the day. Coop also sent her midday text messages just to let her know he was thinking about her, or if something went on in his world, whether it was a problem he needed to deal with at one of his many businesses that included rental properties, two Laundromats, and a car wash, he would let her know. Bernadette also shared her multitude of personnel, administrative, and bottom-line budget challenges that went along with being the second highest ranking member of Bourbon General's executive team. Then, later that night before she wound down from her long day and Coop geared up for his second round—because things at Southern Comfort didn't get going until nighttime—they would share their highs and lows of the day and wish each other a good night until they spoke again the next morning.

By midweek, Bernadette had already grown accustomed to their routine, and she looked forward to the calls and texts that she and Coop shared. She was amazed at his high level of enthusiasm and zeal for life. If she told him that she was having a rough day, he would emphasize all the good things that were going well and help her find a solution for whatever challenge she was facing, always reminding her that she was blessed to be in the position in which she stood. Bernadette respected Coop's view of life because she knew he'd acquired his knowledge from bumps and bruises he'd gained at an early age.

After having been incarcerated while he was young for senseless crimes he'd committed, Coop understood and had learned how to make the most of the opportunities that came with one's freedom, and he was determined to live with appreciation for the life he'd fought so hard to build over the years. If anyone had told Bernadette a year ago that she'd be living in a small Southern town, dating an ex-felon, she would have thought that meant her future was bleak because on the surface it went against the standards she'd set for herself. But as she looked at her life right now, she had to admit that she was the happiest she could ever remember as an adult. In such a very short time, Coop had made her feel special, not just by the words he said but by his actions and deeds.

Yesterday when she'd been so swamped that she hadn't been able to leave her office for lunch, Coop had made sure that food was delivered to her from Sue's Brown Bag, and because she had told him that her cousin was staying with her and was sequestered inside the house until she finished her novel, he'd made sure the order from Sue's was large enough that Bernadette had leftovers to take home to Tess.

Now that it was Friday, Bernadette wanted to see Coop so badly she felt like a kid on Christmas morning who was waiting to open gifts. But she had to be patient because as much as they wanted to see each other, they had to wait. Tonight was going to be busy at Southern Comfort because one of the club's regulars was having a retirement celebration, and Coop was expecting the crowd to be large. Plus, Bernadette knew that Tess had been confined upstairs all week in her makeshift writing cave, and now that it was Friday night, she'd said she was going to take a break and celebrate her steady writing flow. Bernadette had also been in touch with Arizona, who was going through some major intimacy problems with Chris and needed a break from her worries. So Bernadette had planned a ladies' night in with her cousin and her new friend because all three of them needed each other's friendship and advice.

Bernadette was putting the finishing touches on one of her food trays when Tess walked into the room.

"Wow!" Tess said with excitement. "Cuz, this looks like a spread straight out of Martha Stewart's kitchen."

"Aww, thanks, Tess." Bernadette smiled with modesty, and even though she wasn't boastful, she had to admit that she possessed a natural talent for decorating and entertaining. Her den looked more like the setup of a fashionably decorated event space than a room in someone's home. "You know, ever since I was a little girl I've loved decorating and entertaining."

"You sure have, and you certainly have the gift and the skills for it. If you ever get tired of that suited-up corporate life you've been living, you could definitely make a hell of a lot of money as a decorator and event planner."

Bernadette smiled as she surveyed her handiwork, some of which she'd prepared last night and had kept in her refrigerator until she'd come home from work that afternoon. She'd put together delectable trays with everything from fruit kabobs with a homemade strawberry cream cheese dip to both raw and fire roasted veggies and imported and domestic cheeses and crackers, all beautifully displayed on beds of leafy greens. She'd also used cake stands of varying heights and filled them with bacon-wrapped scallops, mini chicken quesadillas, and zesty meatballs. She'd made a bowl of pasta salad and mini cups of garden salads with individual dressing bowls. And last but not least, a chocolate pound cake to satisfy everyone's sweet tooth.

"Thanks, cuz. I'm so glad you approve. I know you go to a lot of fabulous events in the literary world, so I trust your judgment."

"I more than approve, and to show you that I'm serious, I'm going to do the honors of sampling this delicious food." Tess pierced a meatball with a toothpick and popped it into her mouth. "This is so good! Bernadette, I've been telling you for years that you should seriously think about doing a lil' something on the side. Build up a name for yourself."

"Thanks, but right now my nine-to-five pays the bills."

Tess shook her head. "And speaking of your job, how in the world did you find the time to cook all this food and then arrange it like a culinary display?"

"I wish I could take the credit for all of it, but I only put together a portion of the food. I cheated a little and stopped by Sue's Brown Bag for all the hot food. I can't wait to take you there once you get a chance to break away from your writing. That place has the best food I've ever tasted."

"Well, if it's anything like the leftovers from the other day, I'm ready."

Just then they were pulled from their conversation when the doorbell rang.

"That's Arizona," Bernadette told Tess. "I think you two are going to really hit it off."

Bernadette opened the door and greeted Arizona with a warm hug, but when she took her friend's coat to hang in the closet, she was startled by Arizona's appearance. She still looked stunningly beautiful, as usual, but she also looked noticeably thinner. Bernadette knew that wearing black generally gave a slimming effect to one's figure, but as she inspected Arizona, she was sure that it wasn't just the color of the material that had her friend looking as if she'd lost a whole dress size in one week.

"Arizona, you look like you've lost weight," Bernadette said.

Arizona smiled. "I have, and thanks for noticing."

"Only a blind person wouldn't be able to notice. It's been under one week since I last saw you. How did you lose so much weight so fast?" Bernadette asked as they walked back to her den.

"Honestly, and this is gonna sound horrible, but I think it's because of all the stress that I've been under. And this is gonna sound even worse, but whenever I think about Chris I lose my appetite."

"You look good, but losing weight this way is going to negatively affect your health, my friend."

"I know, you're right."

"And honestly, it's not good that you lose your appetite when you think about the man you're going to marry. That's a real problem. Arizona, I'm worried about you."

"You're not alone. My mom is worried, too, and I just don't know what to do. My situation with Chris is wearing me down."

Bernadette shook her head as she thought about the phone conversation she'd had with Arizona a few nights ago when Arizona had described in detail how badly her last sexual encounter with Chris had ended. Bernadette wanted her friend to be happy, and although Chris loved Arizona and she loved him, Bernadette knew that love alone wouldn't sustain their relationship, and over time Arizona's frustrations, mixed with Chris's literal shortcomings, was a combination that was doomed to fail.

Bernadette knew that Arizona was in need of good, sound advice. Tess was in need of healing and a listening ear, and she was in need of reassurance that she wasn't stepping into a minefield in her budding relationship with Coop. Bernadette knew that tonight was going to be therapeutic for them all.

When Bernadette and Arizona entered the room, Tess was already pouring the champagne. "Tess," Bernadette said, "I want you to meet my friend, Arizona. And Arizona, this is my cousin, Tess Sinclair."

Arizona's mouth fell open. "Hold up!" she gasped and looked at Bernadette, then at Tess, and back at Bernadette again. "Tess Sinclair is your cousin?! Oh my goodness! I'm a huge fan." She walked up to Tess with a spring in her step. "My mother has read all your books and that's how I got started reading them. You're a great author. I don't know how you come up with some of your storylines, but I love them and all your characters."

Tess set the champagne back in the ice bucket and extended her hand for a firm shake. "I'm honored, and thank you, and your mother, for your support."

Arizona bypassed Tess's hand and embraced her with a warm hug. "You're welcome."

"Get used to hugs," Bernadette said with a light chuckle. "That's what folks do down here in the South."

"I see." Tess nodded with a smile.

Three hours later the women had devoured the small tray of finger food that Bernadette had picked up from Sue's Brown Bag and were now eating one of the two pizzas that Tess had ordered for delivery. They were on their third bottle of wine and all feeling relaxed and free as they discussed the situations that had led them to where they were at the moment.

"Wait a minute," Tess said as she looked at Arizona. "How small did you say his dick is?"

"Tess!" Bernadette chided. "Don't be so crude."

Arizona gave them both a sad look. "I haven't measured it, but it can't be any more than maybe an inch and a half. And that's when he's fully erect. When he's not, I can't even see it."

Bernadette shook her head because each time she'd heard Arizona describe Chris's tiny penis she cringed, and now that Tess was getting an earful, Bernadette braced herself for the comments that might come flying out of her cousin's mouth.

Tess sucked her teeth. "Damn. Your man is workin' with a gherkin."

Bernadette threw Tess a hard look, akin to how a parent would caution a child about bad behavior.

"Yes," Arizona responded. She closed her eyes and shook her head. "I feel absolutely horrible, but I don't even want to look at him with his clothes off. Ever since last week I've been completely turned off by my own fiancé. He's out of town on business for the next two weeks, so we talk every morning and at night. Every time I hear his voice I get frustrated, and I know that's not right. That's not the emotion I should be feeling when I talk to the man I'm supposed to love and marry."

"No, it's not," Tess said, "but I can see why you feel that way."

"This is the hardest thing I've ever dealt with," Arizona said. "I love Chris, but I'm not attracted to him anymore, and it's all because . . ."

"He has a little dick," Tess said in a blunt tone.

Bernadette pointed her finger at her cousin and tossed her a warning stare. "You're not helping."

"You're right, and I'm sorry," Tess said, motioning to Arizona and then to Bernadette. "But I know what will help." Tess picked up the bottle of Chardonnay and poured Arizona another glass. "You need this, and a whole lot more. If I had some weed I'd give that to you, too."

Bernadette blinked her eyes rapidly. "What did you just say?"

"Calm down, cuz. I was only joking."

Arizona inhaled deeply and then gulped down half of the wine in her glass. "Am I being shallow? I mean, Chris is a good man. He's kind, thoughtful, and respectful. He loves Solomon and he's a great role model for my son. And I can't even begin to tell you how good he is to me. He's everything I've ever wanted in a man."

"Expect for his small dick," Tess said as she took a sip of her wine. "I know that's not something you wanted."

Bernadette spoke up. "Please excuse my cousin. As you can see, the author in her comes out . . . and she has a definite way with words."

"But she's real and she's right," Arizona responded. "If I'da known that Chris had this problem, I probably wouldn't have ever started dating him."

Tess set her glass down on the coffee table and took a slice of pizza from the box as she spoke. "That's why I think the whole 'no sex before marriage' thing is a really bad idea. Before you buy a house you get a home inspection so you can see what kind of problems you'll be dealing with before you move in. I think that sex before marriage is the same damn thing. You have to make sure you're sexually compatible before you say 'I do.' I've heard from so many people that marriage is easy to get into but hard as hell to get out of."

Bernadette rested her hand against her head as she sipped from her glass. "So, I guess the question now is, what do you want to do, Arizona?" Bernadette knew that she was putting her friend on the spot, but she also knew that it was a serious matter, and Arizona needed to make a decision. Her wedding was only a few months away, and given the speed with which time was flying by, June would be here before they knew it.

"I'm still not sure," Arizona replied. "I'm hoping that you ladies can share some wisdom with me because I really need it."

Bernadette almost laughed. "I'm fifty and she's forty," she said, motioning her head in Tess's direction, "and neither one of us have kids or have ever been married. I haven't dated in five years and Tess is in a dry spell."

"But I have booty calls regularly," Tess interjected. "With a hot twentysomething, I might add, who can bring it like nobody's business."

"Ignore her," Bernadette quipped as she continued. "What I'm trying to say is that our advice, at least mine, might not be the wisest, but I'll tell you what I think from my heart."

"From the heart is the best kind of advice," Arizona said. "'Cause I need help."

Bernadette paused for a second. She wanted to make sure that the words she chose were right, and more important, that they would help her friend. "I don't think you're the least bit shallow. You're genuine, and that's one of the things I immediately picked up on about you. You're being honest about how you feel and that's a great thing because a lot of people walk into relationships lying to themselves and to each other, all for the sake of saving face and presenting a picture-perfect image to the world."

"I second that," Tess said. "Folks are all over social media trying to make everyone believe they're living their best life, but ninety percent of the mess they post is bullshit. What they're really doing is out there living their best lie, and I bet that's probably what that bastard, Antwan, is doing right now. The selfish son of a bitch."

Bernadette could see that her cousin was primed and ready to venture down a troubled road, so she steered the conversation back to Arizona's current situation. "It's every woman's right to have good sex . . . and often," she said. "It's an important part of our physical and emotional well-being, and it's a way that you can connect with your partner on a level that no one else can or should. So the fact that it's not what you want is a big concern. But I'll be honest with you." Bernadette paused again and stared directly into Arizona's eyes as she spoke because she wanted to make an even greater impact with the next words she was about to say. "Chris's size and even his lack of skills shouldn't be your biggest concern. The thing you should be worried about is the fact that he seems to be completely oblivious to your wants, needs, and your obvious dissatisfaction."

Bernadette could see that both Arizona and Tess were hanging on her words, so she continued. "From what you've told me, he hasn't even taken the time to acknowledge that you haven't been sexually satisfied each time you two have made love, which tells me that he checked out after his own needs were met, and that's just plain, cut-and-dry selfish behavior."

"You're right," Arizona said. "And he immediately goes to sleep like he's done so much that he's worn out."

Bernadette shook her head. "He might not really be asleep."

"But he snores."

"Arizona, I can fake a snore right now if I want to. Has it occurred to you that he might be pretending to be asleep in order to avoid having an honest conversation with you?"

"She's right," Tess joined in. "Antwan used to do shit like that all the time. Not in the bedroom, but in other areas of our relationship. He'd make up all kinds of excuses for not being able to answer my calls or go out on a date, all so he could avoid having an honest discussion about the messed-up things he was doing. Classic sideline behavior."

Bernadette closed her eyes to avoid rolling them. She loved her cousin, but at the moment she was close to asking Tess to stop drinking and talking because right now, Arizona needed their help. As Bernadette looked at Tess, she was reminded of something that she already knew—Tess relished being the center of attention, and if she wasn't, she'd figure out a way to insert herself into any given situation. Tess had been that way since childhood, and Bernadette knew that she needed to talk to her cousin about what drove her need to always bring the focus back to herself. Bernadette knew that as an author, Tess was often alone, leading a solitary life with the characters she created in her head. But she also knew that real life didn't work that way, and she wondered if her cousin fully understood that at the ripe age of forty. But this moment wasn't the proper time or place to delve into Tess's problems because Arizona's situation was pressing.

"Wow," Arizona said as if she'd just discovered buried treasure. "All this time I've been thinking that Chris was so thoughtful and attentive, but when it comes to the bedroom he's downright selfish. He's always been so giving of everything, whether it's his time, money, or feelings, that I didn't think he had a selfish bone in his body."

Tess smirked. "Sex, good or bad, can bring out a lot of things in a person. Take it from me—"

Bernadette quickly chimed in before Tess could get going. "If you two get married, the things you're experiencing now will only get worse, and eventually his selfish behavior will undoubtedly spill over into other parts of your relationship. When is he returning from his business trip?"

"He'll be gone for another two weeks."

Bernadette nodded. "Okay, as soon as he gets back you need to have a serious talk with him, and it has to happen outside the bedroom because it's clear that trying to have a conversation with him after sex is out of the question."

"I can't even stand the thought of having sex with him," Arizona said with despair in her voice, "so I can promise you that whenever and wherever we talk it won't be anywhere near the bedroom."

Tess finished off the remaining pizza crust from her slice and washed it down with a bottle of Pellegrino. "In addition to what Bernadette said about him being selfish, you also have to consider another side of things."

"Which is?" Arizona asked with curiosity.

Tess leaned forward to emphasize her point. "The fact is this, no matter how thoughtful or understanding he tries to be, not only does he have a small dick, his sexual bag of tricks is empty. You said yourself that he doesn't kiss you the way you like or caress you the way you like. And the big kicker is that he doesn't know how to handle his business downtown. If a man can't do me the way I like, he's got to go because if the dick fails, the tongue can be a great backup. And honey, let me tell you, over time, a little-dick, non-pussy-eatin' man will get on your last nerve."

Bernadette let out a deep sigh. "As lewd as Tess sounds, she's mostly right. Pleasure can be achieved in many different ways, and if you have a really good relationship, the emotional intimacy can bring great pleasure. But sexual pleasure is a whole different ballgame, and it doesn't seem that Chis can take you there on any level."

"No, he can't . . . or he doesn't," Arizona answered.

"I think you were right the first time," Tess blurted in. "But hopefully, and if he loves you, he'll at least try."

Bernadette could see that Arizona was mentally tired and was becoming more and more depressed as they talked. She'd drunk a bottle of wine by herself, but she'd only taken small nibbles of the food that she'd left mostly untouched on her plate. Bernadette knew she needed to change the subject so her friend could have time to clear her head of her worries, and she thought this was as good a time as any to shift the focus to her budding relationship with Coop.

Bernadette knew that having grown up in Bourbon, Arizona could give the real nitty-gritty details on the man. Even though he seemed to be an open book about his life and he was forthcoming about his past, Bernadette was more concerned about his present. She wanted to know about his dealings with women. She wanted to know if he was a love-'em-and-leave-'em type of guy.

She felt that she could take Coop at his word, but she'd also thought she could do the same with Walter and a few others she'd dated in her past, and they'd turned out to be liars, cheaters, and lower than the dirt on the ground. She felt in her heart that Coop wasn't that way, but she wanted to be sure so that she could prepare herself and cut her losses if she needed to. So she began slowly. "Coop and I are going on a date tomorrow night."

Tess clapped her hands. "Up until a few days ago you hadn't been on a legitimate date in five years, and now you're working on two in less than a week. You might get off to a slow start but you damn sure don't let any grass grow under your feet."

Arizona gave Bernadette a sly smile. "I heard that you and Coop got a thing going on."

"What?" Bernadette said with shock and curiosity. "Who's saying that we have a thing going on?"

"Girl, ever since Coop took you to lunch at Sue's Brown Bag, tongues been waggin' all over Bourbon, because like I told you last weekend at my party, Coop doesn't have a steady woman, and as far as

I know that's on purpose. He's had a lot of 'friends,' but nothing real serious. He doesn't even go out in public with some of the women that I know for a fact he's fooled around with. But in your case it's different. He's taking you out in public, during the day, and like I said, that's big for Coop."

Half of Bernadette felt special and tingly inside when she thought about Coop. But the other half, which was practical and rooted in levelheaded logic, felt skeptical and downright afraid of the fact that she was stepping into uncharted territory with a man who clearly had the very real possibility of breaking her heart. She wasn't an authority on love, but she was an expert when it came to feeling the pain of a broken heart. She'd had so many bad experiences with men that she didn't trust her own judgment. And what especially gave her pause about Coop was the fact that no man as good looking as him had ever been genuinely interested in her.

"What have people been saying about Coop," Bernadette asked and then paused, "and me?"

"I can see you're surprised." Arizona said.

"Of course I am. No one in this town even knows who I am."

Arizona laughed. "Honey, this is Bourbon, not DC, so everybody eventually knows everybody. But trust me, people know who you are. When you got that fancy job at Bourbon General, word got around that a sista was runnin' things down at the hospital."

"See, you're a celebrity and you didn't even know it," Tess said with a wink.

Arizona nodded. "Yep. And if you think folks was talkin' about you before, just wait 'til they find out that Tess Sinclair is your cousin and she's stayin' with you out here in the Palisades. Folks in Bourbon gettin' ready to lose their natural minds."

Tess's eyes grew big. "Don't tell a soul that I'm here. I want to be low-key until I finish this book, so that means no distractions. Other than my mother and my editor, I haven't told anyone that I'm staying here."

It struck Bernadette that as much as Tess enjoyed being the center of attention, she was adamant about anonymity when it came to her writing process. When she was in her writing cave she acted as though the outside world didn't exist and was able to block out anything that distracted from or interfered with completing her book. But once her manuscript was finished, she was ready to emerge into the world and spread her wings with all the attention that a blossoming butterfly could command.

"Okay, I understand," Arizona said with slight disappointment.

Bernadette once again knew that she needed to have a separate conversation with Tess, but for now she wanted to move the conversation back to her and Coop, because she knew Arizona could give her the answers she wanted. "So, tell me again, what exactly are people saying about Coop and me?"

Arizona pepped up. "That you're Coop's woman. Not his main woman, but his woman."

"So he's been seeing multiple women?"

"Honey, let's be real. A man as rich and fine as Coop is gon' have women, period. But the thing about him is that he keeps all his personal dealings on the low, and he don't let anybody know what he's doing when it comes to his love life. But he had you up in Sue's, all out in the open, which isn't his style at all."

"But that was only a lunch date."

Arizona nodded. "And that's what makes me know that Coop's really into you. Sue's holds a special place for Coop because it's named after his sister."

"I remember he told me that," Bernadette said.

"Yes, and he was very close to her up until the day she died. Sue used to visit him every single weekend when he was locked up, and after he got out she gave him a chance and a place to stay when no one else would."

"She loved her brother and it's apparent that he loved her."

"Yep," Arizona agreed. "So for him to take you on your first date to the place that's named after someone he loved dearly, that means a lot, and as far as I know, I don't think Coop has ever taken any of his women to Sue's."

"He's that much of a player?" Tess asked with skepticism. She gave Bernadette a cautious side-eye.

Bernadette knew that Arizona's words hadn't swayed Tess's opinion one bit and that Tess was mulling over the very same thing that she'd initially thought; that Coop was a middle-aged playboy with more women than he knew what to do with. Bernadette knew that Coop had had a lot of women because he'd told her that during one of their many conversations. He'd been very open with her about his past and his present, and she knew that he loved the ladies. But he'd told her that a few years ago he'd reached a point in his life that he was finally ready to settle down, and when he met the woman he wanted to share his life with, he'd know it.

"I'mma tell you what my mom told me that Coop told her a few years ago," Arizona said, "'cause you know they go way back, seeing that they both grew up in the Bottoms. Anyway, he told her that he wanted to settle down and get married and when the right woman came along he'd know it, but until then he was gonna have fun and wait for that special one to come into his life."

Bernadette nearly fell off her side of the couch. She thought about the conversation she'd had with Coop about the very same thing. "That's interesting," was all she could bring herself to say.

Tess leaned back into the love seat and looked at Bernadette. "Are you falling for this guy . . . after just one week?"

Arizona jumped in. "One week or one year, what does it matter? At her age," she said, looking in Bernadette's direction, "it doesn't take a long time to know if you're fallin' for somebody. Right?"

Bernadette cleared her throat. "I think it depends upon the individuals and their specific relationship. As for me, I'm not 'falling' for anyone. I enjoy Coop's conversation and his company, and I'm going to keep an open mind about everything. I'm going to take things one step at a time and see where it leads. As a matter of fact, I think that's what all three of us should do; keep an open mind about where we are in our lives, figure out what we really want, and then see what happens."

The three women sat in silence as they pondered Bernadette's words. And even though Tess hadn't said anything, Bernadette sensed that trouble was on the horizon.

# Chapter 17

## TESS

Tess was sitting across from Bernadette at the breakfast table, eating a large bowl of oatmeal and drinking dark roast coffee from her favorite mug that she'd brought with her from home. She eyed Bernadette as her cousin talked in between tiny bites of her veggie egg white omelet and whole wheat toast. The two were deep into a conversation that had started last night, which was the subject of Bernadette's and Coop's new romance.

Tess saw last night and even more this morning that no matter how much Bernadette tried to convince her that she wasn't falling for Coop, her facial expressions, tone, and mood spoke something entirely different. Bernadette's obvious affection for the man was evident in the way her voice changed to a soft pitch when she mentioned Coop's name.

Tess knew that seeing Bernadette happy should have made her happy as well, but it didn't. Instead, she felt cautious and skeptical of Coop because the man simply seemed too good to be true, and her instincts told her that he was hiding something.

"That man is up to something," Tess had said to herself two days ago, "and I'm going to get to the bottom of it!"

Because Tess was experienced at doing research for her books, she had become astute about how to investigate any subject, especially people. So naturally, she did some internet snooping during one of her writing breaks because she wanted to get the low down on Coop.

Tess had typed the name Cooper Anthony Dennis into Google, and what she'd found gave her even more concern about the man that Bernadette was going on a date with tonight. When Tess saw the photo of the handsome man in Google Images, she had to do a double take. To say that Coop was good looking was like saying the Grand Canyon was a cluster of red rocks; it didn't begin to do the description any justice. Coop was fine, even by Tess's hard standards, and if he looked this good in his fifties, she could only imagine the heartbreaker he must have been in his twenties. But Tess had quickly moved on from the man's killer good looks in order to uncover what was behind the magnetic smile, wavy salt-and-pepper hair, and the debonair aura that oozed from her computer screen.

Tess found out that Coop had a criminal record that had started when he was fifteen years old with a charge for petty theft. His illegal activities grew as he became older and eventually led to a ten-year sentence in federal prison when he was just twenty-three years old. He'd been convicted for trafficking drugs from North Carolina to Washington, DC. His sentence would have been reduced, but he'd refused to turn evidence on others involved in the drug ring that he'd been a part of. He wasn't a snitch, but in Tess's eyes, he was a fool. That one act, which had been committed in the black community, had cost him five of the ten years of his lost freedom, and it had kept his criminal friends who should have paid for their crimes on the street.

After Coop had served his time and was released from prison he'd returned to Bourbon. But no matter how much Tess dug and dug, she couldn't find much information about how he'd acquired the apparent wealth he now possessed. According to public records, and articles in which he'd been featured in the local African American newspaper, *The Guard*, Coop owned over half the land and rental houses in the predominantly black section of town called the Bottoms. He also owned two Laundromats, two car washes, and a very popular jazz club called Southern Comfort, which was geographically situated on the racial cusp of the city and drew a large and diverse crowd. She remembered seeing the large billboard advertising the club when she'd driven her rental car from the airport to Bernadette's house.

Tess had to admit that Coop's "pull yourself up by the bootstraps" story was impressive. On paper he seemed to be the model of a reformed citizen who'd paid his debt to society and had given back to the Bottoms, as was evidenced through his charitable giving throughout the community. But Tess didn't completely buy it. She didn't know if it was because of the fact that as a writer of fiction, she had a wild imagination that caused her to create colorful stories in lieu of information, or the fact that the source of how Coop rose to riches was unclear, but what Tess did know was that there was something about the man that wasn't on the up-and-up, and she didn't want Bernadette to get her heart broken again, because she felt this time that her cousin might not be able to recover from it.

"So, what time are you and Coop going out tonight?" Tess asked, before placing a heaping spoonful of oatmeal into her mouth.

"He's coming to pick me up around five for an early dinner, then we're going to catch a movie, and after that we're going to Southern Comfort to enjoy the rest of the evening," Bernadette said with giddy excitement in her voice. "I've been wanting to go to that club ever since I moved here six months ago, and now I can't believe that not only am I finally going, I'm going with the guy who owns the place. How crazy is that?"

"Uh-huh . . . I guess life's full of strange and crazy things."

Bernadette took a sip of her freshly squeezed orange juice and paused. "What's that supposed to mean?"

"Bernadette, you know I love you dearly and I only want the very best for you. But I have to be honest. I'm worried about your involvement with Coop."

"My involvement? You act like I'm deep into a relationship with the man. It's just a date, Tess. And as a matter of fact, tonight will only be our second date, so that hardly qualifies as being involved."

"You said that you two talk and text several times a day."

"And?"

"He's the first person you talk to in the morning and the last person you speak to at night. It may only be your second date, but you start and end your day with the man, and that's serious."

"I know that you create stories in your head, but please leave me out of the plot you're cooking up."

Tess let out a loud, overly exaggerated sigh and folded her arms across her chest. "Who are you trying to convince, me or yourself? I see the way your eyes light up like the sun and your voice gets high like a kite in the wind whenever you talk about Coop."

"You and your words. You're so dramatic."

"No, I'm real, and you know it. Just admit it."

"You sound ridiculous. With the exception of last night, you've been locked away in the guest room ever since you got here, so how would you know?"

"Bernadette, I knew by the way you sounded over the phone last weekend that you were into that man. And now that I'm here and able to see you up close in real time, it's obvious."

"Oh, just stop, Tess."

"No, you stop," Tess countered. "It's obvious that you're into him, and trust me, if I can see it, Coop damn sure can." Tess looked directly into Bernadette's eyes. "I love you, cuz, and I'm only telling you this because I don't want you to get hurt again."

Bernadette took a deep breath and lowered her head. "Why can't you just be happy for me?"

"I don't want this man to take advantage of you."

"Hell, neither do I. But at some point I've got to get back out there and start living again. How am I ever going to find love if I don't open myself up to it? I'm tired of living life in a coffin." Bernadette's chest began to heave up and down. "I closed myself off from the possibility of love or a relationship, and I shut down my feelings for five long years. I threw myself into what I could control, which was my career and my choices. I chose to fill my time with work in order to stay away from any emotional involvement, whether it was romantic or just simple friendships, because I knew I couldn't control anyone other than myself. But you know what I discovered? I couldn't control anything at all. Life moves forward, and you can either quietly stand on the sidelines or jump into it with a big splash. I've been standing on the sidelines for way too long and now I'm ready to start living again."

Hearing her pragmatic, logical-thinking cousin talk like a pie-in-the-sky dreamer made Tess wonder if Coop had slipped Bernadette some drugs. *Maybe he's still dealing,* Tess thought, *and that's how he's been able to accumulate so much wealth.* She'd never heard Bernadette talk the way she was speaking now, and it gave her cause for even more concern. "Did you sleep with him after you two had lunch?"

"What?"

"He either got to you with the dick or some drugs. But he's definitely done something that has you talking crazy. Antwan used to do the same thing," Tess said with a huff. "He used to have my head so far in the damn clouds that I couldn't see what was really going on. Love can blind you to the truth."

Bernadette removed the linen napkin from her lap, neatly folded it, and calmly placed it on the table. Tess could see that her cousin's entire mood had changed, and she braced herself for what Bernadette was about to say.

"Tess, I love you, but right now I'm on the verge of not liking you."

"Don't be mad at the messenger. I'm just telling you the hard truth, and sometimes the truth hurts."

"Will you shut up for once and let me talk!"

Tess couldn't remember Bernadette ever raising her voice at her, and it rendered her speechless as her cousin continued.

"I knew that somehow, some way, the conversation was going to jump back to your relationship with Antwan. Everything always has to revolve around you and how you're the victim. Even last night you couldn't give Arizona advice without bringing up your relationship with Antwan and how he wronged you. Have you ever stopped to think that maybe Antwan wasn't the only asshole in your relationship?"

Tess huffed, leaned forward over the table, and craned her neck. "Excuse me, but did you just call me an asshole?"

"What I'm saying is that Antwan showed his ass one way and you showed yours in another," Bernadette shot back. "Last night you said that love is blind, and just now you said love can blind you to the truth. But honestly, you don't have a clue," Bernadette said as she looked directly into Tess's eyes. "The truth is, love sees what it wants to see. You knew that Antwan was cheating on you and you knew that he was lying about it, but you chose to look the other way and believe his paper-thin excuses even when deep down you knew they weren't true.

"You suffocated that man with your relentless need for attention and your toxic view of life. I remember one time when I went out to dinner with the two of you while I was visiting shortly after you guys started dating, and the entire evening you talked about yourself, and anytime Antwan managed to jump in, you cut him down and cut him off with sarcastic remarks that you thought was funny."

"You're one to talk. How the hell are you gonna sit here and lecture me on how I fucked up my relationship when you've been a doormat that men wipe their feet on and keep steppin'? You might call it bitchy behavior, but I call it taking control, and unlike you, I don't think having control in a relationship is a bad thing."

Bernadette shook her head. "You didn't have control then and you still don't have it now. Besides, what has being in control gotten you, other than ending up frustrated and alone?"

"I'll take being alone and having control any day over being with someone who's gonna walk all over me, use me for what they can get, and then leave me hanging out to dry . . . like a fifty-year-old doormat." Tess knew that what she'd said was beyond mean, but at the moment she didn't care.

"You're exactly right, Tess. But I have to correct you on one thing. You're describing who I used to be. I'm no longer a doormat. I'm walking a very different path that's going to lead me in a new direction, but I can't get there if I continue doing what I've always done."

Tess threw up her hands. "You've been reading way too many O Magazine articles."

"I know that you bleed sarcasm, but can you please stop for one minute so we can have a real conversation?"

"You've already told me that I'm a callous, selfish bitch, and it doesn't get any more real than that."

"Tess, the same way you said that you want the best for me, I also want the best for you, and I wouldn't be showing you genuine love if I didn't tell you the truth. I believe you hunger for attention for the same reason that you talk so much junk, and that's because deep down you're scared. You write books about adventure, love, and faith because you have none of those things in your life, and the reason you don't have them is because you're scared. You're afraid of getting hurt. Well, guess what? You're hurting right now, and that's part of the reason why you're so negative. You're still standing on the sidelines of life, afraid to jump in. Booty calls with twentysomethings is a slow and lonely road that's gonna lead you nowhere, Tess."

Both women sat across from each other saying nothing, but Tess knew that Bernadette was right. Just as Bernadette had buried herself in her work over the past five years, Tess had buried herself in her writing practically all of her adult life. She'd written her first manuscript while she'd still been in college, and one year after graduation that same manuscript became her first book, which went on to top several best-seller lists. By her twenty-fifth birthday, her second novel became a *New York Times* best seller, and since then she'd had a string of chart-topping books that had won her legions of loyal readers from all over the world. She was a big deal in the literary world, but in her own world, she didn't feel nearly as accomplished. She held deep rooted fears of insecurity and self-doubt that she'd been able to mask by act-ing tough, talking shit, and in many instances, acting out.

Bernadette had hit a particular nerve because she'd said some of the same things that Antwan used to say about her behavior.

Tess wanted to come back with an in-your-face response to Bernadette's brutal words, but she couldn't because her mind was overloaded with so much emotion she could barely hold on to it, and she knew she needed to do something before she exploded. A little voice in her head told her, *Put Bernadette in her place, curse her high-and-mighty ass out, then pack your bags and fly back to Chicago so you won't have to put up with this bullshit.* But the calm, more reasonable voice told her, *Take a deep breath, then listen and learn from your cousin's words because she's telling you what you need to hear.*

Tess looked out of the big floor-to-ceiling window beside the breakfast table and wished that she could fly away like the bird that had just breezed by. Being on the receiving end of criticism wasn't something she was used to, and it hurt. She knew she needed time to think things over before she spoke another word or made any impul-sive decisions.

She pushed her now-lukewarm bowl of oatmeal to the center of the table and rose from her chair. "I'm going upstairs to get back into my adventurous love- and faith-filled writing."

It was seven o'clock, and Tess was staring at a blank screen, trying to gather the strength to focus so she could write. "Damn," she whispered. She was startled by how angry her voice sounded. Her mind had been cluttered with complicated thoughts that had put her heart through a variety of emotions ever since she and Bernadette had their conversation that morning at the breakfast table. They had each said things that had hurt the other's feelings, but Tess knew that Bernadette's words had been rooted in truth and love, while hers had been based in love mixed with anger. "How can I love if I'm angry?" she asked aloud.

Tess typed the word "love" into her online dictionary.

*Love: noun: **love**; plural noun: **loves***
*    1. An intense feeling of deep affection; synonyms: deep affection, fondness, tenderness, warmth, intimacy, attachment, endearment*
*verb*
*verb: to feel a deep romantic or sexual attachment to (someone).*

Tess read the definition over and over as she stared at the screen, digesting what the words meant. For the first time in her life, she realized the immense power those four letters carried, and she once again knew Bernadette had been right.

Tess rose from the desk and walked over to the plush armchair near the window in the corner of the room. She smiled and nodded as she looked around the room. "This is just like my cousin."

Bernadette had decorated and designed the room with the comfort of her guests in mind. From the basket filled with bottled water and snacks to the closet containing extra sheets and blankets, to the fluffy towels and toiletries packed with essentials such as shampoo, toothpaste, body gel, and cotton balls, her cousin had put thought and care into anticipating the needs of her guests.

Tess settled into the comfortable chair and thought about the meaning of love and about the things that Bernadette had said to her earlier today. It was true that Tess's books were filled with adventurous characters who loved deeply and had faith that their lives would be better because of it. "I'm such a fucking phony," she said. "There's nothing about me that's adventurous, or loving, and I certainly don't have faith. I guess I'm writing about what I want but don't have." As Tess thought about the state of her life she felt defeated, and she knew she needed to leave the confines of Bernadette's home before she went stir-crazy.

It was just evening, but Tess felt as though it was midnight. Bernadette had left two hours ago—Coop had picked her up at exactly five o'clock—and although she hadn't spoken to her cousin since their breakfast blowout, the house felt empty and cold. "I've got to get out of here."

Tess sprang from her chair and walked over to the chest of drawers where she'd stored her clothes. She'd only packed sweaters, sweatshirts, and leggings because she hadn't anticipated getting out much. But now that she was looking through the boring selection, she wished she'd packed more stylish outfits. If Bernadette was her size she could go downstairs and search her closet, but Tess was nearly five inches taller, so nothing of her cousin's would be a good fit.

Tess pulled a black sweater over her head and stepped into a pair of black and white checkered leggings. She went into the bathroom and rummaged through her makeup bag. After applying foundation, brow liner, mascara, and lipstick, she slathered curling mousse through her medium brown tresses and then headed downstairs.

It was frigid outside, but unlike the Windy City, there was no snow on the ground. Tess couldn't believe that the grass still had a semblance of green color, even during the winter. "I guess the South refuses to yield to Mother Nature," she said. She was hungry, so she set her GPS for Sue's Brown Bag. She'd devoured the food that Bernadette had brought home and she hoped that a good meal would squelch her bad mood.

"This place reminds me of a mini version of South Side Chicago, only cleaner," Tess said as she navigated her way through the Bottoms.

After circling the block two times, she finally found a parking space down the street from the restaurant. Normally, she would have been leery about walking around a strange neighborhood by herself, especially at night, but given the mood she was in, she knew that if anyone approached her it would be them who'd be in trouble. Tess grabbed her handbag from the passenger seat and braced herself for the cold walk to the restaurant.

"Welcome to Sue's Brown Bag," the hostess said.

Tess nodded, noting how bubbly and friendly the woman seemed to be. She looked beyond the hostess stand and into the restaurant, which was much more stylish and modern than the exterior implied. The place was packed, which was why it had been so hard for her to find a parking space.

"Are you waiting for the rest of your party to arrive?" the hostess asked.

"Um, no," Tess responded. "It's just me."

The woman looked confused and surprised. "You eatin' all alone?"

"Yes." Tess ignored the hostess's comment. "How long is the wait?"

"Why you all alone on a Saturday night? You pretty, tall, and classy lookin'. I know you could get a date if you wanted one."

"Excuse me?" Tess couldn't believe the nerve of the woman.

"I'm just sayin' you could easily get a date."

"I know that, but tonight I want food. So I'm gonna ask your nosy ass again, how long is the wait?"

The server rolled her eyes. "You ain't got to be rude, cursin' and whatnot."

"You're calling me rude?" Tess scoffed. "You're asking me questions that's none of your business when you should be doing your job."

The woman huffed. "We have seats at the bar." She pointed across the room. "Help yourself."

If Tess wasn't so hungry she would have strutted straight out the door and into the cold night to find another restaurant, preferably back on Bernadette's side of town where manners mattered. But the fact was that she was hungry, and the aroma floating through the restaurant was so mouthwateringly good that she was willing to put up with rudeness in favor of a delicious meal. "I'll seat myself, but trust and believe, I'll be back."

Tess walked over to the bar and sat on a stool that was tufted with the softest leather she'd ever felt in a restaurant. The bar in front of her was brightly lit from the floor to the ceiling and was filled with shelf after shelf of premium alcohol.

"Hey, pretty lady," the bartender said with a big smile. "How can I help you tonight?"

"I'd like a glass of Chardonnay, a menu, and a conversation with the manager."

"Is everything aw'right?" the tall, chubby man asked. He had a clean-shaven face and his smile was genuine and friendly. "You too pretty to be upset. Is it somethin' I can help you with?"

"Thank you, but no. I need to speak to the manager about the way I was insulted by the hostess."

"Oh, you must be talkin' 'bout Sandy. She good people, she don't mean no harm, she just put her foot in her mouth all the time."

"It's great that you have team loyalty, but I still want to speak to the manager."

The bartender smiled. "I understand." He reached for a bottle and a glass and then handed Tess her Chardonnay, as well as a menu. "I'll go get the boss for you, ma'am. In the meantime, do you want somethin' to eat on while you wait?"

Tess was so hungry that her stomach jumped. "An order of wings, please."

"Comin' right up. I'll put in your order when I go back to get Maceo."

*Maceo? That name sounds like a pimp from a 1970s black exploitation movie,* Tess thought to herself. Now it made perfect sense as to why a rude, loud-talking hostess with no couth was employed there, and as someone who was charged with greeting people, no less. As a writer by profession, Tess always observed her surroundings because any location, person, or situation was fair game to be included in her stories.

As she looked around the restaurant she found it strange that an establishment this nice would have a rude hostess and a pimp managing the place. With its leather chairs, custom-made tables, and modern pendant lights and chandeliers, Tess was impressed by the ambience and sophisticated feel of the place. And the fact that it was packed to capacity was no surprise, given the great food and atmosphere.

As Tess observed, she discovered another interesting contradiction. The overwhelming majority of the patrons looked like blue-collar working-class folk, which matched the outside of the building, but certainly not the inside. Tess looked down at the menu and saw that the prices were unbelievably low. She knew that things were less expensive in the South, but the prices on the menu were just a step above what one would pay for a combo meal at a drive-thru window. It made Tess wonder how the establishment could possibly earn a profit. Her mind immediately went to work trying to figure out what was really going on. She knew that organized crime—which was big in Chicago—often used restaurants as a front through which to launder money, and she wondered if Bourbon had its own tiny version.

"Here you are, ma'am," a server said to Tess as she placed a platter of chicken wings in front of her.

The minute Tess smelled the delicious aroma of Southern fried chicken smothered in bourbon sauce, her mind moved from amateur sleuth into attack mode. She hadn't eaten since she'd abandoned her oatmeal that morning, and now she was ready to tame her hunger. When she bit into the wings all she could do was close her eyes and smile. One dozen wings came out on her plate, and within a matter of minutes Tess had eaten half of them. "These are the best wings I've ever had," she said as she gave a sheepish smile to the bartender, who had been eyeing her.

"You can thank Maceo for that," the bartender said. "That man can burn in the kitchen, yes siree."

Tess stopped chewing her food. "The manager is the cook?"

"Yes, at times," a deep voice said, coming up behind her.

Tess turned around to see who was attached to the voice that sounded like a cool drink of water on a hot summer day. The smooth Southern drawl mixed with crisp diction caught her attention.

"I'm Maceo," the man said with a nod of his head. "I'm the manager, and I do a lil' sumthin' sumthin' in the kitchen."

Tess was so mesmerized that she didn't have the forethought to wipe the wing sauce from the edges of her mouth. Although he was average height, the man possessed a towering presence that gave him command of the room. He wasn't what most would consider handsome, but his easy smile, deep dimples, and smooth skin made him look downright dreamy in Tess's eyes.

"I hear you have concerns about the way you were treated when you came in," the manager said.

"Um, yes."

"Can you tell me exactly what happened?"

Tess was a wordsmith by profession and a trash talker by nature, but right now she was so captivated by the manager/cook that she couldn't gather the words to explain herself. "The hostess was rude to me," was all she could manage to say.

Maceo chuckled and nodded his head again. "Ma'am, I'm so sorry and I apologize for Sandy's behavior. Why don't you let me take care of your meal tonight."

"Well, thank you."

"Do you know what you'd like?"

*A roll under the sheets with you between my legs*, Tess wanted to say. "What do you suggest?"

Maceo smiled. "I think I know exactly what you'd like."

Tess didn't know if he was flirting with her or if he was just naturally sexy, given his Southern charm, but she was enjoying their conversation nonetheless. She smiled back at him and said, "I'm sure you do."

Maceo's easy smile flatlined, changing into a serious look that made Tess's heart beat fast, then before she could blink, he turned and headed back into the kitchen. Tess couldn't finish the remaining wings on her plate because her appetite had suddenly left and was replaced by a strange feeling.

"You aw'right, ma'am?" the friendly bartender asked.

"Um, yes. I think so."

Tess felt her body tremble and her heart was still beating fast. She'd written about this feeling in books, she'd longed for it in real life, and ironically, she'd looked up its definition tonight. As improbable and crazy as it felt, Tess knew that the emotion she was feeling was love at first sight.

# Chapter 18

## ARIZONA

Arizona was sitting on her couch feeling sick to her stomach with worry. Her mother had just left a half hour ago with Solomon, who was staying at her parents' house tonight in order to give Arizona and Chris privacy to talk. Chris had been scheduled to be out of town through next week, but this afternoon he'd boarded a flight headed back home.

Chris had called Arizona last night when she was on her way home from Bernadette's house, and she'd known that he'd sensed something wrong by the tone and shortness in her voice and responses. She'd told him she was fine, but Chris had pressed her, insisting to get to the bottom of what was bothering her. Finally, Arizona had told him that she was having serious second thoughts about getting married, and the conversation quickly became heated.

"Chris, I'm not gonna have this conversation over the phone."

"You can't leave me hanging like this," he'd said. "I deserve to know what's going on."

"I told you that I didn't want to talk in the first place but you didn't listen, you just kept pressing and pressing. The things I want to say need to be aired out in person," she'd told him.

She'd awoken to a text from Chris this morning that said he was coming home and he would be at her house at eight o'clock that evening.

Arizona looked at her watch. It was now seven forty-five. Chris would be there in fifteen minutes because he was always on time. It was one of the many qualities she loved about him. He was a man of his word and if he told her something she could count on it.

The doorbell made Arizona jump off the couch. Chris was early, which meant he was serious and anxious. She took a deep breath and opened the door. The cold air rushed into the entryway and made her shiver. But her chills were quickly replaced by the warmth of Chris's body. Without saying a word he stepped into her house, closed the door behind him, and pulled her into his chest, holding her tightly.

Arizona was so overcome with emotion that she couldn't breathe. She felt Chris's body tremble against hers. But as they clung to each other she realized that he wasn't trembling, he was about to cry. She slowly pulled away and looked into his red-rimmed eyes.

"Chris, baby . . ." Arizona had never seen Chris in this state. She could see that he was trying to hold back tears, trying to be tough. But his trembling body gave him away. They stood in the middle of her entryway holding each other for what seemed like an hour but was really only a few minutes. And within those few, quiet moments, in the safety of Chris's arms, Arizona knew she was loved.

After they gathered themselves, they walked over to the couch to talk. Arizona saw small bags resting under Chris's eyes, a definite indication that he hadn't slept.

"Are you hungry? Do you want anything to drink?" she asked.

"No, I'm good."

"Are you sure? Have you eaten anything today?"

"No."

Arizona rose from the couch. "My mom dropped off some food when she came to pick up Solomon. I'm gonna fix you a plate."

"No," Chris said, barely above a whisper. "I don't want to eat. I want to talk."

Arizona sat back down in the spot where she knew she was about to have a very uncomfortable but much-needed conversation. "Let me start by saying—" Arizona was cut short when Chris raised his hand, motioning for her to stop.

"Arizona, please. Let me start." Chris cleared his throat. "I've been doing a lot of thinking since we spoke last night, and on my two-hour-long drive from the airport tonight. I thought about what you said, and about the things that have happened over the last week. As a husband, it's going to be my responsibility to protect you, honor you, and give you what you need. As a fiancé, I've failed you, Arizona. And I feel horrible about that. I was selfish and insensitive, and there's no excuse for that."

Arizona could see that Chris was sincere, and he seemed to be on the verge of tears again. But as she looked deeper into his eyes, she could see that he wasn't about to cry at all. What she saw was something that she'd never seen, at least not in Chris. She saw fear.

Chris shifted in place and cleared his throat. "This is hard for me to talk about, but I need to say it." He paused, then cleared his throat again. "My condition is called microphallus. Some people call it micropenis—I hate that term. But it is what it is. I guess I should've told you, but, Arizona, I honestly didn't know how, or what to say. My size has been an embarrassment for me my entire life. It's always been a cause of shame in me and disappointment from women. People look at me and see a tall muscular guy, and they automatically think I'm hung like a Mandingo, but I'm the opposite."

Arizona noticed that Chris was barely making eye contact as he spoke. She wanted to ask him to look at her, but she also knew that right now he was avoiding eye contact so that he could get through what he had to say, so she refrained and listened.

"As a teenager, I wanted to experiment like most guys do. But I knew if I did it would only take one girl to spread the word and I'd be the butt of jokes all over the school. It wasn't until I was in college that I had sex for the first time, and it was humiliating. What I'd feared in high school happened in college. It was so bad that the next semester I transferred schools. Over the years I've dated plenty of women, but I've only slept with three, including you, Arizona. Until we met, I didn't think I'd ever find a woman who would accept me for who I was, that's why I've been celibate. But from the moment I met you, I knew you were the one."

Arizona smiled and thought about their first meeting. She'd thought he must be full of himself because of how good looking he was. But after their first conversation she'd known there was something different and very special about Chris.

"I wanted to tell you so many times," Chris continued, "especially after we became engaged. But like I said, I didn't know how to start the conversation. Then, last week when we made love, I lost it." This time, Chris looked directly into Arizona's eyes. "I felt so much physical and emotional love for you that I was completely overwhelmed. I knew you weren't satisfied, but I was too embarrassed and scared to talk about it. I was embarrassed for obvious reasons and I was scared you were going to break up with me and call off the wedding."

Arizona swallowed hard because she'd been thinking about doing exactly what he'd feared, and that was the reason Chris had cut his trip short and was sitting on her couch this very moment.

"So instead of having the difficult conversation, I pretended to be asleep so I wouldn't have to talk to you about it, because I feared you would look at me differently . . . as less than a man. That scared me, Arizona. I don't want to lose you or your love and respect. When you told me that you wanted to call off the wedding and end our relationship, that was my worst nightmare come true, and it's something I've thought about every day since I proposed to you . . . what would happen when we did make love and you saw who I really am. Part of the reason I wanted to make love to you last week was to just get it over with and deal with whatever happened. But when I was faced with the reality of not being able to satisfy you I still couldn't handle it. I'm so sorry, baby. I want to be the man of your dreams."

Arizona reached out and touched Chris's hand. "Baby, you are the man of my dreams and I love you. And yes, I've had thoughts of calling off the wedding and reevaluating our relationship because I've been frustrated, angry, hurt, and downright mad. But through all those up-and-down emotions, the one thing that has remained consistent is that I love you, Chris. I love the man you are, I love the father you are, and I know I'll love the husband you'll become."

Chris moved closer to Arizona and engulfed her in his arms as he'd done when he'd first entered her house.

"We're gonna have to be completely honest with each other from here on out," Arizona said. "And no matter how upset, confused, embarrassed, or angry we think the other might get, we need to talk about our concerns instead of avoiding them, otherwise they'll become problems." Arizona surprised herself with how levelheaded and mature she sounded, and she knew that her conversation last night with Bernadette and Tess had helped her.

Chris nodded. "Yes, I agree one hundred percent."

"Sex isn't the most important part of a relationship, but it's up there," Arizona said. "I heard once that when the sex is good it's only ten percent of the relationship, but when it's bad it's ninety percent because it spills over into everything else and intensifies problems that already exist."

Chris nodded in agreement.

"I don't want sex to be ninety percent of our relationship, Chris."

"Neither do I, and that's another thing I was thinking about on my hour long drive tonight."

"What's that?"

"That we should go back to being abstinent until we're married."

Arizona gave him a quizzical look. "You want a do-over?"

Chris laughed and shook his head. "No, baby. What I'm saying is, I think we should spend this time understanding what each other's sexual needs are and what we like and don't like."

"The only way to do that is through experiencing it, which is what we've been doing."

"Yes and no. I say yes for you and no for me. You know what I like, which is everything you do because you turn me on. But I haven't taken the time to talk to you about physical intimacy so I can understand what you want, sexually, which I think goes back to your emotional needs as well."

Arizona didn't know if Chris was trying to throw her off course or not, but she wasn't clear about what he was saying and she desperately wanted to understand because this was serious. "You're confusing me, Chris. On the one hand you want to know how to please me, but on the other you want to wait until we get married to see if you can. I think that's unfair to me."

"I'm not trying to be unfair to you, Arizona. I'm trying to love you, the right way. I want to listen and really hear what you have to say, and respect how you feel. I want to practice touching you, caressing you, kissing you, and holding you the right way. I know those things set the stage for the main event. If I can get those right, I know I'll be able to please you in other ways."

Arizona thought about what Chris said, and she had to admit that he'd just made solid points. She was big on touch and feel, and the sensation of flesh against flesh had always excited her, especially if the man knew how to touch and caress her just right. Arizona nodded.

"Here, let me show you." Chris turned the palm of Arizona's hand up and began delicately caressing her skin, and with each stroke of his fingers he ever so slightly flicked the tip of his nail against her flesh as he spoke.

"I love you and I intend to honor you every day by showing love to you and our son. I'm going to be the strong post that you can lean on when you can't stand on your own, and I'll be the example that Solomon looks to as I guide and teach him how to be a man. Through honoring and loving you, I'll show our son how to treat women and be responsible and respectful in his relationships. And I want us to have more children so we can spread more love into this world."

Chris spoke all those words while continuing to caress Arizona's hand in the most tender and loving embrace she'd ever felt. Her lips formed a smile, her knees trembled, and the soft spot between her legs grew wet with desire. With just the touch of his hands and the words of his mouth, Chris had made Arizona feel passion, desire, and love. She was so turned on that she wanted to go a step further. Then, slowly, Chris decreased his pressure until his fingers came to a stop before gently releasing Arizona's hand.

Chris looked into Arizona's eyes. "This is just a taste of what our intimacy can be. I want to create a delicious feast that we can both enjoy."

All Arizona could say was. "Me too."

Chris smiled back at her. "I know I let you down, and you have every reason to feel unsure. But I'm asking you to give me another chance. Please trust me, baby."

Arizona thought about all the things Chris had said and about how he'd just made her feel, which was a stark contrast to their encounter last week. She also thought about the more practical, real-life implications of breaking up with Chris, and high on that list was Solomon. He was only in elementary school, but she knew the years would fly by and it wouldn't be long until he'd be interested in girls, and that would lead to dating with a whole other set of dynamics.

Arizona knew that her father was a good male role model for Solomon, as well as a few of her uncles. But she wanted her son to have a man in his life on a daily basis who would pick up the slack where she was lacking. She could always see the difference in how Solomon acted when Chris was around versus when he wasn't. When it was just her and Solomon hanging out at the house he tended to be more clingy and stubborn and not as willing to comply. But the minute Chris was around Solomon became more focused, energetic, and self-directed. She knew it was because she coddled him.

Arizona also knew that Chris brought a much-needed balance to her own life as well. He was the calm, sensible, and tactful side to her exuberant, in-your-face style. He'd also shown her the importance of financial investments, how to create and stay within a budget, and how to manage work and personal business. She knew that if it had not been for Chris helping her over the last two years, she'd still be working at Bourbon General instead of having taken the leap of faith to follow her passion as a full-time makeup artist. She was realistic about her current situation, and she knew that in the coming months if things got lean, Chris would be there to make sure all her bills were paid and she wouldn't have to worry about a thing.

Then there was her family and friends as well as Chris's to consider. She knew that she shouldn't worry about what others thought, but she did. Earlier that afternoon she'd talked to Bernadette about Chris when her friend had called to get advice about where to find an outfit for her date with Coop.

"I want an outfit that has the class of Angela Bassett and the sass of Beyoncé," Bernadette had said.

"Well, you gotta have booty to wear anything close to Queen B."

"I don't need your commentary about my flat behind, I just need you to tell me which store you recommend."

"Go to Mint Julep. It's on your side of town and they have quality pieces that keep up with the current trend. You gonna pay a lil' grip, but you'll come out lookin' like a million bucks and Coop won't be able to take his eyes off you."

"Thanks, Arizona. I just finished getting dressed from my jog and I'm going to head there now. By the way, are you okay? You were so distraught last night. I know you have a tough decision to make."

"I've already made up my mind. I can't do it, Bernadette. I'm calling off the wedding."

Bernadette let a long pause rest in the air before she spoke. "I want you to be one hundred percent sure before you do that, Arizona."

"Oh, I'm sure," she'd said with half confidence.

"I'll just say this. I obviously don't know him very well, but from what you've told me and from what I've observed on my own, Chris is a good man who loves you, and that's like finding a proverbial needle in a haystack."

Arizona felt it was Bernadette's subtle way of telling her, without really telling her, not to let a good man get away. Arizona could tell that just like everyone else, Bernadette liked Chris because he was a nice, likable guy. She also knew it was rare to find a person who got along with your people and you got along with his, and she'd found that in Chris. He was originally from New York but had moved to Atlanta, Georgia, to attend Morehouse College after transferring from North Carolina Central University in Durham, NC, which had made him fall in love with the South and convince many of his family members to relocate there. From the moment she'd met them, it had been a mutual love fest. His parents loved her and she adored them. Their extended families and friends all approved of their relationship and were supportive, which Arizona knew would be a plus for their relationship.

Breaking off their engagement and ending things with Chris would affect a lot of people in Arizona's and Chris's world, but most important, she knew that she was better off with him being in her life than without. And right there, sitting on the couch, Arizona decided she wasn't going to do what she'd told Bernadette earlier today. Instead, she was going to walk in faith and marry Chris.

"I'm going to trust in you," Arizona said.

"Baby, I'm going to work hard so you won't regret becoming Mrs. Pendleton." Chris rose from the couch. "I'm going to open that bottle of wine I bought you last week. I think we both need and deserve a drink."

Arizona watched Chris as he walked into her kitchen, then suddenly, her entire mood changed. She couldn't explain why, but as she looked at her handsome fiancé, she got a sinking feeling that she'd just agreed to walk off a cliff that had nothing but rugged dirt and rocks below.

# Chapter 19

## BERNADETTE

When Coop rang her doorbell at exactly five o'clock on the dot, Bernadette's heart raced with excitement and appreciation. She was excited because this was the first time a man had come to her house to pick her up for a date in over five years, and she felt appreciative that Coop was a man of his word who respected the importance of showing up when he said he would.

She'd debated what to wear for the better part of the day. After her blowout with Tess that morning, Bernadette had gone for a run because she felt the cold air would help her clear her mind as well as come up with the right outfit for her date with Coop. He was a stylish man and she could tell that he spared no expense when it came to quality, but he also had a flair that danced on the edge of daring. She wanted to wear something that said she was sophisticated but also knew how to turn up the sexy. But unfortunately, almost everything in her closet screamed board meeting meets after-hours business mixer.

She'd wanted to ask Tess for her recommendation, but she'd known they each needed time to cool off, plus Tess needed uninterrupted time to finish writing her book, so she'd called Arizona to get her advice. Four hours and a few hundred dollars later, Bernadette stood in the middle of her closet, admiring herself in a backless black jumpsuit. The sheer, thin chiffon-like fabric of her sleeves highlighted her sculpted arms, and the stretchy Lycra material of the jumpsuit hugged her body, emphasizing her flat stomach and svelte physique, and the darting at the back gave her the illusion of an hourglass silhouette, complete with a bump of her derriere. She accessorized her outfit with bling chandelier style earrings and a bling cuff bracelet.

Bernadette had also agonized over how to apply her makeup so that it would enhance her features. Arizona had switched their call to FaceTime so she could give Bernadette a real-life tutorial.

"Coop likes you for who you are," Arizona had said. "He's not shallow like a lot of men out here, and I'm willin' to bet he won't be thinking about whether your face is contoured or if you've created the perfect smoky eyes. The man just wants to get to know you."

Arizona's words had given Bernadette a little comfort, and when she'd opened the door and greeted Coop, he'd smiled wide and told her that she looked beautiful.

Now, they were riding in Coop's black Escalade, listening to the sounds of Earth, Wind & Fire, softly floating through his truck's speakers as they drove down Bernadette's street, heading out of her neighborhood.

"How do you like living here?" Coop asked.

"I guess it's okay. As I said the other day, I work so much that I haven't really gotten out to see much of the town."

"No, I mean how do you like living in the Palisades, and in your neighborhood?"

"My answer's pretty much the same."

Coop nodded and glanced at her. "I admire you, Bernadette."

"Why?"

He winked. "I'll tell you later. Right now I want to know if you want to eat dinner first or go to a movie?"

"I'm kind of hungry, so dinner and then a movie, if that's okay with you?"

"Sure. What do you have a taste for?"

"I know it sounds very generic, but I've been craving spaghetti all week."

"It's my favorite dish."

Bernadette's forehead wrinkled. "Two nights ago you told me that fried chicken, collard greens, and mac and cheese was your favorite."

"It is, right after spaghetti."

Bernadette laughed. "Okay, so Italian it is."

"I'mma take you to a place I think you'll really like."

In less than ten minutes Coop navigated his truck into the parking lot of a small building that was nestled inside the same shopping center as the Mint Julep boutique where Bernadette had found her outfit. She hadn't noticed it earlier today, but now that it was dark and the bright lights were illuminating the shopping center, it looked similar to the shops lining Mazza Gallerie, back in her beloved Washington, DC. With its luxury stores and a mix of retail and residential properties—much like her neighborhood—it was the type of area that catered to a specific clientele.

Coop opened the door for Bernadette and walked in behind her as she took in the upbeat ambience of the space. Music by Italian crooners thumped through the speakers while the smell of buttered garlic bread filled the room. After Coop put his name on the list they walked over to the crowded bar area to pass time during their thirty-minute wait. "Do you eat here often?" Bernadette asked, practically yelling over the crowd of noisy patrons.

"Nope. This is only my second time."

"The food is good?"

Coop nodded. "Yeah, it's pretty good."

"Then why have you only eaten here one other time?"

"It's not my cup of tea. Don't get me wrong, the food is top notch, it's just not my kinda scene, ya know?" he said as his eyes scanned the crowd.

"Then why are we here?"

There were so many people standing, practically squished on top of each other that Bernadette felt uncomfortable. She also noticed that the crowd seemed stuffy and highbrow, not at all an environment she pictured Coop to be in. Between the thirty-minute wait, which she knew was going to be torturous in her three-and-a-half-inch stilettos, and the noisy, overpopulated room, Bernadette was slowly losing steam.

As if reading her mind, Coop said, "Let's get outta here. I'm gonna take you to my stompin' grounds."

Twenty minutes later, Bernadette and Coop entered Ramone's, a quiet little restaurant that sat at the border of the Bottoms community. With its soft music, low lights, and sparsely patronized interior, Bernadette felt it was just right for their evening.

After they were seated and their server had taken their drink order, a glass of Merlot for Bernadette and sweet iced tea for Coop, they settled into their seats in the cozy booth and perused their menus.

"Is the food good here?" Bernadette asked.

Coop nodded. "It's the best Italian restaurant in the county. The food is always good and the service is quick. When you taste the garlic bread you might end up wishing you could leave with the chef instead of me."

Coop's statement made Bernadette curious. "From what you've shown me, you're a man who's very direct and you have a purpose and reason for everything you do," she said as Coop nodded in agreement. "So why did you take me to the other restaurant?"

Coop chuckled. "Honestly, I wanted to impress you."

Bernadette blushed. "Oh . . ."

"This is our first real date and I wanted to take you some place that I thought was more in line with you and your style."

"That place was crowded, noisy, and probably way overpriced,"

Bernadette said as she glanced down at her menu. "And the clientele reminded me of the buttoned-up folks I see from nine to five in corporate meetings every day. Do you really think that's who I am?"

Just then their server returned with their drinks. Bernadette studied Coop's face as he nodded his thanks to the server and moved his sweet tea to the opposite side of where the woman had placed it. She could see that his expression was intense, and now she was slightly apprehensive about hearing his answer to her question.

"I owe you an apology, Bernadette. You're a sophisticated woman with great style and taste, and I wanted to take you to a restaurant that I thought matched who you are. But I forgot to take into account that you're more than just window dressing, like the folks you pegged in that restaurant. You have substance behind your style, and a genuine heart to match your taste."

Bernadette was so flattered that all she could do was smile. Men in her past had showered her with kind words that had made her feel good for the moment but had left her feeling empty over time. But when Coop delivered his compliments, the tone in his voice and the genuine look in his eyes let her know that what he'd said was straight from his heart. He was sincere. "Thank you, Coop."

"No, thank you for accepting my apology. I should've known better."

"It's okay, really."

"No, it's not. I've communicated with you more over the last week than I have with any woman in a few years. And when I say communicate, I mean really talk and listen. When we talked Tuesday night you mentioned in passing that you liked Italian food, so right then and there I knew where I wanted to take you for dinner. But Thursday night when we were talking about voter rights, and you said that politicians in this state are tryin' to roll back progress, I knew you had passion and respect for humanity, and a person like that wouldn't be interested in hobnobbin' where I took you. I wanted to impress you, but you're the one who impressed me."

At that moment their server came to take their order. Bernadette gladly selected the spaghetti that she'd been craving and Coop ordered the Italian pot roast. After the server left, they resumed their intense conversation.

"Remember when I told you that I admire you?" Coop asked.

Bernadette nodded. "Yes. You winked instead of telling me why."

"When I drove into your neighborhood and down your street, I thought to myself, she's probably the only black person on her whole block."

Bernadette nodded affirmatively. "Yes, I am."

"But that didn't stop you from buying that big, beautiful house. You moved from the comfort of everyone you knew to a small Southern town where you don't know a soul and you bought one of the best properties in town. You run a hospital where most of the employees who look like you are pushing a broom. But I heard that one of the first things you did was analyze the pay scale of all the employees so that those very folks who look like you got a raise, and now employee morale is through the roof."

"How did you know that?" Bernadette asked in amazement.

Coop smiled.

"Oh, I forgot, you know everyone and everything that goes on in this town."

Coop laughed. "You're a class act, Ms. Bernadette Gibson."

Bernadette had never blushed so much in her life. Coop was not only staggeringly handsome, he was charismatic, and as she was beginning to see, genuinely sincere and humble.

Once their food came out and Bernadette took a bite of her spaghetti and garlic bread, she knew that Coop was telling the truth and that this was probably the best Italian restaurant in the county because it was the best she'd ever had, period. She knew she was going to have to up the intensity of her workouts because food in the South tasted better than anywhere she'd ever eaten, and at this rate if she wasn't careful she'd be a dress size bigger by spring.

For the next three hours they ate, drank, laughed, and capped off their dinner with the most delicious tiramisu that Bernadette had ever tasted. But the delight of the food didn't compare to the high she felt being in Coop's presence. He paid attention to her and remembered the tiniest of details, as he'd proven earlier when he'd recounted the conversations they'd had throughout the week. No man had ever shown that much concern for her. Coop wanted to know how her day had been, if she'd eaten a proper meal, if she was getting enough sleep at night, and if she was happy.

She also found out a lot more about him that she'd been hesitant to talk about over the phone. From past experience, Bernadette knew it was important to have the benefit of looking into a man's eyes when difficult questions were asked. The eyes were truly the window to the soul, and Bernadette had become a trained professional in discerning whose eyes were telling the truth.

She discovered that Coop's drug dealing had led to his ten-year prison sentence, and during the first five years of his incarceration he was still dealing drugs, inside the prison. But his wayward days came to an end when one of the oldest inmates in the prison, Mr. Ray, passed away. Mr. Ray had been sentenced to life without parole when he was twenty years old. He'd been convicted of first degree murder, and at the age of eighty-five he'd spent his entire adult life locked behind steel bars for a horrible, drug-fueled fit of rage that he'd regretted. Mr. Ray had befriended Coop when Coop had entered prison and he'd constantly warned Coop about the dangers of continuing the life that had sent him to prison in the first place. Before the man died he'd asked to speak to Coop on his deathbed. During Mr. Ray's final hours he'd told Coop things that changed his life and had set him on the road to becoming a completely changed man.

Once Coop was released he had to adjust to a world that had changed while he'd been away. If it hadn't been for his sister, Sue, and her kind and loving spirit he knew he wouldn't have survived. She took him in and offered him a place to stay, but more than that, she provided love instead of judgment, which was what he'd so desperately needed.

Slowly, Coop began to build his empire. He started by purchasing as much real estate as he could. He bought abandoned houses that no one else saw value in, then fixed them up and rented them to folks in need of a good, solid home to raise their kids. Soon, he purchased land as well, more houses, and then businesses. As Bernadette listened, it was clear that Coop was even wealthier than she'd originally thought. But she was puzzled because she couldn't figure out the root of how he'd come into the money to purchase real estate in the first place. She knew the money couldn't have come from his sister because she'd barely been able to make ends meet, and she knew he didn't get a loan from the bank because he had no established credit or work history to qualify for a loan. But the thing that really stood out was that Coop didn't secure a formal job. It was as if the money fell from the sky.

Because they'd spent so long at the restaurant, they missed the movie. Bernadette hadn't really wanted to sit in a cold dark theater, so she was happy when Coop suggested they go straight to Southern Comfort to cap off their date.

On the short drive over to the club, Bernadette couldn't contain her curiosity any longer. She wanted to know where Coop had gotten the money to begin building his empire. He'd told her everything else, and now she wanted answers to calm her presumptions and quell her worries. So she asked.

"Coop, I want to ask you a sensitive question, and I hope you won't be offended by my asking."

"You can't offend me, so go right ahead and ask."

"Where did you get the money to start buying real estate after you were released from prison?"

Coop paused for a very long time. Then said, "Are you sure you want to know?"

As much as his answer scared her, she wanted him to give her the truth, no matter how hard it would be to have knowledge of what he could have possibly done. "Yes, I want to know."

"You're the first woman, or person for that matter, who's asked me that."

Bernadette looked into his eyes and did her best to act unmoved, because she actually was. She didn't let his words throw her off; she was focused on finding out the truth.

"I used to run with a rough crew, but we were always down for each other. The feds were trying to get me to turn evidence on my buddies in exchange for a lighter sentence, but I refused. Some people thought I was a fool for not taking the deal because it doubled my sentence, and from some I received the ultimate respect because I didn't snitch. The truth is that I was offered a deal from my crew because in exchange for my silence they made sure I'd be taken care of when I got out. I kept my word and so did they. That's how things worked back then."

By this time they were parked in the reserved space for Coop's vehicle behind Southern Comfort. The well-lit exterior showcased the impressively large brick building that looked almost identical in back as it did in the front, with its ornate pillar columns etched in an antique gold patina. It was clear by the design and expert workmanship of the building that Coop had put careful thought into making his jazz club a standout establishment. As Bernadette surveyed her surroundings, she thought about the things that Coop had just told her, and what it all meant.

Bernadette looked at the designated parking sign in front of them that read *Cooper "Coop" Dennis* in bold, gold-colored letters. It was all very impressive, but it also seemed wrong. Bernadette didn't know any other way to ask the question that was swirling around in her head, so she did something uncharacteristic. She blurted out her thoughts. "You built all of this with drug money?"

Coop took a deep breath. "I know it sounds bad, but hear me out."

"I'm not judging you, Coop. I'm just trying to understand."

"I knew that drug money was dirty money back then, but I didn't care. For me, it was about survival. I knew my father, and my mother was an addict. My older sister, Sue, and I grew up so poor that some nights we went to bed hungry because it was more important for our mother to feed her habit than her kids. When I was ten years old my mother, who never seemed like one, died from an overdose. After that, Sue and I bounced from one relative's house to the next. I started dealin' drugs in eighth grade, and once I got a taste of how money could allow you to live and feel a certain way, I wanted more, and I was willin' to do whatever I needed to in order to get as much as I could.

"I was young and foolish back then and I did so many things that I regret. I wish I could change the past, but I can't. The only thing I can do is move forward and do better in the here and now. Before I was released, I knew I was gonna be comin' out to a whole lot of money and I needed to do the right thing this time around. I wanted to make that dirty money clean, not just for myself, but for my community, and because I promised Mr. Ray that I would.

"While I was still in prison I took online courses and earned my bachelor's degree in business. Then I studied and did a lot of research into real estate and economic development because I wanted to use the money that was waitin' on me when I got out to help people. I wanted to provide housing to families and build businesses in our community. I was determined to do better and be better."

Bernadette listened carefully because she could see that Coop had been speaking from the heart. "Thank you, Coop. I appreciate your openness and your honesty. I believe you."

"It means a lot to me that you do, and that you even cared enough to ask. Most folks don't question or care about where my money came from, they just want to know how they can get some of it. But you're not like that. You're not concerned or fazed about how much money I have because you have your own. You're independent, confident, and you have standards. I like that. I like it a lot."

Bernadette sighed and tilted her head in a moment of reflection. "I've been used in my past relationships, so I know what it's like to be taken advantage of. I know what it's like to be involved with someone whose only concern is what they can get out of being with you, then once they get it they're gone. It's a hurtful feeling. And if you get pushed too far you can eventually snap. It happened to me in my last relationship and I don't ever want to be in that kind of situation again."

Bernadette didn't want to drag the good time they'd been having into an uncomfortable place, but she also felt it was important that Coop understand exactly what she'd been through. Her vulnerable admission was not only her truth, it was her warning to him that if he hurt her there was a real possibility that she would hurt him.

The two sat in the silence of Coop's truck, thinking about the weight of each other's words. Bernadette knew that she and Coop were moving fast because they were talking about intimately personal things that most people waited to discuss once they moved further along in their relationship. But she had to remind herself that she could no longer operate under conventional standards. She was different now, and Coop was unlike any of the men she'd dated in the past. She knew if there was any chance of her finding happiness, she needed to step outside of what was familiar and leap into the unknown.

Coop broke the heavy silence by quieting the truck's engine with the turn of his key. "Let's go inside."

Bernadette smiled and nodded. "I've been waiting for this all week."

Coop opened his door, then walked around to Bernadette's side of the truck, opened her door, and extended his hand to help her step out of the vehicle. Bernadette shivered from the rush of cold air that whipped around her body, and from Coop's firm grip. The wind had picked up considerably, making it feel twenty degrees colder. But even through their winter gloves, Bernadette could feel warmth in his touch. "Thank you," she said.

"My pleasure."

To Bernadette's surprise, Coop didn't let go of her hand as they walked toward the back door. He inserted his key, then punched a code into a digital pad that granted them access into the building. She walked closely beside Coop as they made their way down a short hallway that led to a set of double doors. Once inside, there was a small lobby area with a desk and two loveseats. Two offices sat to the right, and there was one large office to the left that had Coop's name on the door.

"This is where I spend most of my time," Coop said as he opened the door and turned on the light.

Bernadette could see how Coop could spend all his time at work because his office was set up with all the conveniences of home. As she walked inside she noted the kitchen area to her left that was out-fitted with a sink, stove, microwave, refrigerator, and a small dinette table for two. Beyond the small kitchen was a sofa, chair, and coffee table that provided the feel of a living room. And a few feet away was Coop's large work desk, credenza, and file cabinets. There was a room to the right that Bernadette knew had to be the bathroom.

"I spend more time here than I do at my house, so I made sure I have everything I need in my office. It works for me."

"You give working around the clock a new meaning," Bernadette said. She could see that Coop's office definitely served its purpose as a home away from home. "Does that sofa pull out into a bed?"

"Bingo! But the only difference is that my bed at home is a king-size and this one's a queen."

"How many nights do you spend here per week?"

"Four or five," Coop answered. He motioned toward Bernadette's wool coat. "Let me help you outta this."

Bernadette enjoyed the feel of his hand as it brushed against her shoulder.

"Did I tell you that you look beautiful tonight?" Coop said with a slow, sexy drawl.

Bernadette knew that Coop was inspecting her from head to toe, and she was glad that she'd put in the extra time and attention to look good tonight. She'd also known that she'd be stepping into Coop's world, which was most likely filled with stiff competition from other women, so upping her game wasn't an option, it was mandatory. Her stylishly put together outfit, dazzling accessories, coiffed hairdo that was fashioned into a neat chignon, and carefully applied makeup gave her the extra boost of confidence she needed.

Bernadette reminded herself that one's physical appearance was a superficial fallacy that could come and go, and that if Coop was the type of man who put great emphasis on looks, he wouldn't be with her in the first place. She knew she needed to keep her mind in a positive place and concentrate on enjoying the moment she was in.

"Are you aw'right?" Coop asked with gentle concern.

Bernadette tried to paint a smile on her thin lips. "Yes, I'm okay."

"You sure? You seem distant all of a sudden."

"I'm fine, really."

Coop looked directly into her eyes. "I observe everything, especially when it comes to somethin' or someone that I'm interested in. Now tell me, what's wrong?"

"I'll tell you later, but for now let's go into the club and listen to some music."

Without saying another word, Coop took Bernadette's hand into his and walked into the world of Southern Comfort.

It was close to one in the morning when Bernadette and Coop walked back to his office. The club was still going strong, even though the doors would be closing in another hour. Bernadette couldn't remember the last time she'd danced and laughed so hard. From the moment she and Coop had walked hand in hand into the club, she'd been on her feet; meeting people, dancing with Coop, meeting more people, and dancing some more. She knew that all eyes would be on her because of Coop, but she hadn't anticipated the sheer magnitude of what being with him would mean.

Bernadette appreciated the fact that Coop had made it clear that they were there as a couple because throughout the evening he either held her hand or rested his on the small of her back while pulling her close to him. Coop's public and very obvious show of affection toward her had drawn curious stares from men and envious glares from women. But none of that had bothered Bernadette because Coop had made her feel as though she was the only person in the room.

Now they were sitting on the sofa in Coop's office drinking bottled water from his refrigerator.

"Did you have a good time?" he asked.

"I had a great time. The music was phenomenal and the atmosphere was electric. This is the best evening I had in a very long time."

"I'm glad you enjoyed yourself." Coop leaned back into the sofa. "Now tell me what was botherin' you earlier?"

Bernadette knew she should have prepared herself for the question and the fact that Coop hadn't forgotten about her sudden change in mood before they'd entered the club a few hours ago. "You don't forget anything, do you?"

"Nope. Like I told you, I pay close attention to things I'm interested in."

Bernadette didn't want to tell Coop the truth because it would uncover her insecurity, and she didn't want him to look at her as anything other than the strong, confident woman he knew. But she had to remind herself that if she wanted to have true honesty in their relationship, she had to be willing to expose the good and the bad. She had to be transparent and vulnerable. So she told Coop the truth. "I felt a bit insecure."

Coop furrowed his brow. "About what?"

"Being with you. I know when we're together people wonder why you're with me because you could be with anyone you want."

The same silence that had engulfed them when they'd been in Coop's truck earlier that evening had now returned. Bernadette wanted him to say something, but she was also hesitant about hearing his response because she could see the wheels turning behind his dreamy eyes as he processed her words.

Finally, Coop spoke. "I'm sure Arizona told you that I don't date much and that there's no one special in my life, right?"

Bernadette nodded.

"You're right, I could pretty much have my pick of women if I wanted. But the only woman I'm interested in is you. I walked into the club holding your hand because I wanted you to know it, and I wanted everyone else to know it, too. Bernadette, I've traveled down a lotta roads to get to where I am at this point in my life. When I look at you I see nothin' but beauty."

Part of Bernadette was on top of the world after Coop's declaration, but the other half still had doubts. "Coop, I hear what you're saying, but it's just hard for me to trust. I've been through so many heartaches, and unless you could stand in my shoes you couldn't possibly understand."

Coop shook his head. "Let me tell you sometin', from the moment I saw you struttin' down the hallway in those sexy, high-heel shoes at the St. Hamilton last Saturday night, I knew there was somethin' special about you. I was sittin' in the lobby, checking my phone when you came in. You didn't see me but I saw you. You walked into that hotel all alone and breezed through the lobby like you owned the place. I remember walkin' behind you thinkin', I gotta meet this woman, and from that moment, I was hooked."

Bernadette could feel the heat of Coop's body as he moved closer to her on the couch. He leaned in and once again took her hand into his. "May I kiss you, Bernadette?"

This was new territory for Bernadette because no man had ever asked for her permission to kiss her. But here Coop was, handsome, strong, successful, and sexy as seduction itself, and he was the one pleading with her. She felt empowered, so she nodded and said, "Yes."

Coop's kiss felt as vibrant and intense as the summer sun against her skin. He held her close to his body as one hand massaged her shoulder and the other rested gently on her thigh. His kiss was soft and tender, and it made Bernadette feel like a flower in bloom. She relaxed, allowing her body to wilt in his arms as their kiss grew deeper and stronger. When she felt his tongue graze her lips and then slowly find its way into her mouth, she trembled with excitement.

Coop leaned back onto the sofa and gently pulled Bernadette on top of him until she was resting on his chest. She automatically spread her legs so she could assume a comfortable position as Coop lowered his lips to the delicate skin on her neck. His hands caressed her hips in a slow, rotating motion that made her roll her pelvis to his rhythm as they began a slow grind.

Bernadette could feel herself getting lost in the moment as his large, rock-hard erection rubbed against the side of her thigh. His slow, thrusting hip movements simulated what Bernadette had no doubt would be the best sex she'd ever had. She knew from the large bulge in the front of his pants and the sharp throbbing between her legs that things were about to get serious and she had one of two choices. She could either unleash five years of pent-up sexual frustration right there on Coop's couch, or she could pull back and make him earn the right to experience what she was beginning to realize was a treasure; and that was her body and her love. Slowly, she pulled back.

"Coop, I'm not ready."

Coop's eyes widened, then narrowed as he studied her face. Bernadette knew he wasn't used to a woman telling him no, given the completely bewildered look on his face.

"Like I've said, I've been through a lot." Bernadette swallowed hard and then continued. "And like you, I've traveled some hard roads to get to where I am as well. I'm far from perfect, but I like who I'm becoming, and I need time to see where this is going before we take the next step."

Coop smiled and looked deep into Bernadette's eyes. "I've never met a woman like you, Bernadette." His smooth voice was filled with emotion. "I don't want to rush a good thing, so you take all the time you need 'cause I ain't goin' nowhere."

And just like that, lying atop Coop's chest on his soft, leather grain sofa, Bernadette began the first true relationship she'd ever had.

# Chapter 20

## TESS

Having grown up in Washington, DC, and having spent most of her adult life in Chicago, Tess was accustomed to brutally cold weather and unrelenting snow. She'd become so familiar with weather patterns that she didn't have to check the local forecast to know when the temperature was going to drop and the frozen stuff was going to fall, be it sleet and freezing rain or a hard pounding snow. But she was beginning to realize that weather patterns and Doppler radar didn't mean a thing in the south. It was early Sunday morning and as she walked over to the guest bedroom window and looked up at the sky, she didn't know what kind of weather the day was going to bring.

The clouds hovering above hinted of a winter storm on the horizon, but after being in Bourbon for one day short of a full week, Tess knew that the weather was like a dog's breakfast; it could be anything. She'd thought it was going to snow yesterday, but not a single flake had fallen from the sky. She usually didn't care if the fluffy white stuff blanketed the ground because plows kept things moving in the city. But this was Bourbon, and if there was a hint of inclement weather, everything would be shut down for miles around, and she didn't want that to happen because she had a date with Maceo tonight.

Tess smiled when she thought about the down-to-earth, smart, and dangerously sexy man she'd met last night. If anyone had told her that she'd meet a man who would make her believe in love at first sight, she would have thought they were completely out of their mind. And even though the books she wrote oozed with romance, she'd never really believed in it, or real love at all, for that matter. It had been the reason Bernadette's words had stung so badly during their blowout. Tess wrote about what she didn't have but secretly longed for. She wanted adventure, faith, and love, but deep down she'd always been too afraid to go after it because the risk of disappointment was a hill she didn't want to climb.

Tess sat down in the chair beside the window and thought about Maceo's wide smile, the sexy charm of his Southern accent, and his combination of intellectual heft mixed with edgy swagger. It was clear that his degree from Howard helped shape his mind, but it was his upbringing by a single mother tackling life in the Bottoms that made him the man he was today. Just thinking about him caused the temperature between Tess's legs rise. "I wonder if he can cook between the sheets like he can in the kitchen," Tess whispered aloud.

Last night after Maceo had filled her plate with the most tender slow-cooked barbecue ribs she'd ever eaten, along with a side of tasty apple cider coleslaw and savory molasses baked beans, Tess could barely contain her satisfaction with the meal or her instant and strong attraction to the man who'd prepared it. She'd flirted shamelessly with Maceo, seductively licking the barbecue sauce off her fingers so he could see how agile her tongue movements were. She knew he'd tried his best to appear unaffected because his employees and customers at the bar had all been looking, but when he'd smiled and told her to stick around for dessert, she'd known she'd hooked him. After an hour the crowd had dwindled down, and Sue's Brown Bag was empty by ten o'clock, which was shocking to Tess because that was the time that things got jumping back home. But as the bartender had explained, "Ma'am, folks is tryin'a get home 'cause it's cold outside and they say it might snow." She'd had to once again remind herself that things operated differently in the south, on just about every level imaginable in her eyes.

After Maceo had closed the restaurant and dimmed the lights, he'd joined Tess at the bar for dessert—warm brown butter pound cake and a glass of milk. Over the next two hours she'd learned that Maceo was five years younger than she was, and at thirty-five years old he'd been divorced for several years. His ex-wife and her twelve-year-old daughter now lived in his ex's hometown of Los Angeles, California. Maceo and his ex had a permanently fractured, nonexistent relationship that had ended after fights, accusations, and a DNA test that revealed the daughter he'd raised from birth wasn't really his, the result of his wife's infidelity that had persisted throughout their troubled marriage. His emotional openness had touched Tess and made her even more attracted to him.

Tess had been flirting but she'd also been guarded at the start of their conversation because she'd been nervous and unfamiliar with the butterflies flickering around in her stomach, a sensation she'd only experienced during her book signings. But Maceo had given her that same feeling as he'd continued to share what she had seen and felt were honest and candid details about his life and the struggles he'd overcome. He hadn't let the bitterness of a failed marriage turn him against the possibility of one day having a loving relationship. His vulnerability had given Tess the motivation to open up about her own romantic debacles, and in particular, her dysfunctional relationship with Antwan, and the fact that he'd been one of a long string of men who'd disappointed her.

Tess was in amazement by how easy it had been to tell Maceo about the deeply personal details of her life. She'd told him how she wanted to get married, have babies, and settle down into a traditional relationship, despite her over-the-top antics. She'd also admitted that after turning forty last week, she was more aware than ever that the hands on her biological clock were moving so quickly, she was afraid her time was running out. And to her surprise, Maceo had echoed that he also wanted children, especially because he'd been robbed of that opportunity by his cheating ex-wife.

As Tess continued to reminisce about last night she had to shake her head at life's irony. She'd had to suffer a near breakdown and travel from the big city known for wind to an obscure town named after liquor to find someone who wanted exactly what she did. She was about to rise from her chair when a vehicle coming down the street caught her eye.

Tess peered out the window as the shiny black Cadillac Escalade came to a stop in front of the house, and she nearly fell out of her chair when she saw Coop step out of the vehicle and walk around to the passenger's side. "What the hell?" Tess drew in a sharp breath of surprise. She'd figured that Bernadette had stayed out late, but she'd had no idea that her cousin hadn't come home at all.

Tess watched closely as Coop slid his arm around Bernadette's waist as they walked to the front door and entered the house. Tess jumped out of her chair and moved close to the door so she could hear what was being said downstairs. She knew she shouldn't be spying on her cousin in her own house, but she wanted to know what was going on because this was completely out of character for Bernadette. Tess knew that her cousin had never been the type to sleep with a man on the first date, but she also knew that lately, many things had changed. Turning forty had made her go through changes, so she could only imagine what turning a half century had done to Bernadette's psyche.

As Tess listened closely she heard the deep mumbles of Coop's voice and the light giggles of Bernadette's, then there was complete quiet. She knew the silence meant they were kissing. A few minutes later Tess heard the door close and Bernadette's heels click across the hardwood floors, headed to her bedroom. "I know I need to mind my own business," Tess said as she slipped on her bedroom shoes, "but I need to know what's going on with my cousin."

With the speed of a track and field athlete, Tess sprinted downstairs, startling Bernadette to the point that she jumped.

"You scared the heck out of me," Bernadette said as she turned around and faced Tess. "Have you been waiting up for me?"

"No, I actually thought you were home. I got up a little while ago and was sitting at the window in my room, gathering my thoughts, when I saw you and Coop roll up."

"Oh," was all Bernadette said.

Tess could see that her cousin had bags under her eyes, most likely the result of sexing Coop all night.

Bernadette turned and began walking toward her bedroom. "I'm going to shower and get in bed because I barely got any sleep last night."

"Do tell," Tess teased as she followed on Bernadette's heels.

"I don't kiss and tell, and besides, I'm still mad at you."

Tess could tell that Bernadette was joking because of the smile that spread across her face. "You know you love me, cuz. Now give me all the hot and dirty details, and don't leave out a single thing."

"You must think I'm crazy. Anything I tell you might end up in that book you're writing, so my lips are sealed."

"Under any other circumstances I would say you were right, but not this time." Tess sat on the tufted velour bench at the foot of Bernadette's bed as Bernadette walked toward her bathroom.

"I'm going to take a shower," Bernadette said. "And if you're still here when I get out . . . I might tell you about my evening."

Ten minutes later, Bernadette emerged fresh from the shower, her skin scented with the delicate smell of L'Occitane bath products. Tess shook her head at the fact that her fashionable cousin bathed in up-scale toiletries, yet she was wearing a red and black flannel night-gown.

"And don't say a word about my granny gown," Bernadette cautioned. "It's warm, comfortable, and I like it." She walked to her bed and slid under her damask comforter.

"Coop must've put something on you last night," Tess teased.

"You talk too much."

"But you know I'm right."

"Oh, but you're not, Ms. Know-It-All."

Tess kicked off her fuzzy slippers and climbed atop the bed, sitting cross-legged as she stared at Bernadette. "Cuz, you better give me the details before I start making them up in my head."

Even though Bernadette was clearly tired, she sprang to life as she told Tess about her romantic evening with Coop. From the moment he picked her up, to the fancy restaurant they'd both been glad to leave, to the Italian hole in the wall with great food, to the incredible time they had at Southern Comfort, to the meaningful conversations they'd shared until they fell asleep in each other's arms just a few hours ago, and finally, the romantic kiss he'd planted on her lips when he'd dropped her off.

"I know you're not a lovey-dovey kind of person, and you don't believe in soul-mate connections, but Tess, as crazy as it sounds, I believe I've found my soul mate."

Before last night, Tess would have agreed with Bernadette's assessment of her dismal outlook on relationships and life in general. But today it was as if she was looking at everything with a new pair of eyes, and she was beginning to understand why Bernadette had made a 180-degree transformation.

"No, cousin, I don't think it's crazy at all, and I'm so, so happy for you. I haven't seen you smile like this in what seems like forever." Tess looked into Bernadette's eyes and leaned forward. "I'm sorry for the way I've been acting. Everything you told me about myself was true. I've been unhappy and bitter for so long that it's become a way of life, but I know it's not healthy and it's not right. I admire the change you've made and I want to get to where you are, Bernadette."

Bernadette looked at Tess with surprise. "I hear the words coming out of your mouth but it's hard to believe." She tilted her head in wonder. "What caused your change of heart?"

Tess blushed. "I met someone."

Bernadette sat up in bed. "What? Who? When and where?"

Tess laughed. "I went out to get something to eat and, Bernadette,

I truly got a treat! Girl, this man is so sexy it's a shame, and he's a gentleman, plus he can cook his ass off."

"Wait a minute." Bernadette blinked hard. "I'm gone for one night and you meet a man who's cooking for you?"

"I know, right!"

"Who is he?"

"His name is Maceo and . . ."

Bernadette's hands flew to her mouth. "The manager of Sue's Brown Bag?"

"Yes, you know him?"

"Girl, he's Coop's nephew!"

Tess looked startled. She quickly replayed their long conversation that covered music, food, love, literature, and their families, but she couldn't recall Maceo mentioning that Coop was his uncle, especially since Coop seemed to be a big deal in town. But as she thought harder, something that Maceo had said suddenly rang a bell. "Oh my goodness, it makes complete sense now."

"What makes sense?" Bernadette asked, eagerness filling her eyes.

"Maceo and I were talking about relationships, and how hard it is to find love once you reach a certain age. He said that his uncle recently met someone and he told Maceo that he was in love for the first time in his life. His uncle was Coop, and Coop had to be talking about you."

Bernadette fell back onto her pillow with a happy grin on her face. "This is surreal."

"See, if I wrote this in a book, readers would say it was too far-fetched. But let me tell you, I've come to learn that real life is far more outrageous than anything I could write in a book."

"This is unbelievable," Bernadette said. "What are the odds?"

"I've always heard that everybody knows everybody in small towns, but this takes things to another level."

"So . . . Maceo said that Coop told him he's in love?"

"Yep. That's what he said."

Tess could see that Bernadette was processing everything in her analytical mind. In Bernadette's world, things were black or white with no in-between shades of gray because it was easier for her to deal with situations that didn't involve ambiguity.

"Bernadette, don't overanalyze this and drive yourself crazy trying to figure things out, or run that man off. Just enjoy the feeling and see where it takes you."

Bernadette blinked hard. "You'll have to bear with me if I stare, because I can't believe I'm hearing these words come out of your mouth. What in the world did you and Maceo do last night?"

"I understand your skepticism because it's the same way I felt last week when I talked to you over the phone, and then once I got here I honestly thought that you were going through some kind of midlife breakdown."

Bernadette laughed. "If I wasn't already on this journey I'd think the same thing about you."

"It's amazing how life can change once you start thinking differently."

Bernadette nodded. "Tell me about you and Maceo."

For the next hour, Tess delighted in recounting her evening with Maceo that had lasted until the wee hours of the morning. She could see that Bernadette was tired, but she kept going because her cousin was hanging on every word she was saying.

"Do you two have plans to go out anytime soon?" Bernadette asked.

"He's picking me up this afternoon for lunch and then we're going to catch an early movie. Sundays and Mondays are the only days he takes off from the restaurant, and even then he checks in on things."

"Coop told me that he's a really hard worker."

"What else did Coop tell you? And, girl, don't hold back anything."

Bernadette propped her head on her hand as she spoke. "Not

much. Just that he was very close to his mother, and he'd had a hard time when she passed away a few years ago." Bernadette paused and then remembered something. "It's coming back to me now. Coop said that his nephew's life revolved around the restaurant because after losing his mother and then divorcing his wife, he'd shut down. I remember thinking, wow, that's how I'd been living my life."

Tess and Bernadette sat in silence as they each thought about how their lives were changing at record speed.

Bernadette laid her head back on her pillow. "Love is powerful."

A few hours later, Tess was fresh from the shower, standing in front of the bathroom sink as she applied her makeup. Maceo would be there to pick her up in another hour, and Tess could hardly wait. Once she put the finishing touches of mascara on her lashes, she walked to the closet to select what she was going to wear. "I think he'll like this," she said as she reached for her brown turtleneck sweater dress. The cut of the garment complemented her shapely frame and disguised her bloated belly. She was about to slip it on when a jarring pain gripped her stomach with the sharpness of a knife. The throbbing was so intense that all Tess could do was double over in pain.

She dropped her sweater dress to the floor and limped over to her bed. Her face became hot and her skin grew clammy to the touch as beads of sweat erupted like a volcano. Her head was pounding as though someone was jackhammering bricks against her scalp. "These fucking fibroids and endometriosis," Tess mumbled through clenched teeth. The intensity of her pain had made her sweat just a minute ago, but now she was shivering as though someone had opened the window and let the thirty-degree air ease into the room. She could tell right away that this bout was going to be bad.

Tess crawled under the thick comforter and rocked back and forth, grimacing in pain. "Why now?" she nearly cried.

She pulled the comforter up to her neck as a tear rolled down her cheek, and once again, she thought about her bleak prospects for having a baby. Even though she lived a nonconventional lifestyle, there were certain things she was very traditional about, and family was one. As she'd shared with Bernadette during her first night in town, she wanted to get married, have children, and build a family. But with each stab of pain she knew the inevitable was coming.

A few minutes later, Tess managed to crawl out of bed and slough herself over to the bathroom where she had placed her medicine inside the sink drawer. She put a pill in her mouth and then cupped her hands under the running water from the faucet as she swallowed the painkiller. By the time she made it back into bed she was out of breath, feeling as though she'd just jogged around the block.

"Out of all the times for a flare-up, why now?" Tess moaned. She reached for her phone on the nightstand and saw that she had fifteen minutes before Maceo was supposed to be there, and because he had to drive from across town in the Bottoms, he was probably already on his way. Tess knew that as badly as she wanted to go out on a date, there was no way she was in any condition to go to lunch, much less a movie. She didn't want to cancel, but she also didn't want Maceo to see her in her current state, which was a mess. When she'd caught a glimpse of herself in the mirror after taking her medicine, she could only shake her head at the fact that her neatly applied foundation and concealer looked blotchy, her lipstick had faded, and her expertly applied mascara had smudged so badly that she looked as though she had raccoon eyes.

Reluctantly, Tess dialed Maceo's number, and he picked up on the first ring.

"Hello, beautiful," Maceo said with a smile in his voice. "You must have spies watching me because I just turned onto your cousin's street. I'll see you in about two minutes."

"Oh, Maceo, I'm so sorry," Tess said, barely able to talk.

"Tess, what's wrong?"

"I don't feel well."

"Are you coming down with something?"

Tess didn't know how to tell him that her fibroids and endometriosis were playing kickball in her stomach, and she was losing the match. So instead of getting into the complicated business of her reproductive system, she told him something that she thought sounded better. "Yes, I think I am. It hit me all of a sudden and I can barely get out of bed."

"A couple customers were sick last week, so there's definitely something going around."

"I feel awful," Tess moaned. That part of her story wasn't a lie.

"I'm so sorry you're under the weather, Tess. Is there anything I can do?"

Tess wanted to tell him that he could slide under the sheets with her and hold her until her pain went away, but instead she simply said, "No, I guess it just has to run its course."

"Do you have a fever?"

"No, I don't think so."

"Okay, good. You need to drink plenty of fluids. Do you have soup and crackers or anything to eat? You know you have to starve a fever and feed a cold, right?"

If Tess's stomach hadn't been hurting so badly she would have laughed at Maceo's old-fashioned saying, but all she could do was grit her teeth and nod as though he could see her on the other end of the phone. "I'm not sure what Bernadette has in her kitchen," Tess answered, "and right now I don't feel well enough to even go downstairs to see."

"You sound like you're in pain."

"If only you knew."

"Wow, this doesn't sound good. Do you think you need to see a doctor?"

"No, like I said, it probably needs to just run its course." Tess paused. "I was looking forward to having lunch and spending time with you, but I need to ask for a rain check."

"Listen, I know this is gonna sound crazy, but let me feed you."

"What?"

"You need to eat, regardless of whether we go out or you stay in, and since I'm already here I can make you something if your cousin won't mind me in her kitchen."

Tess tried to smile, but a sharp pain stole it from her lips. Maceo was truly a Southern gentleman, and the fact that he wanted to take care of her touched her in a way that temporarily dulled the ache coursing through her body. She'd barely been able to get Antwan to get take-out for her, let alone offer to cook her a meal, especially when she was in need.

"I know how it is when you're under the weather," Maceo said in a comforting voice, "and you don't feel like having company over, so trust me, I get it. But you don't even have to see me. I'll make you some homemade soup and then I'll be on my way."

"You're so sweet. Maceo, I don't even know what to say."

"Say 'yes, Maceo. You can cook for me,'" he said, raising the pitch of his voice to mimic hers.

Tess could hear the smile in Maceo's voice, and it made her smile, too, so she repeated his words. "Yes, Maceo. You can cook for me."

"That's what I wanted to hear."

"I'll call my cousin and let her know you're outside."

After Tess called Bernadette's cell and explained what was going on, she called Maceo back and gave him the go-ahead to ring the doorbell. Less than an hour later, Bernadette was bringing up food on a neatly prepared tray.

"How're you feeling?" Bernadette asked.

"Like a knife is stabbing my stomach."

Bernadette placed the tray on the nightstand and handed Tess the bowl of soup. "Try to eat a little of this, it might help you feel better."

Tess looked at the bowl of soup. "Maceo is quite a man."

"That he is. And he looks so familiar," Bernadette said. "Like I know him from somewhere."

"The restaurant?" Tess offered in a weak voice.

"No, he never came out from the kitchen when Coop and I had lunch there."

"Well, Coop is his uncle, so maybe you're seeing a family resemblance."

"No, he doesn't look anything like Coop, but he still looks familiar. I'm not the best at remembering faces, but I'm almost certain that I've met him before."

"You're that sure?"

"Yes," Bernadette said with conviction.

"Well, I hope it wasn't under any bad circumstances. Did he mention that you looked familiar?"

"No, he didn't. I don't think it's anything bad. But like I said, I believe I've seen him before."

"I hope not, because to me, he looks like the man I've been dreaming of."

Bernadette gave Tess a surprised look. "Girl, this is too much for me. You're already sprung and so is he. I don't know what you did to that man, but he's clearly taken with you."

Tess wanted to smile but she couldn't, and she could see that Bernadette's eyes rang with worry once she focused in and saw the grimace etched on Tess's face.

"Do you want me to take you to the ER?" Bernadette asked.

"No, I just need to lie here until the pain eases off."

"Like I said, I can call my doctor and get you scheduled for a visit."

"That's nice of you, Bernadette. But I've been through this drill so many times that I know what to do, which is exactly what I'm doing now—taking meds and staying in bed until the pain subsides."

"I'm sorry you're going through this, and that you missed your date with Maceo," Bernadette said as she looked at the delicious bowl of soup and freshly baked bread that Maceo had prepared.

"Me too. It seems like every time I think things are looking up, a cloud hovers over and rains on my head."

"Don't say that, Tess. You have to look on the bright side of things. Even though you don't feel well you have people to take care of you and a warm bed to lie in while you recover. And even though you weren't able to go out with Maceo, the man still came by and made you food to eat so you can feel well enough to go out with him at another time. So smile and appreciate your blessings."

Tess knew that Bernadette was right, and instead of rolling her eyes at her cousin's idealistic optimism, as she'd done yesterday morning, she embraced Bernadette's words. "Thank you for saying that. I needed to hear it."

"Anytime."

Tess looked at her bowl of soup. "This smells and looks wonderful."

"That man is a genius in the kitchen. I didn't even know I had the ingredients to make what he put together, but once he looked around and started pulling things from the refrigerator, cabinets, and pantry, he ended up with this."

Tess saw that the chicken noodle soup had been made with carrots, celery, and onions, along with freshly chopped herbs. Maceo had even baked what looked like a homemade dinner roll. "How in the word did he pull this together so fast?" Tess asked.

"I'm still asking myself that question. I watched him in amazement. I had forgotten that I had fast-acting yeast in the pantry, and I certainly didn't know you could make homemade rolls that quickly."

"I don't even know what fast-acting yeast is, but I'm glad you had it on hand." Tess laughed and then moaned in pain again.

"I don't know what it's like dealing with fibroids and endometriosis," Bernadette said, "but menopause is right around the corner for me. My days of dealing with a monthly period will soon be replaced with hot flashes, night sweats, and weight gain," she said and then paused. "But like you said the other day, I'll miss the fact that it means the end of any hopes of having a child. I know that at this stage in my life, I simply don't have the patience for diapers and sippy cups, or homework and carpools. But if I'd known ten years ago what I know now, I would've had a child, with or without a husband."

"Really?"

Bernadette took Tess's hand into hers. "Yes, it's my one regret. But when I look at you . . . you still have a shot. And despite your current condition, like you said, there's always the possibility that anything can happen, and if you can't have a child biologically you can adopt. You can still have your happily-ever-after."

Tess wanted to cry because despite Bernadette's positive words, deep down she knew that her window of opportunity had likely closed.

# Chapter 21

## ARIZONA

*Four Months Later*

The last few months had raced by so fast that Arizona had barely been able to keep up with the whirlwind of activities and emotions around her. With a steady and growing list of clients, her days were busier than ever. Between the demands of her bourgeoning business, raising her precocious young son, and trying not to feel overwhelmed by her mounting concerns about marrying Chris, most days she felt as though she was holding on by a prayer. If it hadn't been for the incredible bond she'd formed with Bernadette and Tess, Arizona wasn't sure how she would have managed it all.

Ever since that cold February night a little over four months ago when they'd had their girls' night in at Bernadette's house, the three women had been inseparable. They got together once a week for lunch and once a month for what had become their girls' night in, rotating between Arizona's and Bernadette's houses. In between those get-togethers they conference called each other regularly, offering support, advice, and a listening ear. And because Bernadette and Tess were in new relationships and Arizona was in limbo about hers, they all appreciated having someone to talk and vent their problems to if they needed.

Arizona was more thankful for her friends than she could put into words because Bernadette and Tess were her sounding boards for clarity and stability, and they offered different perspectives laced with wisdom and experience. Arizona didn't know if it was because Bernadette and Tess were older, or because they were from different parts of the country, or because they were just wired differently, but they were able to give her better advice and insights than friends who'd known her all their lives, and unlike those very friends, neither Bernadette nor Tess allowed their romantic relationships to steal time away from their sisterhood. Arizona knew that life was a balancing act and between work, family, and everyday living, it was a challenge to fit in anything extra. Ever since Solomon had been born, and most of her girlfriends had started families of their own, her girls' fun time had been practically nonexistent. But now she was happy that things had changed.

Arizona was also happy for her two friends because they were involved in loving relationships that had ironically begun around the same time. She thought it was a twist of fate or maybe even divine order that two cousins were dating an uncle and nephew, and they often joked that the four were in a family affair. Bernadette and Coop were like an old married couple even though they'd only been dating four months. And Tess and Maceo were like love-struck teenagers who'd just discovered they had libidos. Watching her friends' happiness unfold made Arizona look at her own relationship with Chris and continue to question whether she should marry him.

Over the last few months she and Chris had gone back to practicing celibacy, which Arizona saw as a blessing and a curse, and in each instance it was for reasons that she knew were detrimental to having a healthy marriage. She felt it was a blessing that she didn't have to engage in unfulfilling sex with her fiancé, but the curse was that abstaining would only prolong the fact that Chris was in bad

232

232

232

need of practice, and he had a lot of learning to do. Either way, Arizona had a sense of doom, and she knew that wasn't the feeling a woman who was getting married should have.

It was clear to Arizona that she and Chris needed help, so she suggested seeing a clinical therapist who had come highly recommended by one of Arizona's clients. She'd been ecstatic when Chris had agreed to attend their first session a little over two months ago.

But Chris had called the morning of their session and told Arizona that something had come up at work and he needed to reschedule for another time. Arizona had been frustrated and disappointed, but she'd still remained hopeful because Chris had told her how much he loved her, wanted to please her, and would do whatever it took to make sure their marriage started off right. However, he had canceled the next two sessions, using the same excuse about work, and it had left Arizona feeling as though she was hanging at the end of her rope.

Feeling torn about what she should do had caused Arizona to fall behind on her wedding plans, and now with just two weeks left before the big day, she was meeting with her event coordinator and her assistant to finalize the plans. She was on her way to the St. Hamilton to meet Brittany and Sharon of B. Vaughn Events, so they could quickly get back on track with Arizona's neglected plans. Initially, Arizona had thought it was a big plus that the wedding would take place at Chris's hotel because it would save them tons of money and they would be able to customize their wedding to their liking without a lot of red tape. But now she didn't care one way or the other because her biggest concern was what would happen after she said "I do."

Arizona took a deep breath and walked into the hotel restaurant to meet her wedding coordinators. She tried to paint on a happy face when she saw the two women smiling at her as she approached the table. After they exchanged pleasantries, Brittany got down to business.

"As I mentioned in my emails, texts, and phone calls, because I hadn't heard from you I took the liberty of securing most of the vendors and services we'd talked about a few months ago," Brittany said. "But now we're down to the wire, and with just two weeks to go I need your final okay, as well as payment for a few of the services."

Arizona felt terrible about not following up with Brittany because the young woman was always pleasant, professional, and on her game. "I apologize for being MIA." Arizona looked at Brittany and Sharon as she continued to speak. "I've had a lot going on in my life with my new business and adjusting to a lot of change. Plus, Chris and I . . ." Arizona stopped herself short of finishing her sentence, which was that she and Chris might not make it down the aisle.

Sharon smiled at Arizona. "It's normal for brides to feel overwhelmed, and that's what we're here for," she said with confidence. "Even though we're a little behind, Brittany and I will make sure that your big day will be organized and beautiful."

Arizona knew that Sharon was a methodical woman who was adept at handling crises to minimize stress at events, which was one of the reasons Arizona had been excited to hire the duo to handle her and Chris's wedding. But now, she felt underwhelmed, and as much as she tried to hide her anxiety, her body language revealed the truth. "Thanks," was the only word Arizona could say.

"Sharon is right," Brittany reiterated. "We've got it handled. The only thing you need to concentrate on is how much fun you and Chris are going to have on your honeymoon night," she said with a smile and a wink.

Arizona wasn't a person prone to tears, but the thought of her honeymoon night made her cry as if she'd just received bad news.

"Oh my," Brittany said with alarm. She scooted her chair close and gently placed her hand on Arizona's shoulder. "It's going to be just fine. Sharon and I understand the kind of pressure you feel, and like she said, that's what we're here for."

Arizona glanced at Brittany and Sharon through tears and wished she could tell them that planning the wedding wasn't causing her stress, it was what she was going to have to deal with after the wedding that had her upset.

Sharon placed a glass of water in front of Arizona. "Drink this," she said calmly.

"I'm sorry," Arizona choked out in between sobs. "I don't usually cry, but lately my emotions have been all over the place."

Brittany nodded. "We know, dear. But like I said, just focus on life as Mrs. Pendleton."

The thought made Arizona burst into more tears. She knew Brittany and Sharon were at a loss, given the confused looks on their faces. And as if they could read her mind, Brittany spoke up. "We'll do whatever you want us to do. You run the show and you have the power to decide the next step."

Sharon agreed by nodding. "Go home and relax and we'll check on you tomorrow."

Later that evening during a three-way call with Bernadette and Tess, Arizona told her friends about her disastrous meeting with her wedding coordinators. "I know Brittany and Sharon probably thought I was a crazy woman."

"No," Tess said, "They see shit like that all the time and they probably knew what was up."

Bernadette jumped in. "Anytime a woman cries at the thought of her honeymoon or the mention of life with her new husband, it's a sign that something's wrong."

"You're right," Arizona said with sadness in her voice. "What am I thinking? I can't possibly marry Chris if the thought of it makes me this unhappy and full of anxiety."

Bernadette let out a sigh. "It's normal to feel nervous, because you're getting ready to make one of the biggest decisions of your life. But the reason you're having doubts is a serious one. You need to talk with Chris and lay everything on the line, Arizona. And I mean everything."

"Yeah," Tess interjected. "Because once you say 'I do,' there's no turning back."

Arizona knew her friends were right. After her and Chris's big confrontation a couple months ago they hadn't talked about the sexual elephant in the room, and Arizona feared that Chris had put it out of his mind and didn't think it was a big deal because he carried on as normal. Meanwhile, she was living day to day with the heavy weight of second thoughts. "He's coming over in an hour and I'm gonna have a long talk with him."

"Good," Tess said. "You can't keep tiptoeing around his little dick because it's not gonna get any bigger, but your problems will."

Bernadette sighed heavily. "Tactful Tess has a point."

"Damn right I do," Tess echoed.

Arizona felt that her friends wanted to say, "Girl, don't do it," but they didn't want to make the decision for her. She didn't think Bernadette or Tess would marry Chris if they were standing in her shoes. Bernadette had said that Coop was the best lover she'd ever had and that he took his time making sure that she was satisfied each and every time they made love. Arizona knew that Bernadette was telling the truth because Coop's reputation for being a good lover had been verified by one of Arizona's mother's friends back in the day when Coop used to get around. And from what Tess had said, good love-making was in the family genes, because Maceo had blown Tess's mind so much that she was in the process of relocating to Bourbon next month.

Arizona had been careful not to put her friends on the spot, but she was coming down to the wire and she needed help. "I want you two to be honest with me," Arizona said before clearing her throat. "If you were in my shoes, would you marry Chris?"

The line was silent.

"Bernadette . . . Tess . . . please, I need your advice," Arizona nearly begged.

Finally, Tess spoke up. "No, I wouldn't."

"Tess!" Bernadette hissed. "We agreed that this decision would be Arizona's alone, and we would give advice, not a verdict."

"Listen, the girl needs help. She asked and I told her the honest truth. Now, what would you do, Bernadette? Would you marry Coop if he had a small penis and didn't know how to go down on you or please you in any way?"

"Sex isn't the most important part of a marriage."

"Says someone who's gettin' her back blown out every night," Tess shot back. "Let Coop start falling off and see how you'll feel then."

Bernadette sucked her teeth. "Pleasure can be achieved in other ways."

"But that's the problem." Arizona jumped in. "I don't get pleasure from anything he does, physically or otherwise. I used to love just sitting, talking, and cuddling with Chris. Now he irritates the stuffing out of me, and the thought of him touching me makes my head hurt."

"I've said it before and it bears repeating," Bernadette said, "I still believe that sex isn't everything in a relationship, but according to what you just said it means a great deal to you, and your future with Chris is going to be filled with problems if you don't confront this head-on."

Arizona sighed. "Bernadette, I know you pride yourself on being diplomatic and impartial, but you still haven't answered my question, and I really need your help." Arizona held her breath in anticipation of what Bernadette might say.

Bernadette spoke without hesitation. "If you love him, marry him. If you don't, give him the ring back, call your coordinators, and have them send out your cancellation notices."

"You didn't tell her what you would do," Tess said. "Answer her question, cuz."

"No, I didn't, and I'm not going to," Bernadette said in a serious voice. "I can't say what I would do because I'm not in Arizona's situation. And honestly, Tess, you don't know what you would do if you were put into a situation with Maceo that required you to make a decision about a part of him that fell short. Chris is a good man who loves Arizona and her child, and he treats her with respect and dignity. He's kindhearted and generous, and he supports her one hundred percent on anything she tries to do. You and I both know how hard that is to come by."

"True, but a big hard dick isn't easy to come by either, especially someone who knows what to do with it," Tess said.

Once again the line went silent and the tension was thick.

"Arizona, have you been praying about what you should do?" Bernadette asked.

"Of course I have."

"Then be still and let God move you to your decision."

"That's easy to say," Arizona responded. "But until you're faced with making a decision that could either make or break your happiness, you have no idea how hard it is. One minute I think God is moving me in one direction and the next minute I feel like I'm being pushed toward the opposite."

"I will say this," Bernadette offered. "If you marry Chris and you continue to be sexually unsatisfied, he's going to have to go to counseling with you, otherwise you have no chance of overcoming your problems."

"And I'll leave you with this," Tess added. "I strongly believe that if Chris doesn't learn how to bring it, you're gonna eventually step out on him."

"No, I wouldn't do that," Arizona said. "The one thing I'm not going to do is be a cheater, ever again."

Now it was Bernadette's turn to reply with brutal honesty. "Arizona, I want you to think about what I'm getting ready to say. Tess is right."

"Well damn, cuz!" Tess said. "I can't believe you actually agree with me."

"How can you say that, Bernadette?" Arizona asked.

"Because I know human behavior." Bernadette paused, and then spoke slowly. "People don't change what they want, they change where they get it from. You want good sex, and if Chris can't give it to you, eventually you'll seek and find someone who can."

Bernadette's words sank in like thick mud, and Arizona didn't know what to say because she knew that Bernadette and Tess were right. Over the next few minutes Bernadette tried to lighten the mood by talking about how she was still trying to adjust to North Carolina's wishy-washy weather. They ended their call with Tess, of all people, saying a quick prayer, asking God to give Arizona the words and direction she needed.

As Arizona sat on her couch, waiting for Chris to come over, she hoped that God would hear Tess's prayer as well as her own.

# Chapter 22

## BERNADETTE

Bernadette was amazed at how well she'd been handling the chaos around her, and she knew she had age and time to thank for being able to deal with the twists and turns she'd experienced that week. But right now, her head hurt as if she'd been hit with a hammer after listening to loud music. The conversation she'd just had with Arizona and Tess had been difficult and emotional, but in no way did it compare to the private hell she'd been internalizing since her shocking discovery a few days ago. It was as if life was repeating itself, taking her back to the day when Walter had shattered her illusion of happily ever after.

Bernadette was still numb from the devastating revelation she'd uncovered about Coop, and that knowledge had ironically put her in the same situation with Arizona, forcing her to make a decision about the fate of her relationship with the man she loved, and more important, the only man who had ever truly and deeply loved her back.

"What am I going to do?" Bernadette whispered aloud as she looked down at the framed photo of her and Coop sitting on her nightstand. "I told Arizona to pray and be still, and I need to do the same."

Until meeting Coop, Bernadette hadn't thought it was possible to experience unconditional love from anyone other than her mother. And after all that she'd been through, the thought that she could actually trust anyone enough to allow them into her life and love them the way she loved Coop was something she'd all but given up the hope of feeling. But she'd found love when she'd least expected it, and now she couldn't imagine life without the feeling it gave her when she woke up every day. Over the last four months she and Coop had fallen into a rhythm that felt more natural and more loving than anything she'd ever experienced.

She'd initially been nervous about getting too attached to Coop so quickly. But after only two weeks of dating Coop, he'd told her that he knew she was the one, and he hadn't been discouraged by her skepticism. "I'm gonna earn your trust, and you're gonna be my wife," he'd said.

Bernadette loved the fact that Coop went out of his way to show and prove to her that he loved and cared for her. He thought about her needs over his own—whenever they shared a meal he always gave her the last slice of pizza, or piece of bread, or sip of wine, or whatever it was they were eating. He paid close attention to the things she said during their conversations—he knew her favorite color, where she liked to shop, and that she preferred generous scoops of natural brown sugar in her coffee. He was the calm in the middle of her storms, and that was one of the many things that made Bernadette admire Coop the way she did. She'd been so used to always being the strong, levelheaded voice of reason for family, friends, and coworkers, but now Coop was that person for her.

And if all those wonderful qualities weren't enough, Coop was hands down, without a shadow or hint of a doubt, the best lover Bernadette had ever had. He knew how to be gentle when she needed tenderness and bold when she needed more. His touch and caress made her weak in the knees and wet between her legs. The first time they'd made love she'd nearly been in tears it had felt so good. He'd pleased her with his tongue, his hands, his lips, and with his well-endowed manhood. She loved looking down at his handsome face nestled between her thighs during oral sex, and it always gave her a jolt when she saw him lick his lips and smile. But beyond the physical pleasure he gave her, Bernadette loved that Coop showed her his love and kindness through words and actions. He made her feel beautiful, wanted, and deserving of love.

Now, as Bernadette sat on the edge of her bed trying to figure out what she should do with the information she'd found, her mind took her back to a few days ago when she'd been in Coop's home office and had accidentally come across a discovery that jeopardized her relationship with him and their future together.

Coop was in the process of moving a portion of his office at Southern Comfort into his home, where he now spent most of his time ever since he and Bernadette had started dating. Through Bernadette's urging, Coop was undertaking the laborious task of purging to make room for the papers, boxes, documents, and office equipment he'd soon be moving into his home. Bernadette had gone over to Coop's house straight from work, and they'd been packing up what had seemed to her like thousands of files that were scattered throughout the large space. Coop had left to run an errand and then pick up dinner for them while Bernadette stayed behind and had continued to purge. She'd been in the process of moving papers and folders from his large metal cabinet into one of the many plastic bins they were going to transport to a shredding facility, when she'd made her discovery.

Bernadette had nearly finished unpacking the cabinet when she saw something that caught her eye under a messy stack of papers, buried at the bottom of the large cabinet. "What's this?" she'd asked with curiosity. A piece of paper was stuck in what appeared to be a manmade cut-out at the base of the cabinet. Bernadette reached in, pulled up the flap covering the secret space and immediately got a sick feeling when she realized she'd discovered a small, makeshift hidden compartment. Her heart started beating fast when she saw an old, rusted metal box inside. She didn't have to open the box to know that she'd find trouble inside, otherwise the box wouldn't be in a secret hiding place to begin with.

"Lord, please don't let Coop be involved in drugs again," Bernadette whispered as wild thoughts began to pop into her mind. She picked up the old, rusted metal box that was covered in dust and took a deep breath to brace herself for what she might find inside. Then suddenly she changed her mind. Whatever was in that box belonged to Coop, and he'd hidden it there for a reason. "I'll just put it on his desk and ask him to go through it when he gets back," she said aloud.

Bernadette reached to take the box to Coop's desk when the tiny lock on the box swung open and the papers inside flew out, along with something wrapped in a dusty gray cloth that made a loud thump when it hit the floor. When Bernadette bent down to gather the papers and the cloth she gasped at what she saw—a police report, newspaper clippings, and a gun.

"Oh no!" Bernadette whispered with panic, then looked around as if someone was watching her. A few moments ago she hadn't wanted to pry into Coop's things, but that was before she'd known what was inside. She instinctively recoiled and moved away from the box's contents because there was undoubtedly a bad story behind the things she'd just found, and even though she didn't want to know what she felt was going to be a terrible truth, she knew she needed to have full knowledge of whatever had made Coop keep a gun and criminal documents locked away in a hidden compartment in his home office.

The fact that Coop had a gun didn't alarm Bernadette because she knew he kept one in his truck, as well as one inside the nightstand beside his bed—and she'd learned that many people living in Bourbon did as well. As Bernadette gathered the papers, another bad feeling overcame her. Something told her that if she read the details of the documents in her hand she was going to be sorry, but instead of listening to her gut, she followed her curiosity.

Line by line Bernadette read a police report and newspaper articles that were dated more than thirty years ago, detailing the death of a man who'd been killed by a gunshot wound directly to his heart. His name was Morris Fleming, and he'd been murdered under mysterious circumstances, and in what one of the newspaper articles alluded to as a possible drug deal gone wrong, given that his body had been found in a section of the Bottoms that had been known for drug activity and prostitution.

"Oh, my goodness." Bernadette gasped as reality set in. "I remember this," she whispered in shock.

Shortly after Bernadette had moved to Bourbon, she'd seen an investigative report on the evening news marking the anniversary of a cold case involving a murder that had taken place more than thirty years ago. She'd been drawn to the story because the victim, Morris Fleming, had been a medical student from Washington, DC, who had just completed his residency at Johns Hopkins. He'd come to Bourbon for a visit, and he'd been in the wrong place at the wrong time and had lost his life. To this day neither his family nor the authorities knew the purpose of his ill-fated trip to the small Southern town, where he had no relatives or friends that anyone had known of. Despite the years that had rolled by, Morris Fleming's parents had not given up the fight to solve their son's murder and bring the guilty party to justice.

Bernadette shook her head, and her hands began to tremble as she looked closely at the picture of Morris Fleming, who looked like Maceo's twin. "That's why Maceo looked so familiar when I met him," Bernadette said to herself, remembering the conversation she'd had with Tess. She'd remembered the investigative report on the evening news and the image of the handsome young man with the high top fade and the Members Only jacket, but it wasn't until now, looking at the picture in her hand, that she recognized Maceo through the image of a dead man.

Even though Bernadette's mind was quickly organizing pieces of the puzzle into place, she didn't want to believe what she knew was the truth. "Why does Coop have information about a decades-old murder hidden in a secret compartment in his house?" As her eyes scanned the documents to confirm her thoughts, she found what she was looking for, and it made the faint hairs on her arms stand on edge. She saw Coop's unmistakable penmanship scribbled on a piece of faded loose-leaf paper, and the words that followed answered her question. Coop had written Maceo's name, his birth date, and the words "I'm sorry for what was done. I can't bring him back but I can help raise his son."

The date of Maceo's birth was six months after Morris Fleming had been murdered. "Jesus," Bernadette said as her mind raced. "It all makes sense now."

She remembered Tess telling her that Maceo had grown up not knowing who his father was, but that he'd heard rumors that his mother had carried on an affair with a successful sales executive from up north who'd been married with kids. He'd met Sue while traveling on business and they'd gotten together every time he'd come to town. But once he'd found out she was pregnant he hadn't wanted to risk losing his wife and children, so he'd beaten her in an attempt to cause a miscarriage. After that he'd dropped out of sight and no one had heard another word about the mystery man. Tess had said that Maceo had always been frustrated because he'd never been able to verify whether the story was true because neither his mother, nor Coop, nor anyone in his family would ever talk about what had really happened. But what Maceo did know for sure was that his biological father had indeed assaulted his mother, and he knew this because one of his older cousins who'd passed away several years ago had told him that shortly after Maceo's mother had shocked her family with the news that she was pregnant—by a man whom none of them had met—she had been spotted in town with a black eye and bruises.

Bernadette closed her eyes and wrestled with the truth that had settled in the pit of her stomach. Coop had killed Morris Fleming, and as much as she didn't want to admit it, she knew that the man she loved was a murderer. She knew that Coop had loved Sue dearly, and once he'd found out that Morris had not only gotten her pregnant but that he'd tried to savagely beat the baby out of her, Coop had made sure that Morris never put his hands on another woman again.

Bernadette picked up her smartphone and googled "Morris Fleming Murder." Although it was a cold case, the investigative news feature several months ago had reignited interest, and there was even an 800 number that had been posted so people could leave an anonymous tip if they had information that would help solve the case.

"He got away with murder," Bernadette whispered, feeling numb. She looked at the 800 tip-line number, and she thought about the desperate pleas of Morris's parents, who were now elderly and frail, and only wanted closure and justice for their slain child. Then she thought about the fact that she had information that could give the couple the answers they'd longed for. But Bernadette's stomach knotted at the fact that, that same information could send the only man she'd ever loved to jail.

It was hard for Bernadette to fathom that Coop was capable of murder because he was such a loving, kindhearted, and gentle man. But he'd shared, in his own words, that during his youth he'd been violent, hot-tempered, reckless, and even ruthless about anything or anyone beyond himself and the money he'd made selling drugs. He'd admitted that he'd done a lot of things he wasn't proud of and that he wished he could erase.

Bernadette didn't know what to do, so she carefully gathered the papers and used a Kleenex from Coop's desk to put the gun back into the dusty gray cloth. She returned everything back into the metal box just as she'd found it, then she placed them under the messy stack of papers at the back of the file cabinet where she'd first discovered the horrible truth.

Bernadette nearly jumped into the air when her phone rang, and she became even more nervous when she saw that it was Coop calling her.

"Hey," she said.

"I'm at the restaurant with Maceo and he wants to know if you want chicken, ribs, or both?"

"Oh . . . it doesn't matter."

"Since when?" Coop said with a slight laugh. "I know you love Maceo's cooking, so I'm surprised you didn't say both."

"Either one is fine with me."

"Bernadette, baby, is something wrong? Are you okay?"

"I'm good."

"You sure? You don't sound good."

"I'm just tired, that's all."

"I'm sorry, baby, I know between your demanding work schedule and helping me clean out my cluttered office, you're beat. But just relax. I'm on my way over with some good food and a bottle of your favorite wine, and since tomorrow is Saturday, you can sleep in."

Bernadette loved that Coop was always thinking of ways to please her and minimize her stress. But right now he was unknowingly causing her more worries than she'd ever felt in her life. "Okay, I'll see you when you get here," Bernadette said, trying to sound upbeat.

"Bernadette, are you sure nothin's wrong?" Coop asking again, this time with more concern in his voice.

Coop's concern made her think about how everyone said that she and Coop acted like they were an old married couple because they got along so well and knew each other like the back of their own hand. Bernadette knew that was true because right now no matter how hard she tried to convince Coop that she was fine, he knew that she wasn't. But she didn't want him to worry, or get suspicious, so she injected cheer into her voice to appease him before they ended their call.

Now, back in the present, Bernadette was more torn than ever as she thought about the shocking discovery she'd made a few days ago. She had to choose between doing what was legally, ethically, and morally right, versus pleasing her heart. She knew that as a law-abiding, morally conscious citizen, she needed to call the tip line and report what she knew. But as a woman who was deeply in love with a man who returned that love tenfold, she needed to protect Coop and keep his secret hidden in the past where he'd buried it all those years ago. Bernadette reasoned that Coop had been a different man back then and he was truly a good man now. She wanted desperately to talk to Coop about what she'd discovered, but she feared that any mention of the past would lead to the possible end of their relationship, and she wasn't ready for that.

Bernadette thought it was ironic that even though the nature of their dilemmas was vastly different, she and Arizona were both in situations where they had to make a hard decision about the man they loved.

# Chapter 23

## TESS

Over the last four months Tess's pain from her fibroids and endometriosis had gotten so bad that some days she could barely get out of bed. Yet despite her challenging health problems, her relationship with Maceo had blossomed into nothing short of a storybook romance fit for one of her novels. Tess could honestly say that she was no longer a skeptic when it came to love—she was a believer. She was the happiest she'd been since she could remember.

When Tess had come to Bourbon during the first week of February, she'd been on a mission to finish her manuscript and get her mind right. For the first time in her writing career she'd missed her submission deadline to her editor, which had been due to her frazzled mental, emotional, and physical state. She hadn't realized how off balance her life had been until she'd arrived in Bourbon. She couldn't thank Bernadette enough for inviting her to stay at her house because had it not been for Bernadette's love, support, and generosity, Tess knew she would have continued to wilt in Chicago instead of bloom in Bourbon. And thanks to the new love in her life, she was now happier than she could ever remember feeling. Coming to Bourbon had changed her life, and Maceo had changed her world.

Maceo was supportive of Tess as a person and of her career as a novelist, and she knew this because of the things that he consistently told her and showed her. He offered encouraging words of support when she felt stuck with her manuscript, and he delivered delicious home-cooked meals to her door when she was squirreled away in her writing cave, unable to venture into the outside world for fear that she'd disrupt her writing rhythm. His support had helped her finish and submit her manuscript two weeks ago, and both her agent and editor had told her it was her best book to date.

Maceo was the reason why many things in Tess's life had improved. His genuine love and no-frills, everyday laid-back way of living helped tame the wild, impulsive side of herself that sometimes caused her to make erratic decisions. His strength and vulnerability allowed her to open up her true feelings and accept the love that she had never felt worthy of, and his optimism and drive pushed her to look at life in a more positive way. And although she was still stubborn, quick tongued, and excitable, she'd become more patient, compassionate, and introspective. Tess could hardly believe the change that she saw within herself, and she knew a large part of it was because of Maceo. He'd even begun talking about engagement and marriage.

Tess's new outlook on life and her relationship with Maceo had led her to make the decision to move from Chicago to Bourbon. Two weeks ago when she'd pressed Send and submitted her manuscript, she'd poured a glass of wine and then called one of her Chi-town friends who was a Realtor and begun the process to put her house on the market. Since she'd made that decision, things had been moving quickly. She'd set the wheels into motion to list her home, and in the meantime, Bernadette had told her she was welcome to stay with her for as long as she wanted or until Maceo popped the question and they got married, which it was almost certain to happen soon, given how their relationship was unfolding.

Tess had flown back to Chicago yesterday so she could meet

with her Realtor and start coordinating her move. But she'd also scheduled the trip so she could meet with Dr. Gina, her long-time trusted OB-GYN . . .

Tess had just undressed and she was lying on the exam table, nervously scrolling through her phone as she waited for Dr. Gina to come in and start the exam. Tess couldn't help but smile as she looked at the photos that she and Maceo had taken over the last few months. She knew that her life had become rich and full, but looking at picture after picture brought home the reason why.

Between her stretches of long days and nights in her writing cave, Tess would emerge for the day, and when she did, Maceo was right there to fill her hours with fun and electric energy. She looked at the memories they'd captured, from eating at his restaurant, to enjoying fun at the beach, to triple-dating with Bernadette, Coop, Arizona, and Chris, to selfies as she and Maceo fed each other ice cream. She knew she was truly blessed.

Tess's mind was brought into focus when Dr. Gina entered the room.

"Tess, it's so good to see you!" Dr. Gina said with warm enthusiasm. She leaned in and gave Tess a gentle hug. "How have you been, dear?"

Tess loved Dr. Gina because not only was she one of the best OB-GYNs in the Chicago area, she was caring and took a genuine interest in her patients, which made them feel like a person and not a medical chart full of problems. At only four feet eleven inches tall, Dr. Gina was short in stature but she commanded a giant presence when she walked into a room. Tess smiled. "I'm in love," she said happily.

For the first five minutes of her appointment, Tess told Dr. Gina about Maceo, how they'd met, and the love he showered upon her every day. Tess smiled wide as she scrolled through a few pictures on her phone, showing Dr. Gina photos of Maceo and her. Then Dr. Gina's nurse assistant entered the room and it was time for the exam.

Dr. Gina's assistant placed Tess's phone on the counter while Tess reclined back onto the exam table and braced herself for pain.

"Just relax," Dr. Gina said in a soothing voice. "We'll be finished before you know it."

This was the part of her visit that Tess had been dreading. She scooted her hips to the edge of the exam table, spread her legs, and placed her feet in the hard stirrups. Tess tried to relax as Dr. Gina had instructed, but she'd already been in pain when she'd walked into the office, so she knew she was about to experience even more discomfort. She closed her eyes and saw bright white stars when she felt the cold speculum enter her vagina and then spread her apart.

"Tell me more about the amazing love of your life," Dr. Gina said.

Tess knew that the woman was trying to take her mind off the pain, so she tried to talk about the love she was grateful to have. But she was in so much discomfort that even the thought of Maceo didn't quell the stabbing sensation inside her. Tess knew that if it hadn't been for the grace of God, along with copious amounts of herbal teas, pain medication that she'd occasionally taken, and Bernadette's constant support and encouragement, she wouldn't have been able to have gotten through most days. Her condition was the one thing in their relationship that Tess had kept secret from him. She knew that Maceo had a huge desire to have children and that he looked at her as the woman who could give him at least two and possibly three if they worked fast.

The longer Tess waited to tell Maceo about her fibroids and endometriosis, the harder it was to divulge the truth. She knew he'd immediately ask why she had kept the truth from him, and she didn't want to run the risk of disappointing him, yet every day that she kept quiet she was unknowingly pushing them further apart.

"Okay, we're finished with this part of the exam," Dr. Gina said with a nod. "And you know the routine."

"Yes," Tess responded. "I hope the lab results will come back sooner than they did the last time because I'm nervous, plus, I'm only in town for a few days, so if the results come back and I need to see a specialist . . ."

"Let's jump one hurdle at a time," Dr. Gina cautioned. "I'll put a rush on your lab work and try to get it back before you leave."

"Okay."

"Now it's time for the last part of your exam."

Tess nodded. "I know the drill with this, too." She winced in pain as Dr. Gina inserted a finger inside her vagina while she pressed on the top of Tess's abdomen with her free hand.

"Does this feel sore, tender, or painful?" Dr. Gina asked.

"All of the above."

"I'm sorry, dear. I'm trying to be as gentle as I can," Dr. Gina said as she continued what Tess likened to kneading dough on her stomach. "Your abdomen is clearly enlarged, and it feels like not only have your fibroids grown in size, you have more clusters."

Tess hadn't needed an exam to tell her what Dr. Gina had just diagnosed. Her usually flat tummy now had a little bulge. Maceo had rubbed the tiny bump on her stomach one night and had said that he loved every inch of her body. Tess had wanted to cry because she'd known that he'd meant it, and she'd also known that her stomach stood a better chance of growing from fibroids rather than a baby.

Dr. Gina removed her gloves and told Tess she could sit up straight. "I think we need to do a transvaginal ultrasound."

Tess couldn't bear the thought of another exam or anything else probing inside her. "Not today."

"How long will you be in town?"

"Through the end of the week."

"Your lab results should be back in two days. Can you come then?"

Tess nodded. "Yes, I'll be here."

After her appointment, Tess raced through afternoon traffic, feeling good to be behind the wheel of her Mercedes again after several months of being away. She weaved in and out of traffic until she reached her home. She knew she wouldn't have any problem selling her house because it was in a prime, upscale location, and for the seven figures she would clear after closing costs, she and Maceo could build a mini mansion in Bourbon if they wanted to. But she knew they wouldn't because they both wanted to live a nice but simple life.

Once Tess got home she called Maceo and they talked for nearly two hours.

"I'm thinking about flying out there tomorrow night," Maceo said.

Tess immediately panicked. She had an ultrasound scheduled for the day after tomorrow. She hadn't told Maceo about her OB-GYN visit this morning, and she definitely didn't want him to know that she was having a follow-up procedure. "I thought you were super busy at the restaurant," Tess countered.

"I'm never too busy when it comes to my woman. You've only been gone one day and I already miss you. Now that you're finished with your book we can spend more time together, and besides, I can help you with anything you might need around your house."

"Aww, that's so sweet, and I miss you, too," Tess said with sincerity. "But I know that you're short-staffed, and if you leave right now it could create a worse problem when you get back. I'll be in your arms by the end of this week and we can catch up on lost time."

"I like that last part," Maceo said with a sexy laugh. "Tess . . ."

"Yes?"

"I love you, and I thank God every day that he brought you into my life."

"I thank him for you, too."

Later that evening Tess settled onto her couch with a glass of wine and a deli sandwich. She knew she should be sipping green tea, known for shrinking fibroids, and eating organic veggies and baked salmon, which she'd read could help quell the pain caused by her endometriosis. But that had been her standard fare for the last few months, and despite Maceo's excellent culinary skills that had made eating bland food more tolerable, her condition had worsened.

So tonight she was indulging. She was also looking forward to talking with Bernadette and Arizona in a few minutes because she needed to focus on someone else's life instead of her own. She knew that Bernadette was still trying to adjust to a healthy work/life balance after being such a die-hard workaholic for most of her career. And Arizona was trying to decide if she was going to call off the wedding and lose a good man who loved her or marry him and put up with unfulfilling sex.

When Tess's phone rang she immediately picked up. "What's up, ladies!" she said, happy to be connected with her friends.

"You sound great," Arizona said. "You must be drinking wine."

"As a matter of fact I am, and tonight I'm enjoying a smooth Pinot Grigio and a Chicago-style deli sandwhich."

Bernadette chimed in. "No more organic this and grain-fed that. Now that you're finished with your book you're cutting loose, and I don't blame you because you deserve it. I'm proud of you, cuz."

"Me too." Arizona joined in. "And speaking of cutting loose, I know it's an adjustment to be back in the city after spending so much time in Bourbon over the last few months."

Tess took another sip before she answered. "It's different. And the funny thing is that I thought I'd really miss the city, but now that I'm here, and it's only my first night back, I miss Bourbon."

Bernadette laughed. "You don't miss Bourbon, you miss your man here in Bourbon."

"And more importantly, I miss his magic stick," Tess teased, and then immediately regretted her words. "I'm sorry, Arizona."

"Girl, that's okay. I'm glad to know that somebody's gettin' some good lovin', 'cause I know I'm not. And as you both know, it's not just because we're practicing abstinence . . ." Arizona couldn't finish because of the sadness in her voice.

Tess knew Arizona was at her wits' end. And with less than two weeks to go until she was scheduled to walk down the aisle, she still didn't know what she was going to do.

"Ladies, I know I'm always asking for advice," Arizona said. "But what I really need is prayer."

"You're always in my prayers, Arizona," Bernadette said.

Tess spoke up. "And mine as well."

"Thanks, ladies. I've been praying every night and I'm still so confused."

"Arizona," Bernadette said, "What are you praying for?"

"That God guides me to make the right decision."

"Can I offer some advice?" Bernadette said.

Tess couldn't wait to hear what Bernadette was going to say because she knew whatever came out of her cousin's mouth, it was going to be good, and Tess could probably apply it to her own life.

"Sure," Arizona said. "I'm all ears."

"Me too," Tess echoed.

"I'm not trying to be preachy, but when you ask him for guidance, also ask for the other things you want, and be specific."

"How does she sound asking God for a big one and explosive downtown action?" Tess blurted out.

"Tess, please . . ."

Arizona stepped in. "Tess is right, Bernadette. I don't think God is going to make Chris's penis any bigger than it already is, and at this point I can't even think about his lack of oral skills."

Bernadette sighed. "I agree that God isn't going to make Chris's penis grow, but what he can do is grow your future husband's knowledge of your body and how to truly please you. Chris might not be able to give you oral sex that'll curl your toes, but God may bless him with the ability to make you feel super sexy and excited by his touch and caress. Be specific and ask for what you really, really want rather than praying for things that are out of Chris's control."

Tess wanted to cry because Bernadette had just given her the insight she needed for her own prayers. Instead of asking God to bless her with the ability to get pregnant and bear Maceo's child, she was going to ask him to bless her with the ability to love, nurture, and raise a child—whether that meant having her own or adopting.

After talking for another half an hour Tess said good night to her friends, took her shower, had a good-night phone call with Maceo, and was in bed by eleven o'clock. But before she drifted off to sleep, she said a prayer, and as Bernadette had instructed, she was specific about what she wanted.

# Chapter 24

## TESS

*Arizona's Wedding Day*

Tess sat beside Maceo inside St. Mark AME Zion Church. If ever there was a beautifully decorated wedding ceremony venue, this was it. B. Vaughn Events had artfully executed Arizona's vision of a rustic-themed indoor wedding, with pops of sophisticated and modern elements such as soft lights, tons of greenery, and tall glass cylinders with floating candles beside each pew. She had figured Arizona for a glam-theme type of bride, but this simple style fit in a great and unexpected way. The sanctuary was packed with what Tess felt was every single black person in the city. But she shouldn't have been surprised at the large crowd because Arizona had been born and raised here, and the Bottoms was a tight-knit community.

Tess looked down at Maceo's hand tightly intertwined with hers and thought about their future. Once she'd returned to Bourbon at the end of last week, it was more clear than ever how much Maceo loved her because when she'd arrived at his house he'd prepared a candlelit dinner for them, with soft music playing in the background. After they finished a delicious meal of stuffed chicken, baked sweet potatoes, and herb-flavored broccoli, they'd topped off the evening with a decadent chocolate cake and a proposal on bended knee. Tess had been shocked, happy, and tearful, but most of all, she'd been grateful.

But as much as she'd been overjoyed about her future with Maceo, she was also terrified because of the news that Dr. Gina had given her. The bottom line was that Tess needed to have a hysterectomy. Dr. Gina recommended surgery as soon as possible so Tess would have enough time to recover before her next book tour.

As she listened to the beautiful music, Tess wondered how she was going to break the news to Maceo, and once she did, how she was going to explain the fact that she'd accepted his proposal while being fully aware that she wasn't going to be able to have children, yet said nothing to him.

She knew she had to tell him, and she would. Right after Arizona had her big day.

Tess was drawn from her thoughts when she saw Bernadette and Coop being ushered in to take two of the last seats available at the end of the row behind her and Maceo. She looked at her phone and noted the ceremony was supposed to start in five minutes. Tess thought it was strange that Bernadette was arriving so late because when she'd spoken to her cousin an hour ago, she and Coop had already been on their way to the church. Tess looked down at her phone when she heard it buzz and saw a text message come in from Bernadette.

Bernadette: Arizona texted me this morning and said she's scared!

Tess stared at the message and then looked back at Bernadette, only to see nervous worry on her cousin's face.

Tess: Is she going to go through with it??

Bernadette: I don't know. I texted her back but she hasn't responded.

Tess: This is a mess!

Bernadette: Yes . . . a BIG MESS!

# BERNADETTE

Bernadette's nerves were frayed, and between her own worries and now a possible runaway bride, all she wanted to do was go home and crawl into bed. The truth about Coop's past had been weighing heavily on her mind. After discovering the circumstantial evidence that could implicate Coop in Morris Fleming's death, Bernadette went against her gut and logic and had tried to convince herself that Coop couldn't have killed Morris. But if she was completely honest, she would admit that she was fooling herself.

Bernadette's curiosity had led her to do some investigating on her own, and what she'd discovered had left her disappointed. One of the reasons why the authorities hadn't bothered to fully investigate the case and had let it go cold was because Coop and the "big boss" he worked for in Raleigh had the Bourbon Police Department on their payroll as part of their monthly expenses, and the money the police got every month made them turn a blind eye to crime, especially if it involved a black man killing another black man. Coop's connection to the local authorities explained why he had police reports and even a weapon in his possession.

But even with the heavy weight of worrying that she was in love with a man who might have taken someone's life, the fact that at the ripe age of fifty she was six weeks pregnant made Bernadette's palms sweat, her head hurt, and her mouth dry.

Two weeks ago, what she'd thought had been the early signs of menopause were actually the beginning symptoms of her pregnancy. It had been time for her yearly physical exam and pap smear, so she'd scheduled an appointment with Dr. Vu, the new OB-GYN that Arizona had referred her to. She'd been sitting on the exam table, still dressed in the flimsy blue paper gown, when Dr. Vu came in with a big smile.

"I know most people want sleeping pills," Bernadette had said.

"But I need something that will keep me awake because I can barely make it through the day without a nap."

Dr. Vu nodded. "In your condition, the best thing for you is plenty of fresh fruit, vegetables, lean meats, herbs, and a regimented sleep schedule because, Ms. Gibson, you're pregnant."

Bernadette laughed out loud. "You're funny! Now seriously, Dr. Vu, what can you give me? I've heard that B12 shots are good for increasing energy, so if you can, please give me one that might help me stay awake."

"Ms. Gibson, I'm not joking," Dr. Vu said in a gentle voice. "The standard pregnancy test that we gave you came back positive, and based on the date of your last period, I estimate you're about six weeks."

Bernadette had laughed when Dr. Vu had insisted upon her taking a pregnancy test after she'd told him that she had missed her period. But now, Bernadette's laughter was slowly turning into fear, and the rise and fall of her chest signaled panic.

Dr. Vu pulled up a seat beside the exam table and reached for Bernadette's hand. "Ms. Gibson, I can see that this is a shock. Take deep breaths, inhaling through your nose and exhaling through your mouth."

Bernadette did as her doctor had instructed, and after a few minutes and two cups of water, her breathing returned to normal. "I can't believe this," she told Dr. Vu. "I'm fifty years old. I'm supposed to be going through menopause, not pregnancy."

Dr. Vu smiled. "It's not unheard of for women in their fifties to conceive."

"No wonder I'm so tired."

"I can prescribe some prenatal vitamins, and because of your age, I'd like to refer you to one of my colleagues who specializes in high-risk pregnancies."

That afternoon Bernadette had gone home, crawled into bed, and tried to wrap her brain around the fact that there was a baby growing inside her. Not in her wildest, most outrageous dreams did she think that she'd be pregnant at fifty years old, and according to Dr. Vu's estimate, Bernadette was due March of next year, which meant she'd be fifty-one years old when her baby was born. She'd been experiencing highs and lows ever since. And just as she'd given Arizona advice less than two weeks ago—only a day after finding out she was pregnant—she'd started making her prayers specific.

Bernadette had asked God to show her the way and remove things she didn't need from her life in order to make room for what He had in store for her. She'd given up all hope of ever finding love, and her dream of having children had been left in the dust a long time ago. But now she was involved with a wonderful man who loved her, and that morning he'd told her that she better get ready because their wedding was going to be next, and knowing Coop the way she did, she knew that a ring and a proposal were soon to follow. And if that blessing wasn't enough, the fact that she was now pregnant was nothing short of a miracle.

Bernadette felt both excited and nervous at the possibility of having a child. She was excited because she'd always wanted to be a mother, but that was when she'd been younger. She was much older now, and she was nervous because of all the complications that could go wrong simply because she was a "mature mother," which labeled her a high-risk pregnancy requiring specialist upon specialist. Then she hadn't even broached the fact that she was sure that Coop had no interest in dealing with dirty diapers and sippy cups at fifty-two. He'd repeatedly told her that now that they were together, he was going to stop filling up his time with work and start enjoying life, traveling and exploring the world with her.

Then there was a part of Bernadette that ached for Tess. Her cousin was struggling with the fact that she desperately wanted to have a child, and here she was, not even thinking about getting pregnant, yet she was in her first trimester.

Bernadette's mind was brought into the here and now when the soft wedding prelude music stopped and the church fell into complete silence. Bernadette immediately looked in Tess's direction. Her cousin was staring into her eyes with fright. Bernadette looked down at her phone.

TESS: OMG, Do you know if Arizona is even here?

BERNADETTE: No, but I hope she is.

TESS: Why did the music stop? Are they getting ready to call it off?

BERNADETTE: How the hell do I know!

Bernadette's nerves had been on edge before, and now they had taken a leap off a cliff. A long pause that seemed to last an hour was broken when a soloist walked to the front of the church and started to sing. The doors to the sanctuary opened and the minister, Chris, and his best man walked down the aisle.

# ARIZONA

Arizona was nervously waiting in the designated bridal area trying to calm her nerves before it was time for her to walk down the aisle. She'd been anxious for the last two weeks, and her stomach had been in knots as she'd tried to figure out whether she should marry Chris or call the whole thing off. She'd agonized so much that she could barely eat or sleep, and over the last four months she'd lost a whopping fifty pounds, which ironically was the reason why she'd been late getting to the church. She'd needed to get her dress taken in another inch, and the seamstress hadn't delivered the dress until twenty minutes ago.

But even if she had to walk down the aisle in a pair of jeans, Arizona had made up her mind that she was going to marry Chris. After sleepless nights, endless days, and lots of prayer, her decision became as clear as crystal late last night. She dreamed that when she'd woken up, Chris was nowhere to be found. He'd disappeared and no one knew where he was. In her dream, she'd been alarmed, not because he was missing and might have met with foul play or some other type of catastrophe. She was upset because the thought of living one day without Chris literally made her wake up in a soaking sweat. At that moment, she knew that she was going to marry him.

"Alright, Arizona. It's your time to shine," Brittany told her as she led Arizona to the doors of the vestibule.

When Arizona walked down the aisle arm in arm with her father, she caught a glimpse of Bernadette and then Tess, who both looked worried and relieved, but most of all happy. Then she looked at Chris, standing at the altar with tears in his eyes, ready to love her with his whole heart. By the time she reached the altar, Arizona's face was streaming with happy tears as well, and so was nearly everyone's in the entire church. Even her pastor became choked up as Arizona and Chris exchanged traditional vows and then spoke their own personalized vows that outlined their love, commitment, and promise to each other before God and their family and friends.

"I do," Chris said with a smile.

"I do, too," Arizona said with a happy grin.

The minister pronounced them husband and wife. Chris kissed his new bride, and the entire congregation cheered as the new Mr. and Mrs. Pendleton turned and faced the audience, hand in hand.

One of the ushers walked from the side and placed a broom in front of Chris and Arizona as the minister spoke.

"Chris and Arizona will pay homage to the ancestors by jumping the broom."

"Amen," the church called out in chorus.

The minister continued. "Jumping the broom can be traced back to the Asante people in what is now known as Ghana, West Africa. This rich cultural practice became the only symbol of African slave couples' unions in America.

"As Chris and Arizona prepare to jump the broom, they will leap together into a new life and into their creation of a new family by symbolically sweeping away their former single lives, former problems and concerns, and they will begin a new adventure as husband and wife.

"Now, church, join me in saying 'Harambee!'"

"Harambee!" the congregation called out, in the Kenyan tradition of celebration.

As Arizona walked back up the aisle as a married woman, she, Bernadette, and Tess all thought about the minister's words. They each hoped that the days and months ahead would usher in new beginnings and sweep away the problems of their pasts.